The Advocate

[signed: To Mary!! Enjoy! Teresa Burrell 1/16/2022]

Teresa Burrell

Silent Thunder Publishing
San Diego

This book is a work of fiction. References to real people, events, establishments, organizations, or locales are intended only to provide a sense of authenticity and are used fictitiously. All other characters, and all incidents and dialogue are drawn from the author's imagination and are not to be construed as real.

THE ADVOCATE. Copyright 2009 by
Teresa Burrell.
Edited by Marilee Wood
Book Cover Design Karen Phillips

ISBN: 978-1-938680-03-8

DEDICATION

My deepest gratitude to my friends, Ron and Kim, for their strength, love, and encouragement;

To Marilee, my dear friend, for keeping me on track and for her never-ending words of wisdom;

To my friend, Bob, for his unconventional humor that kept me sane while I practiced law at juvenile court;

To my friend, Patti Ann, for her passion and high expectations;

To my "de facto son," Bobby, for his love and for always making me proud;

To my nieces and nephews for their devotion and admiration that continually drives me to set an example by meeting my goals;

To my brothers, Don, Gene, Byron, and Philip, for helping me learn life's hard lessons;

And especially to my sisters, Sissy, Marjo, Madeline, and Lana, for always having my back, and for loving me, believing in me, and supporting me no matter what I do, because in a world of utter chaos, the power of their love, the depth of their loyalty, and the extent of their confidence provides the path for me to reach my dreams.

THE ADVOCATE SERIES

THE ADVOCATE (Book 1)

THE ADVOCATE'S BETRAYAL (Book 2)

THE ADVOCATE'S CONVICTION (Book 3)

THE ADVOCATE'S DILEMMA (Book 4)

THE ADVOCATE'S EX PARTE (Book5)

THE ADVOCATE'S FELONY (Book 6)

THE ADVOCATE'S GEOCACHE (Book 7)

THE ADVOCATE'S HOMICIDES (Book 8)

THE ADVOCATE'S ILLUSION (Book 9)

THE ADVOCATE'S JUSTICE (Book 10)

THE TUPER MYSTERY SERIES

THE ADVOCATE'S FELONY
(Book 6 of The Advocate Series)

MASON'S MISSING (Book 1)

FINDING FRANKIE (Book 2)

CHAPTER 1

"If I knew he were dead, maybe then I could let go." Sabre Brown's fingers slid up and down the side of her Styrofoam cup as she and her best friend, Bob, walked away from the coffee cart in front of the Juvenile Division of the San Diego Superior Court.

He put his arm around her tiny waist and pulled her closer to him. "I know how much you miss him."

"Not knowing is the worst part. You'd think after five years, I'd quit expecting him to return." She sighed and her voice softened. "The last time I talked to him, he called to wish me a happy birthday. He called me the night before because his plane was leaving early in the morning and he didn't want to wake me. I badgered him about growing up, since waking me in the middle of the night would generally bring him great pleasure."

They stood in silence for a moment. Sabre turned to Bob. "You're a lot like him, you know . . . the same crazy sense of humor, only you're less of a prankster. Once he came to my office with silly putty or something hanging out of his nose, like a booger." Sabre swallowed and cleared her throat. "I don't know what I'd have done without you the past few years. You make it a little easier, you know." She glanced at her watch.

"We have a few minutes yet before the vultures start to circle," Bob said. "By the way, Happy Birthday."

She attempted a smile. "You remembered."

"Sure, kid. I couldn't forget such an important day."

1

"I wish I could."

"I know." He slipped his arm in hers. "We better get into court." They walked arm in arm past the metal detector just as a teenage boy placed his belt on the conveyor, grabbing for his baggy pants as they fell to his knees, displaying his Taz boxer shorts and his warthog tattoo. They chuckled as they entered the crowded hallway.

"I need to talk to my 'methamphetamine gazelle' over there." Bob nodded his head toward a woman with stringy, uncombed hair framing a face with skin spread thinly over her bones. Her missing teeth added a slight whistle to her high pitched voice. She paced up and down the short hallway, rubbing her hands together and complaining to anyone who would listen.

Sabre continued through the crowd in her well-pressed suit, J. Garcia tie, and Cole Haan pumps past one client after another, each with his or her own sad tale. Gang members, druggies of all ages, and men and women charged with all forms of child abuse filled the halls, many of them touched by poverty, others from gated communities. From wherever they hailed, the stories remained the same; only the package differed.

She spotted a client about twenty feet ahead in a clown suit. Her stomach gave a queasy twinge when she saw him. He had the perfect profession for his pedophilia and he flaunted it by wearing his clown costume whenever he came to court, red nose and all. *Not today*, she thought. Sabre squeezed her petite body through the crowd, ducked between two bikers, avoided eye contact with the clown, and stepped into a courtroom where he couldn't follow.

By 11:30 a.m., Sabre had completed her morning calendar. As she stepped out into the hallway, she heard Bob call from across the room. "Hey, Sobs. Come here."

Sobs, his nickname for her, came from Sabre Orin Brown. He had a lot of fun with her initials. When he wasn't calling her Sobs, he called her his little S.O.B. They had started working at juvenile court about the same time and had had their first trial together. Neither of them knew exactly what they were doing, but together they figured it out.

Their first case had involved a five-year-old, who had what appeared to be five cigarette burns evenly placed around one of her ankles. Sabre represented the mother and Bob the father. The parents, adamant they had not hurt their little girl, could not offer good explanations for the little round, infected areas. The attorneys were unable to reconcile the fact that the burns were so evenly placed on the ankle. Neither the attorneys nor the judge bought the testimony from a medical expert who stated a five-year-old child could hold still for five perfectly placed cigarette burns, but no other explanation had been proffered.

After some serious research and investigation and a little luck, Bob found an article about flea bites and how the fleas get under elastic and leave a row of bites which are often in a perfect line. The little girl had been playing in a sandbox and had been wearing anklets with tight elastic at the top. With some help from a couple of medical professionals, he determined fleas had been the most likely cause of the infected area, not cigarette burns. The little girl had scratched them to the point of infection.

They had won their first jurisdictional case in juvenile court, a difficult feat even for a seasoned attorney, as they soon discovered. That began a beautiful friendship and their reign at "Kiddie Court." There had never been anything romantic between them. He remained her best friend and confidante. They enjoyed each other's company and completely trusted one another. Inseparable at court, and on the rare occasion when Sabre socialized, she usually did it with Bob and his wife, Marilee.

Sabre walked toward Bob, standing near the appointment desk. "Hi, honey. What's up?"

"The clerk has a pretty nasty case–an eight-month-old baby with broken ribs, a broken femur, and a subdural hematoma. She's tried to give the case away, but no one will take it. She said if we take it, she'll give us one of those easy domestic violence cases," Bob said.

"But I'm hungry."

"You're always hungry."

"All right, let's get it over with. I have the cards."

Sabre removed three playing cards from her briefcase: a king, a queen, and a joker. "We don't need the joker. Public Defender has the minor."

Sabre put the joker back, shuffled the king and queen, and laid them face down on the table. Bob reached down, drew a card, and turned over the queen. "Sorry, Sobs, it looks like you got the dad. From what I've read, he's the most likely perpetrator."

"I'm sure he's a real peach. What do I care anyway, except it'll be more time consuming."

"Well, you can have the minors on the domestic violence case. You're better with the kids than I am anyway."

Sabre went to find her new client, the child beater. She always struggled with this type of case. She found it difficult to understand how someone could beat up an innocent little baby. *Maybe my client's not the bad guy*, although the information she'd received from Bob indicated otherwise.

She counseled her client and explained his rights and the court process. She looked at the scared, young man, who appeared so innocent, and thought how different he must have been when he used his baby as a punching bag.

After the hearing, Sabre gathered her files and went into Department Four to wait for the other attorneys on the domestic violence case. It had been an easy morning so far with mostly old review cases. Just that new domestic violence case and she could go eat.

Bob came into the courtroom. He and Sabre seated themselves at the table. Another attorney sauntered in, followed by his client, Peggy Smith, an attractive, young, pregnant woman with a bandage on the left side of her forehead. They took a seat on the right side of the table next to Sabre and Bob.

The door opened and the Public Defender entered with Gaylord Murdock, a tall man with sandy blond hair and cutting blue eyes. Murdock stared at Peggy with an intensity that made Sabre shiver. Peggy's face tightened and she squirmed in her seat, unable to tear herself away from his gaze. After about three seconds, Murdock's face softened and his lip curled up in a smile. No sign of remorse or shame emanated from him as he glided to his seat with his broad shoulders straight and his head held high.

Sabre watched their interaction and wondered what she failed to see.

"Excuse me, ma'am," Murdock said, in a strong southern accent as he squeezed between the railing and Sabre's chair. She studied him for a moment. In spite of his obvious good manners, she perceived a hardness about him.

She thumbed through the file and read he had been born and raised in Atlanta, Georgia. She hated when her calendar was so full she didn't have time to read the reports prior to the hearing. This wasn't the first time, nor would it be the last, that she had to read and listen at the same time.

"In the matter of Alexis Murdock and Jamie Smith . . ." The court officer called the last case on the morning calendar.

Sabre glanced at each page in the report to determine the most pertinent information. Her client, a ten-year-old girl named Alexis, lived with her father and Jamie, the two-year-old son of her father's pregnant girlfriend. According to the detention report, a neighbor had heard loud voices, a woman screaming, and what sounded like furniture breaking, so she called the police. When the police arrived they spoke with a very pregnant Peggy Smith, who told them her boyfriend, Gaylord Murdock, had hit her and split her head open.

As Sabre read, she heard the attorneys introduce themselves. When her turn approached, she stood up. "Attorney Sabre Brown appearing on behalf of the minors." She sat back down and continued reading the police report.

Peggy Smith is a white female, 24 years of age,

light brown hair, dark brown eyes, about 5' 4" tall, weighing about 135 lbs., and approximately eight-and-one-half-months pregnant. Smith had some redness and swelling on her right eye and an inch-long laceration that was bleeding and appeared to need stitches. Smith stated her boyfriend became angry because dinner wasn't ready fast enough and he hit her in the face with his fist.

The case continued, with each attorney making statements for the record. Sabre had done this so often she had become quite adept at listening and reading at the same time. It appeared to be a typical domestic violence case. She continued reading.

We talked to the ten-year-old girl, Alexis Murdock, who said her father came home from work and he and Peggy started yelling at each other. She said her dad was real angry but he didn't hit Peggy. She fell and hit her head on the coffee table. Gaylord Murdock gave a similar version of events, but because of Smith's pregnancy, her lacerations and her earlier statements of physical violence, we took Murdock in for questioning. Officer Jacobs called an ambulance for Smith. By the time the ambulance arrived, Smith had changed her story and said she had fallen and hit her head on the coffee table. We proceeded to take Murdock downtown for questioning and the minors, Alexis and Jamie, to Jordan Receiving Home.

". . . so even though my client vehemently denies the allegations, he's willing to attend the programs the social worker is suggesting. In the interim, we'd request the court detain the child, Alexis Murdock, with her father, pending the next hearing," Mr. Murdock's attorney finished his request to the court.

Sabre took her cue. She stopped reading and responded with words she had stated so many times they rolled off her tongue void of any conscious thought. "Your Honor, I'd ask, if the court is so inclined, it only be done with my concurrence. I'd like to speak with the children and see what they have to say."

"Very well," Judge Cheney said. "The social worker has discretion to return the children to their parents under the following conditions: the criminal charges are dropped; the parents are living separately; any other criminal check comes back unblemished; and minor's attorney is in agreement with their return." He hit his gavel on the block. "That ends the morning calendar."

Before Sabre could stand up, Mr. Murdock appeared at her side waiting to pull her chair out for her. As she rose, he stepped forward and opened the gate for her and the social worker to pass through. Sabre thanked him, though skeptical of his southern gentleman manners, something she rarely saw in southern California.

Bob and Sabre walked out of the courtroom together into the hallway. "The social worker seems to like both of the parents, especially the father. This case should settle at the next hearing with a voluntary agreement," Bob said.

"Well, I'm anxious to see what the kids have to say. I'm going over there now. We could stop at In-n-Out Burger for a quick bite on the way. Do you have anyone to see at Jordan?" Lunch together was a daily ritual, limited to a few select restaurants due to Bob's unwillingness to experiment with his taste buds.

"That works for me. In fact, I do have a kid I need to see in Teen Housing. I'll be right with you," Bob said, as he walked across the room toward a client who stood talking to one of the bailiffs.

Peggy and her attorney walked outside, followed by Sabre. Just as they stepped out, a woman flung the courthouse door open, nudging Sabre's arm.

"Son-of-a-bitch," the woman screamed as she stomped

out waving her arms in the air. "Supervised visitation, my ass. I'll see my kids when I damn well please. To hell with that." Bob followed her out. He and Sabre watched while the bailiff escorted her to the bus stop.

"One of yours?"

Bob nodded. "Charming, isn't she?" He removed a pack of cigarettes from his pocket, took one out, and lit it up. "Let's go eat. I'm buying."

Just then, Gaylord Murdock walked out of the courthouse. He looked toward his girlfriend, and once again Sabre spotted a glare from him. She watched the muscles tense up in Peggy's face and then her shoulders slump, as her body tightened into itself.

CHAPTER 2

"Hi, Ms. Brown." Kathy, the clerk at Jordan Receiving Home, greeted Sabre when she came in the door. "Who are you here for today?"

"Jamie Smith and Alexis Murdock. They still here?"

Kathy nodded and raised an eyebrow. "They sure are. Alexis is something else. Wait in Room #3. I'll bring them right out."

Sabre went into the interview room used for visits between the children and their parents or their attorneys. The modest but comfortable room contained a sofa, a table with a couple of chairs, and some brightly colored toys and books for the children. A sliding glass door led to a small square with a patch of well-groomed, dark green grass, a sandbox, and a shade tree so visitors could take the children outside. Offices and other visiting rooms bordered the square, so people couldn't leave without going back through one of the rooms. Occasionally, a parent tried to escape through the square with their child, but they were seldom successful.

Kathy returned with a two-year-old, dark-haired little boy, and a thin, blonde girl, in a pink, cotton dress. The little boy, quiet and solemn, buried half of his face in the side of the girl's leg. The little girl, on the other hand, grinned from ear to ear.

"Ms. Brown, this is Jamie and Alexis."

"Hi, Jamie. Hi, Alexis," Sabre said.

"This nice lady is going to talk to you and explain some things about what's going on. I'll see you in a bit." Kathy left them alone to have a private conversation.

Alexis sat down on the sofa and the little boy immediately climbed up on her lap. She pulled him close to her and comforted him as if she were his mother. As she did, a trace of tranquility crossed his face.

"Your dress is very pretty," Sabre said.

"Thanks. My father bought it for me. He says little girls should look like young ladies, not tomboys, so he makes me wear dresses."

"And what do you think? Do you like to wear dresses?"

"Sometimes."

"Well, my name is Sabre Brown and I'm your attorney. Do you know what an attorney is?"

"Yup, a lawyer. You go to court and say, 'Objection' and stuff."

"True, and sometimes lawyers go to court for their clients so they don't have to, especially when their clients are children," Sabre said. "Alexis, I'm going to ask you a few questions, but before I do, I want to explain something to you. Do you know what 'confidentiality' means?"

"Nope."

"Well, because I'm your lawyer, anything you say to me will be confidential, which means I can't tell anyone unless you give me permission. The law is designed in such a way so you can feel safe when you talk to me. Then I can represent you and protect you better because I know what's going on. It's kind of like a secret. When someone tells you a secret, you're not supposed to share it with anyone, right?"

"Right."

"Well, this is even more powerful than a secret. Lawyers can't tell the secrets their clients tell them or they can get in a lot of trouble and maybe not even be able to practice law anymore. Do you understand?"

"Yup. So if I tell you something, you can't tell anyone?"

"That's correct." She waited to see if Alexis wanted to add anything. When she didn't, Sabre asked, "Alexis, do you know why you're here?"

"Yup," she said, and paused for a moment as if to line up

10

all the pieces. "Peggy was doing that stuff she does that makes Father really angry. He talked to her at first. Then they started yelling at each other. Then Peggy fell and hit her head on the coffee table. Then the police came and brought me here."

"What 'stuff' does Peggy do that makes your Father angry?"

"You know, drug stuff. It can hurt the baby inside her. 'A person who is pregnant should not do drugs,'" she obviously mimicked.

"Have you ever seen Peggy do drugs?"

"Nope, but they argue about it all the time."

"Have you ever seen your father hit Peggy?"

"Nope."

"What about you? Has he ever hit you or hurt you in any way?"

"No," Alexis snapped.

"Alexis, I'm sorry if I upset you, but there are questions I have to ask and sometimes they are uncomfortable for both of us. Just remember they're just between you and me. Okay?"

"Okay," she answered, as she looked down at Jamie and tightened her hold on him. "I'm teaching Jamie his ABCs. It's never too young to learn them, you know. Everyone should know them. I love my father. He's a good father. Peggy shouldn't do those things to make him angry. She shouldn't do drugs. She could hurt the baby. You shouldn't hurt babies. When I grow up I'm going to take care of little kids." She continued to hold on to Jamie while she babbled.

"You love your little brother very much, don't you?"

"Yup, he's the best. He's real smart, not like . . . ."

"Not like who, Alexis?"

No response.

"Alexis," Sabre spoke softly, "can you tell me what happened before the police arrived the other night?"

"I heard them yelling at each other."

"Where were you?"

"In the bedroom doing homework and watching Jamie. When I heard them yelling, I came out. I don't like it when they yell. It scares me."

"Did you hear what they were yelling about?"

"Yeah, about drugs. My father hates it when Peggy uses drugs."

"Then what happened?"

"My father got real mad, but he didn't hit her," Alexis said. "She was screaming real loud. She tried to hit him with that soup thing, you know, the thing you dip soup with. He tried to take it away from her, and she fell and hit her head on the coffee table. She acted real crazy. I've never seen her act that bad before."

"Alexis, did you tell Marla, the social worker, what you just told me?"

"Nope."

"Why not?"

"I don't know."

"Do you mind if I tell her what you just shared with me? Remember, I can't tell anyone what you tell me unless you agree."

"You can tell her."

Sabre observed Alexis' discomfort. She needed Alexis to trust her, so she tried a subject less threatening. "Alexis, I hear you do really well in school. Do you like school?"

"Yeah, I love going to school. At least, I did in Atlanta. I haven't made any friends here yet because we just started."

"What's your favorite class?"

"I like music. I love to sing, and Father says I sound like a canary when I sing."

"Wow, maybe you could sing for me sometime. I can't sing at all. I sound more like a sick cow than a canary."

A little smile spread across Alexis' face. "Maybe, but I don't feel like singing right now."

"That's okay. You don't have to sing now. Some other day." Sabre felt like she'd made progress, but she could see it wouldn't be easy gaining the little girl's confidence.

"What was it like living in Atlanta?"

"Fine," Alexis responded, but her chin dropped into her chest and she pulled Jamie closer to her, as if she needed to protect him.

Sabre sensed something terrible had happened to Alexis, more than just the fighting between her father and Peggy. "Do you have family in Atlanta?"

"My Grandma Ruby used to bring me Christmas and birthday presents, but she doesn't anymore."

"Is she your father's mother?"

"Nope, she is my mother's mother. My father's parents are Grandma and Grandpa Murdock. They're real nice and they live in a really big house."

Sabre remembered reading in the detention report how Alexis' mother had left when Alexis was about five years old and had never returned. "Alexis, do you remember your mother?"

"Yup. She was real pretty, but I was a bad girl."

"Why? What did you do?"

"I don't remember, but if I wasn't bad she wouldn't have left us. So I try real hard to be good. Maybe she'll hear about it and come back to me."

"Did someone tell you your mother left because you were bad?"

"Sometimes Peggy says she'll leave like my mother did if I'm not good. And she'll take Jamie with her. I don't want Jamie to leave." Alexis squeezed Jamie tighter.

Sabre wanted to take her in her arms and just hold her and make her feel loved, but when she reached over and touched her on the shoulder to comfort her, Alexis pulled away. Sabre removed her hand and looked into eyes filled with sadness. This part of her job pained her, seeing the heartache in these innocent little children. It drove her to continue to work sixteen-hour days, seven days a week.

"Sweetheart, I'm sure your mother didn't leave because of you. Adults sometimes do things that affect the people they love, not because they want to hurt them, but because they have their own problems. Lots of reasons come to mind why she may have done what she did. Maybe some day you'll find out the truth. In the meantime, don't blame yourself. Even though I don't know why your mother left, or why she hasn't returned, I'm absolutely certain it had nothing to do with your being bad."

Alexis looked up at Sabre with eyes that said, "I want to believe you." For a moment Sabre almost connected with her. Then her demeanor changed and she slipped into the little, bubbly girl who had first entered the room. She seemed to put on emotional armor and tune out the rest of the world.

"I got to help this morning in the classroom. The teacher's real nice. She let me tutor the little kids, too. She said I was real smart, and so when I finished my work, I got to work with the others. Most of the kids didn't finish, so she was real happy when I did. And I got an 'A' on my spelling paper, too. I love to help the little kids, especially with their spelling." Alexis smiled and continued her chatter.

Sabre picked up the house phone on the wall to let the front desk know she had completed her interview, and the children could return to their rooms. She continued to chat with Alexis, with the little girl doing most of the talking, until the attendant came back to pick them up.

When they rose to leave, Sabre wanted to hug her and hold her close to let her know someone cared for her, but she didn't. She knew not to impose herself on Alexis, even if she appeared desperate for attention. Enough boundaries had been crossed.

Sabre watched as Alexis chatted with the attendant. Alexis walked towards the door. Just before she went out, she turned and looked at Sabre. "That confidential thing you talked about–you can't tell anyone, right?"

"Right."

"Not even my father?"

"Not even your father."

Alexis turned just as quickly and walked away, picking up her chatter where she had left off.

14

CHAPTER 3

Sabre exited the building in search of her friend Bob, knowing if he had finished his interview he would be outside having a cigarette. She hated his smoking. Sabre couldn't stand the smell of it, but most of all she felt concern for his health. She nagged him about it every day, trying to shame him into quitting.

She spotted his prematurely gray hair above the fence outside the gated area, far enough away so the children from the facility couldn't see him. "I thought I'd find you here, sucking poison into your lungs. You know, if you weren't such a wuss, you could quit that nasty habit," she goaded him.

"Hey, I know I can quit. I've done it a thousand times," Bob retorted. "How did your visit go?"

"I'm not sure. Alexis is a sharp little gal. She's real bubbly and she loves to talk, but she's not letting anyone in right now. It's going to take some time to gain her trust and learn the family secrets. I'm afraid if we don't reach her soon, we never will."

"Well, Sobs, if anyone can do it, you can. You'll win her heart, just as she'll win yours. So what's next?"

"I'm going to speak with the social worker and see if she's come up with anything else. Maybe I'm reading too much into this. It's probably a simple little case we can cover with some classes and a quick reunification." Before Bob could respond, she went on, "It's just . . . I see fear in her eyes. I have no idea where it's coming from. It may have nothing to do with what's going on in her life right now. Perhaps it's just my imagination, but I need to help her if I can."

"Go with your instincts, Sobs. You don't miss many. In fact, my queen, I can't remember your being wrong yet."

"Right," Sabre said with a snicker. "Do you have a trial this afternoon?"

"Yeah, how about you?"

"No, my case settled this morning. I'm meeting with the social worker on the Murdock case in about half an hour. I have just about enough time to drop you back at court before our appointment. We better get rolling."

~~~

Sabre walked into the cubbyhole Marla called an office, partitioned off like the other nineteen, eight-by-ten-foot cubicles surrounding her, her desk piled a foot high with papers and files. On top of one stack sat a partially eaten box of white, powdered donuts and a huge cup of soda.

Amateur drawings wallpapered every wall. A bulletin board of children's photos, from newborns to teenagers, some laughing and playing, and others with sad faces, depicted Marla's life. These were her children. Not her birth children, but the product of her work, and she loved them all. Marla yearned for children of her own, but the doctors had told her she'd never conceive because of the cancer she had had at the age of four. Marla was twenty-nine now, single and looking, her dream of marriage and raising a family fading. She'd always planned to adopt, but her belief that a child deserved two parents made her reticent to be a single mother – and Mr. Right was yet to be found.

"Hi Marla, how's life treating you?"

"Probably better than I deserve." She chuckled. "Are you here about Alexis and Jamie?"

"Yeah, I just came from Jordan Receiving Home."

"So you met them, then? Aren't they precious? Did you get any information you can share with me?"

"I hoped you'd be able to fill in some of the blanks for me. I'm not sure what it is, but there's definitely something wrong. Alexis appears to be afraid of something. By the way, does Peggy have any drug history?"

"I don't know. We're still waiting on the records from Atlanta."

"What about Murdock?"

"Nothing on him yet, either. Same story; we're still waiting. You'd think, in this information age, we could obtain things a little quicker. If we don't come up with something before the next hearing, we aren't going to be able to keep those kids in the system. Maybe we shouldn't – maybe they're safe at home – but I sure couldn't stand to see one of them end up in the morgue like . . . " She stopped mid-sentence, pain evident on her face.

"Marla, you have to quit blaming yourself for the death of the Sanders boy. It wasn't your fault. There's nothing you could've done."

"But I made a home visit the day before, and I didn't remove those boys. I keep thinking that little boy would be alive today if I'd made the right call."

"You made the only call you could. You didn't have a legal basis to remove those children at the time. You had no way of knowing the parents had a meth lab in their van and it would blow up and kill him. The police didn't even know. How were you supposed to? Everyone, except you, realizes you're not at fault. The investigation by the Department completely cleared you. You need to stop beating yourself up.

"Anyway, this case is totally different. We have these children now, and we'll keep them safe. When we have all the puzzle pieces, we'll figure out this family secret, if there is one, and we'll make the best decision we can. You know you can't return the children without my concurrence, and I'm not giving it until I know it's safe. So if you have a problem with your department head, or with the parents, just blame it on me."

"I may just do that." Marla smiled. "So do you think you can get through to Alexis?"

"I'm not sure. She did tell me her father didn't hit Peggy

17

that night. She said they argued about Peggy using drugs and Peggy came after him with a soup ladle. When he tried to take it away from her, she fell and hit her head. It'll be interesting to see what we find in the police report from Atlanta. I'm going to put in a call to them and see if they can help."

"Sounds good. I'll follow up with what Alexis said. If Peggy uses drugs, it's interesting Murdock didn't tell us or the police about it. Please keep me informed if you hear from Atlanta, and I'll do the same."

"Will do. Listen, Marla, you take care of yourself. If you ever need someone to talk to, I'm a good listener." Sabre gave her a hug and headed down the hallway between the cubicles, toward the exit, greeting other workers as she passed. She knew almost everyone in the building, most of them diligent workers who really cared about their clients, but few as dedicated as Marla.

Sabre drove back to her office to catch up on some paperwork and the slew of phone calls she knew she'd have to respond to.

When her cell phone rang, Sabre looked at her watch. It read 3:03 p.m. "Hi, Mom. I'm glad you didn't give birth to me in the middle of the night," Sabre said as she answered the phone. Her mother always called exactly on her birth minute.

"Happy twenty-eighth birthday," her mother said. "I hope you plan to do something fun today. Remember, this is your special day."

"Yeah, Mom. I'm going out with my friends this evening," she lied. In reality, she never told anyone her birth date except her best friend, Bob, and she made him promise not to make a big deal of it. Sabre hadn't celebrated her birthday for the last five years. Birthdays had always been such a family affair, but things were different without her brother Ron. It had been bad enough when he had moved to Dallas, but his disappearance was almost unbearable.

Back at the office, Sabre dialed the phone and heard a pleasant voice say, "Atlanta Police Department, how may I direct your call?" She gave her name and briefly explained what she needed. "One moment please, I'll connect you to Detective Carriage. Have a pleasant day, ma'am."

"Thank you," Sabre responded, amused at being called "ma'am." She heard the phone ring and then a deep, southern voice came on the voice mail. "This is Detective Joe Carriage. Please leave a message, and I'll get back to you just as soon as I return."

CHAPTER 4

Ring, ring. Sabre bolted upright in her bed early on Saturday morning, too early for light to be shining through the window. *Ring, ring.* The bright red numbers on her clock read 5:32 a.m.

"Hello." She cleared her throat.

"Good morning, ma'am. May I please speak to Ms. Brown?"

"This is Sabre," she said, trying to sound awake. "Who is this?"

"Oh, ma'am, I'm so sorry. Did I wake you? I just realized how early it is in California. I'm calling from Atlanta, Georgia, and it's 8:30 here. I was returning my phone calls and this one came up next. I'm so sorry. Go back to sleep, ma'am. I'll call you later. Oh, this is Detective Carriage, Joe Carriage. I'm sorry, ma'am," the smooth, southern voice continued.

"No, no. It's fine. It's time to get up. It's a good thing you called," she fibbed. "I called you about a case I'm working on here in juvenile court. I'm a defense attorney, and I represent the children in a dependency case."

"And how do I fit in?"

"The family is from Atlanta and I need some background checks. I know the Department of Social Services has asked for them, but I wanted to take it a step further. We need the information very soon. I don't want to keep those children out of the home if they're not at risk."

"I'll see what I can do. I'll be delighted to follow up on the background checks to see what the holdup is. I'll need a little information, names, etc."

"The names of the adults are Gaylord Murdock and . . .."

20

"Did you say Murdock?"

"Yes. Why? Do you know him?"

"Murdock is a well-respected name in these parts. They've been around for years, practically built this city. I apologize, ma'am. I didn't let you finish. Who else is involved?"

Sabre provided him with an overview of the case and gave him the details he needed to run a check on both Peggy Smith and Gaylord Murdock.

"Sounds like a simple domestic violence case. Do you know something you haven't told me?" Detective Carriage inquired.

"Just some things Alexis said made me uneasy. It may be nothing."

"You said you wanted more than a background check. Is there anything in particular you want me to be on the lookout for?"

"The usual stuff – criminal history, drug involvement, family background. If you wouldn't mind, would you see what you can find out about Alexis' mother? She left the picture approximately five years ago, and Alexis hasn't seen her since. Her folks may be still living there. Perhaps they can shed some light on the situation. I sure would appreciate any help I can get."

"My pleasure, ma'am. I owe you one, just for waking you up at 5:30 in the morning. I'll sure see what I can find out. I have to run, but I'll get to this as soon as I can."

"Thanks, Detective."

Sabre hung up the phone and leaned back on the propped-up pillows. She needed to plan her day so it didn't slip away, but first she reached into her nightstand and pulled out a little red, tattered notebook. She held it as one might a precious piece of artwork. She brushed her hand across the top of it and pulled it close to her heart. She thought about how her eight-year-old brother Ron had saved his nickels intended for the church collection plate. Instead, he had bought her the notebook for her sixth birthday. So, at six years and two days old, Sabre started to create a list of things she planned to accomplish in life.

As she did every morning when she first woke up, she read through her list, checked a few things off, and reviewed what she had accomplished and what she still had yet to do.

The list had grown over the years. The items had become more realistic and defined. Every single entry, except one, developed into some form of manageable dream. Some of the "kid's fantasy" ideas, like *become a famous movie star* had been adjusted to fit Sabre's life. She didn't actually aspire to be a star, but she did want a part in a movie, so that remained as her focus. Only one entry did she ever actually cross out and that was *Marry Victor Spanoli*, the little boy who had lived next door. Sabre chuckled to herself every time she read that part of the list. She remembered the day Victor had moved into the neighborhood. Two days after her sixth birthday, they'd met. His name had been her first entry in the notebook. Sabre wondered whatever had happened to Victor – if he still played his sax and what he looked like today.

She continued to read through the list of things she hadn't yet accomplished: *play a part in a movie; learn to oil paint; take a dance class; visit every state in the U.S.* The list went on. She'd been busy the past few years getting an education and establishing a stable home. Soon she could start doing the fun stuff, not that she hadn't done a lot in college and law school. She managed to travel quite a bit, but it only made the list grow because she discovered new things she wanted to do or see.

Sabre looked at the notebook. She had tried so hard over the years to protect it, but time had taken its toll. Once a deep red, now almost without color, the cover was partially off the wire spiral. Several pages had been taped back in because they'd been torn completely out. Only half of the back cover remained intact.

The notebook served as a checklist of her life – what she had accomplished and what she had yet to do. It acted as a guide for her and helped get her back on track when she strayed. Most of all, the notebook provided her a lifeline to Ron. She thought of him every time she saw it. Sabre wondered if he knew just how much it meant to her and how it helped her achieve her dreams. When she wrote something in the notebook, it represented a commitment to her brother, and with the exception of her goal to marry Victor Spanoli, she was determined to meet her commitments. Tears swelled up in her eyes and she murmured, "I sure do miss you."

Sabre rose from her bed, slipped into an old pair of gray sweats and a t-shirt that read: "I wonder what wine goes best with guilt." She headed out on her Saturday routine of visiting minor clients in their relative's or foster home placements, group homes, or mental hospitals.

By seven in the evening, she had finished her visits. She drove to her office to check her messages and to write a de facto parent status motion that needed to be filed by Monday. Her office, located in an old Victorian style home downtown, had its parking lot in the back alley. Sabre parked as close as she could, approximately twenty feet from the back door. The only illumination came from an adjacent office building and the sixty-watt bulb above her office's back doorstep, making it difficult for Sabre to see. Fog had started to set in, blocking any light from the moon.

She opened the office door. A familiar odor caught her attention – faint, but recognizable. Her brother's favorite cologne, *Kantor.* It had been years since she had experienced the smell of his cologne, unsure if they even still made it. She'd check with the other attorneys on Monday to see who in the building wore the cologne. She started to dismiss it when she noticed that her brother's photo, on the credenza behind her desk, was facing the wall. She knew she hadn't moved the photo.

Putting it out of her mind, she sat down and began to work. The silence in the office provided the perfect atmosphere to write the motion she needed for Monday. No phones ringing, no interruptions from clients or delivery persons. Sabre found it difficult to focus, though; she still felt a little uneasy about the cologne and the photo.

She tried to bury herself in her research and drafting of the motion. As she delved into the legal issues, she forgot all about her concerns until the phone rang. Sabre jumped.

She took a deep breath and answered the phone, "Law Office." No one responded. "Hello." Still silence. "Hello," she repeated. She hung up the phone and went back to work.

Ring, ring . . . She picked it up again. "Law Office." Still not hearing anyone on the line, she hung up the phone. She began gathering up her cases, waiting for the phone to ring again. This time she didn't answer it. She picked up her files, shut off the lights, and walked to the back door. She stood sideways as she locked the office door, glancing from side to side, and looking over her shoulder. She hurried to her car, each step picking up the pace. She hit the button on her keys to open her trunk and tossed her files into it. As she reached her car door, she heard a rustling across the parking area in the bushes. A shadow moved across the pavement. Her hand shook as she hit the button to unlock her door. She jumped in her car, locked the door, and drove off, skidding as she left the parking lot. Several miles down the freeway, the nervousness in her stomach began to dissipate.

CHAPTER 5

Sabre could see the sun streaming in through the window. It promised to be another beautiful day in San Diego. No time to waste on negative thoughts. She leaned over, opened the drawer in her nightstand, pulled out the little tattered notebook, and commenced reading through her list. She felt good about her life, in spite of the struggles she had encountered along the way. It had been a long, hard road, but she had finally made it. The majority of her dreams had been accomplished. College had been tough, working two jobs and attending school full time, and law school even tougher, especially the last year without Ron, but things seemed easier now.

She picked up a pencil and read from the notebook: *Home with an ocean view*. She had lived in her first home for a week now, "*a spacious two-bedroom condo with an office, three bathrooms, an ocean view, within walking distance of the beach*," or so the ad read. The ocean view was a stretch, but she could see some water from one little corner of her living room window. She checked it off.

Sabre got up and opened the shade to let in more sun. She dashed downstairs, plugged in the coffee pot, jogged back upstairs, and took her shower while her decaf coffee brewed. She fluffed her dark hair in front of the mirror. It had finally grown almost to shoulder length.

The smell of the coffee beckoned her to the kitchen. She picked up the cranberry scone she had bought the night before, cut it in half, poured her mug about half full of skim milk, and filled the rest with coffee. She stepped through the sliding glass door to sit on the front porch in the early morning sun. Perusing the newspaper's headlines, she found nothing but sadness and crime. She saw enough of that at work. She laid the paper down and watched the mourning dove in a nearby magnolia tree.

As Sabre sipped her coffee, she reflected on her life. Others may not have found it ideal, but she chose this life. She mulled over what she had to do today: several hearings this morning; the trial on a drug baby case this afternoon; and a visit to Jordan Receiving Home to meet with a four-year-old client who had been found sleeping in the bushes in a cemetery and now suffered from post-traumatic-stress syndrome, as evidenced by her total lack of speech. Then to the office to respond to the phone calls, write a couple of letters, and open those two new cases from yesterday . . . a pretty normal day, probably ending about midnight. Putting in full days didn't matter much since she had no social life. Being a lawyer often proved to be hectic, frustrating, even demanding, but never boring. Now she had her new condo to come home to. What more could she ask for?

Sabre opened her closet door and picked out a very expensive black suit she had purchased the day she received the news she had passed the bar. Up until then, her wardrobe had consisted mostly of jeans and t-shirts. She used her one suit for job interviews. When she received her first paycheck as an attorney, she spent the entire check on power suits and silk blouses, but her black suit, still her favorite, made her look as good as she felt. She added two inches to her height with her black-leather Gucci pumps, which brought her up to five-foot-three-and-a-half-inches.

Sabre picked up her calendar and a huge stack of files, threw them in the trunk of her car, and drove to court. She felt the same kind of exhilaration she remembered from junior high school, excited to get there to see her friends. The juvenile court attorneys were a different breed, not like Domestic Court where she had started her career in law. She had quickly tired of the conflict and backbiting she experienced handling divorce cases and soon found her

26

element in "kiddie court."

Her mood dimmed as the events of Saturday night at her office crept back into her mind, especially the smell of the familiar cologne. She pulled into the parking spot adjacent to her friend Bob's car.

"Good morning, Sobs," Bob said as he exited his car. He always sounded so pleased to see her. "How's my post-pubescent nugget of love and carnality this morning?"

She smiled. "Hi, honey. You sure know how to change a girl's mood."

He walked over, put his arm around her, and gave her a little hug. "What's the matter?"

"I'm not sure anything is, but it feels like I've entered the twilight zone." She explained what had happened in her office on Saturday night. "I'm sure there's a perfectly good explanation for each thing that happened, but all together they made me uneasy."

"Well, let's look at it. The phone ringing and no one there, that happens all the time. It could've been someone on a cell phone unable to make a connection, or someone who dialed wrong and just hung up. There are a thousand possibilities. The photo being turned could have been the janitorial crew."

"They only come on Wednesdays."

"Okay, but you could've bumped it when you turned around or, you said yourself, you may have looked at it, been distracted by something, and then placed it back down askew, right?"

"Right," she acquiesced.

"And as for the cologne, it probably belonged to someone who had come in with one of the other attorneys in your office. A strong smell can linger awhile."

"Yeah, that bothers me the most. I checked with the other attorneys. No one had been there. Do you think I just imagined the smell?"

"I doubt it, but I'm sure there's a perfectly good explanation. Maybe someone walked past the office wearing the cologne, or maybe someone in the offices upstairs had it on and the fragrance came through the vents. It's an old building. It's not exactly air tight."

"You're right. It just made me really miss my brother. I guess a part of me expected him to walk in the door. Five years and I still haven't accepted he's dead."

"It's harder when you don't get closure." Bob appeared to be empathetic, but Sabre knew he had never lost anyone close to him.

"He must be dead, because I can't believe he wouldn't have contacted me somehow if he were still alive. Maybe he was hit over the head and he has amnesia." She chuckled.

"Stranger things have happened."

"You know, we had a conversation the night before he disappeared. At the time it seemed perfectly normal – normal for Ron, anyway. But afterward it made me wonder if he knew he was in some kind of danger."

"Why? What did he say?"

"Well, he made me promise to visit our mother more. He said, 'She needs you, and she's going to need you even more.' At the time, I just thought she'd been complaining about me not spending enough time with her, but I think he knew he might not be around much longer."

"Did he say anything else that struck you odd?"

"Ron always said odd things, just to drive me crazy. I've played that conversation over in my head a thousand times, and I haven't come up with anything else. He was going fishing the next day. He lived in Dallas at the time, but he loved to go to Seeley Lake near Missoula, Montana. We'd go there every summer when we were kids and stay with our grandparents for a couple of weeks. Anyway, that's where he said he was going, but they found his car abandoned at the airport a few days later, in short-term parking. The police checked with all the airlines, but his name didn't appear on any of the passenger lists."

"So, if he flew out of there, he used an assumed name. Why would he do that? Why would he not contact the people he loved? It doesn't make any sense."

"I agree. We were really close, and it's impossible to believe he wouldn't have done something to contact me."

They reached the courthouse and waited in line to go through the metal detector. "Good morning, Mike," they both said, almost at the same time.

"Well, if it's not the king and queen of juvenile court!" Mike joked.

"Yeah, we're going to Burger King today to pick up our crowns. I hear they have some with our names on them," Bob responded. "I see they fixed the metal detector. It's amazing we don't have more trouble than we do with fathers in the same room with some pervert who molested their kid."

"If anyone ever dared to molest my little girl, he wouldn't live to appear in court," Mike said.

Mike often helped out at the front door until the hearings began in Department Four, his regular station. Sabre admired most of the bailiffs who worked at juvenile court, but Mike was her favorite. He loved to tease, but she knew he meant what he said about the child molesters hurting his seven-year-old daughter, Erin. Mike went through some hard times when his wife filed for divorce, but fortunately for him, she seemed more concerned about flying around the country with her airline pilot than about staying home with their daughter. Consequently, she didn't fight his pursuit of custody, and Erin fared better for it. Everyone knew Mike lived for his little girl. He attended all her gymnastic events, her dance practices and recitals, or whatever she happened to be involved in at the moment.

"You two have a good day. I'm here if the bad guys get out of line. Just yell and I'll come running and perform my Clint Eastwood act. You know how I love to play Dirty Harry."

Sabre picked up her bundle of files from the belt on the metal detector and walked over to the side of the room to lay them on the ledge protruding from the south wall, so she didn't have to carry them from courtroom to courtroom. Some of the attorneys had huge briefcases. If Sabre tried to pack all of her files in one of those, she wouldn't be able to lift it, much less carry it around all day. She hated those goofy little carts you stack things on and pull around. Besides, they'd slow her down. Her stack of files approached nearly a foot in height. She had eight hearings scheduled. With the exception of two fairly new cases, each file measured between one and three inches thick, all labeled and color coded.

Bob, on the other hand, had an equal number of hearings, but all of his files together were about as thick as one of Sabre's. She eyed his files. "How do you do that?"

"Do what?"

"All you have in your files is the report for today's hearing, and it's not even fastened in. It's just thrown in there. I could never function like that. Besides, I always need to look back in the file to find some bit of information in the middle of a hearing."

"It's all up here." He pointed to his head with his index finger. "Anyway, you're on most of my cases, so if I need something, I can always have you look it up."

"I don't know how you function when I'm not around," she said. She admired his intelligence and his memory. He seldom wrote anything down. Sabre wished she could do that, but she didn't trust herself enough to rely on her memory, so she made sure everything stayed at her fingertips.

Sabre picked up three of her files and walked with Bob down the long corridor to Department Five, past the counter in the middle of the room with the big "Information" sign hanging overhead. Bob and Sabre thought the space could be put to better use as a coffee stand. Unfortunately, the court administrators didn't agree.

A line formed at the information counter, and the hallways filled with people waiting to see what would happen next in their dysfunctional lives. On a bench near the wall, a mother sat next to a ten–year–old boy facing burglary charges. Most of the delinquent minors were detained in

Juvenile Hall, located behind the courthouse. They would be brought through a tunnel from The Hall directly into the courtroom when the judge called their case. The majority of the clients were there for dependency hearings, which consisted of child abuse or neglect, and stretched across all races and professions. Abuse didn't seem to have any real boundaries. It found its way into all walks of life.

"Hey Sabre, Bob. Wait up." Thomas Gilley, the public defender on the Murdock case, called from within the crowd about ten feet behind them.

"Hi, Tom, how goes the war?" Sabre asked, as he caught up to them.

"I need to talk to you about the Murdock case. Do you have a minute?"

"Sure."

"You should hear this too, Bob. Don't you represent Jamie's father?"

"Yeah, for what it's worth. The guy's in some institution. I've tried to talk to him, but he's a few French fries short of a Happy Meal," Bob said. "Why, what's up?"

"I had a long talk with Gaylord, my client. He seems like a pretty nice guy. I don't have the police report back yet, but it appears his girlfriend, Peggy, has drug history. He's very worried about his baby she's carrying. His version of the incident last week differed from hers. When he came home, he could tell she'd been using and a fight ensued, an argument actually. When he confronted her, she flipped out. She started screaming at the top of her lungs and swinging at him. She picked up a soup ladle from the kitchen and started hitting him with it. When he tried to calm her down and restrain her, she pulled away and fell and hit her head on the coffee table."

"His story fits with what Alexis told the police," Sabre said, "but why didn't he just tell the police Peggy was using? Why did he let them arrest him?"

"Because he didn't want Peggy taken into custody. She's so close to having the baby, he feared she might give birth in county jail. He didn't want his child born in jail. Besides, the cops weren't exactly open to any scenario except domestic violence. They didn't give any credence to what Alexis told them. You know as well as I do men are always the ones arrested when there is a hint of domestic violence."

"Here, look at this." Tom handed her an album covered with bright, Barbie-pink fabric. The cover contained the words "Alexis Murdock" in big block letters. Underneath her name in slightly smaller letters, it said "My Pride and Joy."

"I thought you might find it interesting. My client was reluctant to give it up, even for a second, until I impressed upon him the importance of your viewing it. Why don't you hold onto it this morning so you can look it over. I'll get it back from you before we break for lunch. Just be very careful with it; I had to promise him my firstborn if I didn't return it in perfect condition."

"I'll be careful. I'm going to be in pokey Judge Kaylor's courtroom. As slow as she is, I'll have plenty of time to review it between hearings." She took the album and walked to Department One.

Sabre found a seat in the back corner of the courtroom where she wouldn't be interrupted while she waited for her case to be called. She looked at the bright pink cover, untied the ribbon, and opened it. On the first page she saw a sonogram and the words, "Alexis' first photo." It had her footprints, her first artwork, and a photo of her every year on her birthday. It contained awards ranging from "The Sandbox Award" through "Best Citizen." The album held spelling-bee conquests, ribbons from sporting events, and poems Alexis had written. It captured Alexis' life from birth to present.

As Sabre studied the album, Bob walked in and took a seat next to her. She handed it to him. "Have a look at this. A lot of effort and love went into this album. Murdock obviously cares a great deal about his little girl, his 'pride and joy.'"

"Hmm . . . . He seems genuinely concerned about his

unborn child as well. If what he said about the fight is true, he has good reason for concern. Unfortunately, in this state, there isn't anything a father can really do until his baby is born. He certainly has no means to keep the mother from using if she decides to. He can't lock her up or place any kind of physical restraints on her to protect his child."

"I guess his frustration is understandable . . . if it's true."

CHAPTER 6

The sun had set and twilight faded enough to make the lights inside Sabre's office visible. After her experience on Saturday night, she felt relieved to have company. She entered through the back door, dropped her files on her desk, and walked to the front of the building to say hi to Elaine, the receptionist.

Sabre's office, furthest from the front entrance and the least desirable of the three, seemed perfect to her. Jack Snecker occupied the front office. He had first pick since he discovered the building, leased it for himself, and then sublet the office space to other attorneys. The building had once been a beautiful, old Victorian home. Fortunately, someone had the foresight to convert it to office space rather than tear it down. Jack's office, the largest, had once been the living room. It had a beautiful bay window across the front providing him a view of the street from his huge, antique mahogany desk and chairs. In front of the fireplace, a little settee and a couple of chairs created a cozy sitting area for guests.

"Hi Elaine," Sabre greeted the receptionist. "How has your day been going?"

"Not bad, actually," she responded with her dry sense of humor. "The copy machine broke down again, I spilled coffee on my desk and made a big mess, I accidentally hung up on Jack's wife when she called, but the good news is we've only had eight calls today from your favorite Looney tune, Crazy Carla. I don't know how you can deal with that woman. She ranted and raved about some nonsense. I couldn't make any sense of it."

"She has problems we can't even imagine, Elaine." Sabre sighed. "I'll call her in a minute and calm her down. Did you hear anything from the Atlanta Police Department?"

"Oh yeah, here's the fax and your mail." Elaine handed her the police report on Peggy Smith and the stack of mail she had opened for her. "One of the pages is not legible, though. I called and left a message, but it's late in Atlanta so you'll probably have to wait until tomorrow. I didn't speak to Detective Carriage. I left a message with some night clerk."

"Thanks, Elaine." Sabre took the report, along with the twenty-two pink slips containing phone messages, and went to her office. She shuffled through the pink slips as she walked down the hallway, pulling out the ones from Carla. When she returned to her desk, she called Carla. This task always took some time, but Sabre wanted it out of the way. It was a daily routine, not one she particularly enjoyed, but it had to be done even if every call was the same. Sabre would call; Carla would scream for a little while making no sense. After she rambled for five minutes or so, Carla would take a breath and Sabre would start talking to her about butterflies and green pastures. It always soothed her. Sabre couldn't remember when she had discovered how to do it, and although uncertain if it was the words or the way she had learned to deliver them, it calmed Carla down.

Today's call was no different. Sabre called her, and while Carla yelled, Sabre turned the volume down on her headset and started thumbing through her mail. Sabre hated that some tree had to die for all the junk mail. She separated the mail into stacks of bills, checks, correspondence needing to be filed, personal items, and the junk. Even though Elaine opened all the mail, Sabre still wanted to view everything coming in so she could decide what to keep and what to throw away.

She tossed the junk mail into the recycle trash bin, put the bills in a basket on her credenza, clipped together the checks and correspondence and placed them in a box for Elaine, and set her personal items in another basket on the corner of her desk to take home and look through later.

She heard Carla take a breath. Sabre turned up her volume and started to speak. She had to be quick or she would miss her opening. "Butterflies, green pastures, and butterflies," she began. "Carla, imagine yourself walking through the field and a beautiful purple and blue butterfly lights on your arm. You look around and you see little dots of color–pink, blue, red, and yellow–the tall, green grass moving ever so slightly in the light breeze, and a rainbow of multi-colored butterflies dancing across the pale blue sky. There's no one else in your world, just you and your butterflies wandering through your green pasture . . . ." Sabre went on until she heard Carla breathing comfortably and then she said, as she always did, "Don't worry, Carla. I'll take care of everything."

She hung up the phone and turned to the police report, anxious to see what it said. She read through the report twice, first to see if it contained anything significantly affecting the case, the second time, more slowly, looking for details she might have missed the first time. After the second reading, she called Marla.

"Marla, it's Sabre, your favorite attorney."

"True, but that's not saying a whole lot," she responded. "Whatcha got?"

"Did you get the report from Atlanta on the Murdock case?"

"It's somewhere on my desk here, but I haven't had a chance to read it yet. Anything exciting in it?"

"Well, Peggy does have a drug history. It looks like she's had a problem for some time. She's been arrested a couple of times for possession, once for pot and most recently for meth. . . . .a little over a year ago, about the same time she hooked up with Murdock. Do you happen to know how they met?"

"No, but I'll see what I can find out."

"By the way, I have an illegible page – page eight. It looks like it might be Peggy's family history sheet. Will you look at yours and see if you can read it?"

"Sure. I know it's here somewhere." Marla said. "Is there any bad news in there on Murdock?"

"No. He has no convictions, not even a traffic violation. He comes from a well-respected family in the area. The Murdocks own a good portion of the city and have been in local politics for generations. Gaylord Murdock has lived there most of his life. He left twice, once to go to college – to Harvard, no less – but returned right after graduation. It appears he may have left about five or six years ago and returned after about a year. I don't know for certain exactly when he left the second time."

"Any idea where he went?"

"No, not yet. I'll see what I can find, though, and maybe you could do the same. It's probably nothing, but he's so squeaky clean in Atlanta, I wonder if his political connections have something to do with it, or if he really is the 'good guy' he portrays. I've become so skeptical; I don't believe anything I read anymore and only half of what I see."

"I know the feeling, but you have good instincts, Sabre. I know you'll dig until you find what you're looking for. Just keep me informed if you can." Sabre could hear Marla shuffling through the papers on her desk. "Oh, here's the report. Let's see . . . page eight. No, sorry; I can't read mine either."

"By the way, how are Alexis and Jamie doing? Have you seen them recently?"

"Yeah, I went by this morning. They seem okay, but Alexis won't let Jamie out of her sight. She nearly panics when they're separated. She can't focus until she can see he's okay. I've seen siblings attached before, but this goes beyond that. You can see the fear in Alexis' eyes when she doesn't have a visual on him."

"You have to wonder what she's seen or heard that has made her so 'parentified.'" Sabre paused. "I think I'll go by and see her when I leave here. Maybe I'll take them for a bite to eat. Do you think I can get a car seat at Jordan? I don't expect I'll be able to take Alexis without Jamie."

"That's a given. I'll call over there and make sure they have one for you."

Sabre hung up the phone and read through the police report again. She jotted down a few questions she needed answers to.

Where did Gaylord Murdock go when he left Atlanta?
Does he have a record anywhere else?
How did he meet Peggy Smith?
Why does Alexis seem so protective of Jamie?
How did Peggy get hurt the night of the arrest?
Is she using drugs now while she's pregnant?

Finally, the ultimate question:

Is it safe to send the children home with Murdock?

She put down her note pad and dialed the Atlanta Police Department, "Detective Carriage, please."

"I'm sorry ma'am, but he's gone for the day. May I take your name and number and have him return the call tomorrow?" the person at the other end of the line responded in her sweet, southern accent.

Sabre gave the woman the information she requested along with her home and cell phone numbers. "If he calls in, please ask him to contact me. Oh, and please tell him not to worry about waking me up. I don't sleep much anyway."

Sabre took out her calendar and gathered together the files she needed for court the next day. As she started to go through the first case, Elaine walked into the office with her purse and jacket in her hand. "I'm calling it a day, Sabre. Jack and David have already gone. As usual, you are the last to leave."

"Goodnight, Elaine. See you tomorrow." Sabre heard the back door close and lock as Elaine left for the day. She buried herself back in the case.

She wrote a few notes on a form she'd designed for her hearings. She had a different color for each type of hearing so she could find things at a glance. It became especially helpful in the middle of a hearing. Everyone at court ragged on Sabre about her anal organizational skills, but whenever someone needed information on a case, they checked with her first.

She clipped the pink form on the right side of the Sanders file, closed it up, and started a separate stack of "ready files." She picked up the next case; pulled a green form for the disposition hearing and filled in the date, case name, and department number; and proceeded to read through the file to see what she needed to cover in court. She started to write something in the "requests" section of her form when . . . THUD. Something hit the wall. She muffled a scream. She stood and pulled the curtain back a bit. Total blackness. She grabbed her cell phone and dialed 9-1-1, ready to push "Send" if needed. Her heart pounded as she tiptoed to the back door. She lifted one slat in the blind very carefully and peered out into the parking area. The dim porch light provided little help. Sabre couldn't see anything and detected no movement. She stood still, watching for a few minutes. She took a deep breath, tried to dismiss it, and went back to her desk to finish preparing her cases for court.

Sabre reached for a pencil, but her trembling hand dropped it. She let it lay there and gathered up her files to leave. She peeked out the window again before she slowly opened the back door and looked around. When she decided everything was okay, Sabre stepped out, locked the back door behind her, and jumped in her car to leave. Once on the road, she began to breathe easier thinking how silly she had acted.

Sabre called Jordan Receiving Home to remind them she was taking Alexis and Jamie on a little excursion. Though her office was located only a few blocks away, by the time she parked and entered the building, the children were ready to go.

"Hi, Alexis, remember me?" she asked the little girl

standing there in a pretty yellow dress.

"Yeah, you're the lawyer and your name is Sabre. Are we really going to McDonald's?"

"Yes, we are. Do you like McDonald's?"

"I love their French fries. Can we get a kid's meal? Jamie likes to go there, too. He can have my toy if he wants." She turned to Jamie, "Come on, Jamie. Let's go."

"Okay, Alexis, we're ready. You bring Jamie and I'll get the car seat for him." Sabre saw Alexis gently take the hand of her little "brother." Sabre buckled Jamie in the back seat and Alexis watched as if to make sure it was done correctly. She sat down in the front seat, listening and responding whenever Jamie spoke.

"I'll show you where my office is," Sabre said. "We drive past it on the way." They drove three blocks, made a right turn, and half way up the block Sabre said, "There it is, on your right, the one with the bright lights in the front."

"You have a pretty office," Alexis said.

"Thank you."

They continued their conversation at McDonald's, Sabre being careful not to interrogate her. "Tell me about school in Atlanta. What did you like best about it?"

"My friend, Mattie," Alexis said. "She's my best friend in the whole world. We played with our Barbie dolls. She has more than I do, and she has lots of doll clothes, too. But mostly, we played school and I was the teacher. We didn't play with the other kids because they would tease Mattie and call her names because she couldn't hear and she talked kinda funny. I wonder who she plays with now. I sure miss her." Alexis always spoke fast, like she needed to make sure she could get it all in.

"Maybe you could write her a letter. Do you know her address?"

"Yeah, I'll write her a letter. She'd like that."

Sabre picked up her briefcase and took some paper, an envelope, and a stamp and handed them to Alexis. "Here's everything you need." Sabre pointed to the upper left corner and said, "You put your name here above mine and Mattie will know who the letter came from. If she writes you back, I'll bring the letter to you. Here's where Mattie's name and address go." Sabre wrote Mattie's first name on the envelope for her so she would know where to write it. "What's her last name?"

"Sturkey," Alexis said with a smile. "It's turkey with an 'S' in front. It's a funny name, but she can't help it. The other kids would gobble around her. She couldn't hear them, but she could see and she knew they were making fun of her. When I grow up, I want to take care of kids who can't hear, like Mattie. Maybe I can teach them things. I can sign, you know. Mattie taught me." Alexis spelled out her name in sign language. "A-l-e-x-i-s. That's my name. I can say other things too, like 'Good morning,' 'I love you,' and lots of other stuff. Mattie taught me something new every day."

"How long have you known Mattie?"

"Since we came back to Atlanta from . . .." Alexis caught herself and didn't finish her sentence. "She was in my class. I was new and she was real nice to me. We sat next to each other."

"It sounds like Mattie is a great friend. No wonder you miss her."

"Yeah, I miss her so much. She shared my bed, you know . . ." Alexis stopped talking for a second, looking at Sabre with her eyes wide open like she surprised herself. She picked up where she left off. ". . . whenever she would stay the night. She would stay sometimes. We'd have slumber parties, just the two of us."

"Did you ever stay at her house?"

"Nope. She only stayed at mine. Father doesn't like me to stay overnight anywhere. He doesn't like me staying at Jordan. He says I should be going home soon. Will I?" Her voice held little emotion.

"I'm not certain yet. We'll go back to court in a few days, and the judge will decide whether you can go home or if you need to stay out a little longer."

"But I'll go home sometime?" Alexis' expression did not change.

"Do you want to go back home to your father?"

"Sure. Who wouldn't want to go home to their father?" Obviously a canned response.

On the ride back to Jordan Receiving Home, Alexis chattered about things she had seen or heard while in the Home. She talked about new kids who had come in and others who had been there awhile. She seemed to know just about everything going on there.

By the time they arrived Jamie had fallen asleep, so Sabre took him out of the car seat and carried him in. She handed Jamie to one of the workers and turned to Alexis. "You have your paper and envelope to write to Mattie. If you can have the letter done, I'll swing by here tomorrow, pick it up, and get it in the mail for you. It should arrive in a couple of days. I'm sure she'll be happy to know you're thinking of her."

"I'll have it ready. She'll like getting a letter." Sabre detected sadness in her voice.

"Good night, Alexis. I enjoyed our time together."

Alexis took a step toward Sabre, and with her arms stretched out, reached up to hug her. Sabre reciprocated and Alexis held on for a couple seconds, then let go, said, "Bye," and ran back to her room with a staff member.

"She must like you a lot," said the attendant.

"Why's that?"

"Because, as long as she's been here, she has not allowed one staff member to hug her. She's a very lonely little girl."

CHAPTER 7

After court the next day, Sabre stopped by Jordan Receiving Home to pick up Alexis' letter to mail to Mattie. The two of them sat for awhile in the visiting room with Alexis jabbering away and Sabre listening. Alexis appeared to be comfortable at Jordan now, and she knew every staff member and every nook and cranny in the building. In the midst of her chatter, Alexis turned to Sabre and said, "I've been thinking. You know that confidential stuff you told me about. Is that really true? If I tell you something, you can't tell anyone?"

"That's absolutely right. You have my word. Why? Is there something you want to tell me?"

Alexis looked down at her feet and twisted her body back and forth. She remained silent for a few seconds and then said, "Nope. Just wondering."

"Well, if at any time you want to tell me a secret, you can be sure I'll keep it. I need to go now, but I'll see you soon. You have my card. If you want to talk, just give me a call. I wrote my cell phone on the back, so you can reach me any time." Alexis gave Sabre a quick hug, handed her the letter to mail to Mattie, and walked off, babbling to the attendant.

Sabre stopped at the post office and mailed Alexis' letter on her way back to her office. Elaine greeted her when she walked in. "Here's your mail and your phone messages. Detective Carriage just called a few minutes ago. I told him you'd be in shortly. Carla must be taking extra meds; I haven't heard from her yet today."

"Thanks, Elaine. I'll call just the same and make sure she's all right."

Sabre passed David's office on the way back to hers and saw him sitting at his desk. David had moved into the middle office right after Jack leased the building. He and David had known each other in law school and had both worked for the same insurance defense firm after graduation.

She stopped for a minute to chat. She seldom saw him because he spent little time in the office. He had tired of practicing law and stayed away as much as he could, spending his free time helping his wife in her ice cream shop. Sabre listened to David complain about working too many hours and his plan to quit practicing, but she had been hearing the same story since she moved in. She doubted he would ever leave.

Back in her office, Sabre dialed the phone. "Hello, Detective Carriage. This is Attorney Sabre Brown. We spoke last Saturday morning."

"Yes, ma'am, I recall, and I want to apologize again for waking you."

"No need to. I needed to get up anyway. You did me a favor," Sabre reassured him. "You called a bit ago. Did you get any information for me on Murdock or Smith?"

"Yes, ma'am, I did, but I don't know if it'll help. As you know, the Murdocks are very well-liked and respected in this town. There's not a one of them, including Gaylord, with any kind of criminal record. They're pretty powerful, though, so I'm not certain any record would remain if they ever did get in trouble. Gaylord married a beautiful, local woman named Elizabeth Sterling about ten years ago. Some say Gaylord married way below his class."

"Below his class?" Sabre replied, with obvious indignation in her voice.

"Ma'am, you have to understand. This is the South. People here still think that way. Elizabeth didn't come from old money. Heck, she didn't come from any money – not exactly trailer trash, but not a socialite either. Her father taught at a local high school and her mother worked in a bank. Anyway, about five years ago she disappeared. It seems she dropped Alexis off at her mother's house on her way to the gym, but she never made it there. The department investigated every lead they had on her disappearance, but nothing ever materialized."

"Was Gaylord a suspect?"

"No, ma'am. No one thought for a minute he had anything to do with it. Nothing in the file indicated he might be involved, and Gaylord seemed devastated by his loss. He appeared distraught and genuinely upset about the whole ordeal. From all outward appearances at least, he was a very loving husband and father. He and his wife seemed to be the perfect couple. No one ever saw them fight. If they did, it was out of the public's eye."

"Seems almost too good to be true."

"Not really, ma'am. Well-bred southerners don't generally fight in public," he instructed her on their culture. "But here's the odd thing. Yesterday, my boss approached me about looking at the file and told me in no uncertain terms to 'leave the past in the past.' Then later, when I went to look something up in the file again, it was gone. I've had a clerk looking for it all day, but it seems to have disappeared."

"That's odd," Sabre said, but she thought it equally odd he had tried to look in it again after his boss told him not to.

"Well, we'll see if it shows up. In the meantime, I've made an appointment to speak with Ruby Sterling tomorrow afternoon. I'll let you know what I find out."

"Please don't get me wrong, because I really appreciate your help, but why are you doing all this?"

"I just want to make sure those children are safe, ma'am. Isn't that what you want?"

"It sure is. Thanks, and I'll let you know if I find out anything more on my end. Oh, by the way. Would you please check the report you sent us and resend page eight? Mine was illegible."

"Sorry about that. I'll send it again."

Sabre hung up the phone, wondering why Detective Carriage was being so helpful. Maybe that's just more of the "southern way."

Sabre returned the rest of her calls, checked on Carla, then gathered up her files and left for the day. For the first time in months, she left the office before the others.

~~~

On Monday, Sabre spent most of the day in court. She had a jurisdictional trial in the afternoon. She represented a non-offending mother, which meant she didn't have to do much. Her thoughts turned to the Murdock case. About a quarter to three, the court took a recess. Sabre called her office, hoping to have a message from Detective Carriage regarding Ruby Sterling. It had been almost a week since she had last spoken with him. Either he didn't have anything to report, or he was just too busy to call. Elaine read her the list of calls. No message from Carriage.

By the time Sabre returned to the office, everyone had already left. Elaine had placed a stack of phone messages and her opened mail on Sabre's desk. Sabre laid her files down and started through her routine. First, she separated out all of Carla's messages, eleven of them today – not the record of seventeen, but a bad day nevertheless. She punched in number four on the automatic dialer and heard Carla's voice on the other end ranting, as usual. Sabre turned the volume down like she always did and commenced sorting her mail.

On the top of her stack of mail lay Alexis' letter to Mattie, marked "ADDRESS UNKNOWN" across the front in big, red letters. Sabre wondered if Mattie had moved or if Alexis had just written the address incorrectly. Sabre sat, staring at the letter, flipping it over and over again in her hand, tempted to read it in order to learn more about Alexis and hopefully provide her better representation. However, the private, personal letter belonged to her client, and reading it would undermine the trust her client had in her. While those thoughts went through her mind, she realized she had pulled the letter out of the envelope and unfolded it. Her eyes caught the greeting. It read, *"Dear Honey, I'm sorry...."*

"What am I doing?" Sabre said aloud and quickly folded the letter back up, stuck it in the envelope, and set it aside.

She heard the pitch in Carla's voice start to lower and the speech pattern slow down. Sabre knew Carla would take a short hiatus from her ranting soon and she would have a few seconds to cut in so she prepared for her counseling session. "Butterflies and green pastures . . . ." Sabre said. When Carla seemed calm enough, Sabre hung up the phone. She would be all right for a while. She wished she could do more for her.

Sabre tapped the receiver for a dial tone and made another call. "Detective Carriage, this is Attorney Sabre Brown."

"Hello, ma'am, I was just about to call you. Sorry I took so long, but I was hoping I'd have more to report. Ruby Sterling refused to see me. I could've gone over there, but I doubt she would have told me anything. She doesn't have much trust in the Atlanta Police Department. You may want to give her a call. I think she has a genuine interest in her granddaughter's welfare. Maybe she'll talk to you."

"Okay, I'll try," Sabre said. "Detective, would I be imposing too much to ask you to check out one more thing?"

"I'd be delighted, ma'am. What do you want me to do?"

"Well, Alexis wrote a letter to her best friend, Mattie, and it came back. She was her classmate. Perhaps you could see why the letter returned and maybe check with the school as well to see what you can learn about her."

"I can. Has Alexis tried calling her friend?"

"No. Mattie's deaf. That's why I suggested she write to her."

"I'll take care of it right away. What's her name and address?"

"Her name is Mattie Sturkey."

"Are you sure the last name is Sturkey?"

"Yes. Alexis even explained it is spelled turkey with an 'S' on the front. Why?"

"Because Ruby Sterling's maiden name is Sturkey. Something's not right. I'll check out the address as soon as we hang up. First thing in the morning, I'll go over to the school. I'll call you tomorrow. Oh, what's the address?"

Sabre gave him the address, and he gave her Ruby's phone number. Sabre hung up the phone and called Ruby Sterling. A voice on the other end said, "Hello."

"Hello, may I speak to Ruby Sterling, please?"

"Who is this?" the woman said curtly.

"My name is Sabre Brown. I'm the attorney for Alexis Murdock. I'm calling from California," Sabre stated as politely as she could.

"Ruby's not here. Bye."

"Wait!" Sabre said before she hung up. "Please ask her to call me. It's very important. Her granddaughter needs help."

"Okay, what's the number?" the woman said, still sounding agitated.

Sabre gave her the number, thanked her, and hung up. Before she could make another call, the phone rang.

"Hi Marla, what's up?"

"I wanted to give you the latest info on the Murdock case. Peggy gave birth to a baby girl this morning and she was born positive."

"So she was using drugs like Alexis and her father said," Sabre mused. "How's the baby?"

"She's so tiny. She only weighed six pounds. She's going through some withdrawals, mostly restlessness, and she isn't sucking very well. No signs of fetal abnormalities or convulsions, so she could be worse, but she'll have to stay in the hospital for a few days anyway."

Sabre cringed. The baby would likely have severe tremors, eating problems, restless sleep, and a lot of pain. In addition, who knows what damage the drugs would cause down the road?

"What did they name her?"

"Haley. Haley Murdock."

"Pretty name," Sabre said. "So, how's Gaylord reacting?"

"He's pretty upset at Peggy. I can't say as I blame him."

"Do you think he uses?"

"It's hard to say. There haven't been any indications of it so far. He's been drug testing for the past couple of weeks now and has had nothing but clean tests."

"I assume you're filing a petition on the new baby?" It was more of a statement than a question.

"Yes, the detention hearing is set for Thursday. I don't think the baby will be released from the hospital before then, but if she is she'll be detained in a foster home. The mother says she'll get into a drug program, but we'll see what she actually does. The father wants the baby home with him. Since they're not married we'll need to establish paternity first. He seems to be a pretty decent guy from all outward appearances. It looks like he's been a good parent to Alexis. She never says anything bad about him. So, if everything checks out, maybe we can get those kids in his care. The problem is Jamie isn't his child, and it'll break Alexis' heart to separate them."

"And hard on Jamie, too," Sabre said.

"Anything new from Atlanta?"

"Nothing concrete, but I have a call into Alexis' maternal grandmother and Detective Carriage is checking on the school for me. I hope we have some information before the detention hearing." Sabre loathed the tough calls, dealing with people's lives, knowing her decisions could affect them forever. She hated this part of her job, but she hated it even more when people in her position didn't care.

For the next couple of hours, Sabre prepared her other cases, but her mind kept returning to Alexis. Mattie's last name being Sturkey seemed pretty strange. With a name that unusual, she had to be related. If so, she wondered if Alexis knew. If she did, why didn't she mention it? The greeting of the letter really nagged at her, *Dear Honey.* She tried to think of the reasons why Alexis would call her best friend "honey." It must be just some term of endearment. After all, Sabre often used it herself with her buddy Bob. Reading the letter might give her the answer, but she resisted the temptation.

Sabre got ready to leave for court. She felt comfort in the fact nothing odd had happened tonight at the office. It seemed there had been something strange every night she had worked late for the past few weeks.

When Sabre reached the back door to leave, she noticed the porch light was out. She reached for the switch to flip it up, but it was already in the "on" position. She set her files down, walked over to the cupboard, and took out a light bulb and a flashlight. She turned the flashlight on, but nothing happened. "Damn it," she said out loud, remembering she forgot to buy batteries.

Though not afraid of the dark, Sabre felt some trepidation after all the things happening at the office recently. She cautiously opened the door and looked around. Seeing nothing, she reached up to unscrew the bulb; it jiggled. When she tightened it, the light came on. Just then, the phone rang and Sabre jumped. She jerked her arm back inside, slammed the door, and locked it. She took a deep breath, exhaled, and answered the phone. No one responded. Her hand shook as she hung up the phone. Her heart pounded like a drum in her chest, and her muscles tightened. She had to tell herself to breathe.

"Okay, Sabre," she said, as she breathed deeply, "it's time to calm down. It's just a stupid, loose light bulb and a wrong number. Stop acting crazy."

She sat down at her desk for a few minutes to gain composure. Once her hands stopped shaking, she picked her files back up, walked to the door, and looked out again. With her key in her hand she stepped outside. Still looking around, she locked the door and darted to her car, feeling a mixture of fear and paranoia as she drove away.

CHAPTER 8

At 6:43 a.m. Sabre found a parking spot in front of Clara's Kitchen, her favorite breakfast spot. Bob would arrive any minute. His son, Corey, had to be at school at 6:30 on Thursdays for band practice, so Bob would drop him off. He and Sabre met at Clara's Kitchen for breakfast every Thursday before court.

It was a little, family-owned restaurant where the locals ate. The building, an old, two-story house, had once been a bed and breakfast. Clara Johnson, the original owner, began renting out rooms after her husband passed away. Her seven children were mostly grown by then and several of them had moved out, leaving empty bedrooms. Eventually, she stopped renting out the rooms and converted the entire downstairs into a restaurant. Clara continued to live on the second floor with her granddaughter, Maggie, who had come to live with her after the child's parents had been killed in a car accident when she was three years old. She grew up in Clara's Kitchen and learned all her secret recipes, recipes Clara shared with no one else. Maggie, twenty-four-years old when Clara passed away, loved the Kitchen as much as her grandmother had and worked hard to keep it going in her honor.

Sabre walked in and sat at her usual table by the window so she could see Grandma Clara's flower garden. She had a standing reservation. Instead of calling in each week, she only called when she couldn't make it.

When the waitress came over to her table, Sabre exchanged pleasantries with her and ordered a black coffee for Bob and a decaf for herself. "Fill the cup one-third of the way with the coffee and then fill it up with warm, non-fat milk, please." The waitress laid the menus on the table and left to get the coffee. Sabre knew the menu by heart so she seldom looked at it anymore. Instead, she gazed out the window at the rows of snapdragons in yellow, pink, purple, and white, the bright pink petunias, the pansies of every color, and a beautiful patch of blue flowers she couldn't identify, about six inches high and two feet in diameter, surrounded on three sides by rose bushes that seemed to bloom all year long. Lost in the sea of color, she didn't notice Bob until he took a seat across from her.

"Good morning, Mr. Clark. I was just admiring the flowers. They seem particularly bright this morning," Sabre said in her best Katherine Hepburn voice. "Did you get Corey off to school okay?"

"Sure did." Bob took a sip of the coffee. He tipped his cup slightly in her direction, "Thanks," he said. She smiled and nodded. Bob continued on his favorite subject, his son. "Corey really enjoys the band. He's decided he wants to play the saxophone. This is the first thing that has held his interest for any length of time, so I try to encourage him. He has already decided what sax he wants, a Yamaha Professional, but he's not getting it. At least not right now. After he has played for a year, if he's still interested and practicing, we'll get him a good sax, maybe even the Yamaha."

Ahh . . . the sax. Sabre slipped back in time to her childhood and her first encounter with Victor Spanoli, her little saxophone-playing friend, the memory of their meeting as vivid to her as the flowers in Clara's garden.

It was Sabre's sixth birthday. After the gifts had been opened, she and her twin cousins carried them to her room to play with her new toys. They had just started playing a game of "Chutes and Ladders" when Ron burst into the room. "Sabre, come see. We have new neighbors."

The children ran to the porch to see who was taking the place of "Old Man Meridian," the grumpy old goose who yelled at them every time they got close to his yard. They stood out front and watched the new family unload the truck taking up their entire driveway. Sabre climbed up on the edge of the white wooden porch and stretched her neck to see around her brother. "Do they have kids?"

"Yeah, there's an older girl and a little boy, about your age, a mother and father and a dog," Ron replied, as if he already knew them. "And they're Italian." Ron repeated something he had heard his mother say.

"What's an Italian?"

"Mom met the parents the other day. She said their names are Lois and Salvatore Spanoli. They just moved here from New York," Ron said, ignoring her question.

"What's an Italian?" Sabre asked again.

Ron, unsure himself, explained, "It means they eat spaghetti and pizza."

"We eat spaghetti and pizza. Are we Italian?"

"No, dopey, we're Catholic!" Ron pointed toward the truck and a golden retriever. "Look, there's the boy. And look at that great dog! I wish we had a dog."

They watched the new neighbors for a while, but soon got bored with them going in and out of the house carrying boxes. All four of them marched to the backyard to re-join the party just in time to catch Aunt Sallie drag her long, gray pigtail through the punch bowl. The party continued throughout the day and into the evening. The twins and their parents even stayed the night to avoid the long drive back to Bakersfield. Sabre's party was perfect, and she had lots of toys and some new clothes to wear to school.

On Monday morning, as Sabre skipped off to school, she felt special in her new pink blouse and Winnie the Pooh overalls. She spent the day telling her classmates about her party. At 2:25 p.m., just like every other day, Ron waited outside her classroom. He walked her home, dropped her at the front door, then ran off to play with his friends.

Sabre took her jump rope and went out in the front yard to try and see the new neighbors. She gazed into their yard as she skipped around the driveway. When she didn't see anything, she sat on the front porch and played with her jacks, in case anyone came out.

She spotted the skinny boy with black, wavy hair as he came out of his front door carrying something shiny. It threw off flashes of bright light as the sun hit it. He looked straight at her, but just as she stood up to go say "hello" he disappeared into his backyard. A few minutes later he returned. With his head down, he walked across her lawn towards her with his saxophone in one hand and the other hand behind his back. About three feet from her he stopped, pulled his hand from behind his back, handed her a small bunch of dandelions, and said, "I'm Victor."

"I'm Sabre." But before she could say anything else he raised his saxophone to his lips and tooted a few notes sounding a little like "Hot Cross Buns," and turned and ran home. Sabre smiled. She saw his beautiful, dark eyes sparkle when he blew his horn.

She jumped up, ran inside, and placed the dandelions in a vase with some water, as she had helped her mother do many times with their roses. Then she ran to her room and picked up the little red notebook Ron had given her for her birthday. She was going to put all her wishes in it, and she wanted to get started. She went to the desk in the den, found a red pen, and sat down at the kitchen table while her mother fixed dinner. She picked up the pen and said, "Mom, how do you spell marry?"

"That depends, is it the name Mary, or the wedding kind of marry?"

"The wedding kind."

"M-a-r-r-y."

Sabre wrote each letter in her notebook as her mother said them. "How do you spell Victor?"

"Who's Victor?"

"The boy next door. I just met him. He brought me flowers and he plays music."

Her mother chuckled as she spelled Victor and then

Spanoli for her daughter.

Victor and Sabre played together every day. They walked home from school together, with Ron teasing them most of the way. They had their afternoon snack together, sometimes at her house and sometimes at his. Then Sabre would go to her room, do her homework, wait for Victor to finish practicing his sax, and they would play together until dinner.

One Sunday afternoon, a couple years later, Sabre and Victor were walking home from a skating party. A few blocks before they reached their street, a fire truck sped past with its siren blaring. They ran to keep up with it. They couldn't see any smoke, but they saw the truck turn up the street toward their homes.

Out of breath, they arrived at Victor's house and saw the fire truck parked in his driveway. An ambulance, with its lights flashing and siren blasting, pulled up next to it. Neighbors came out of their homes and people crowded around. Men in uniforms ran in and out of the front door.

Sabre's mom met them at the sidewalk and tried to talk to Victor, but he ran past her into the house. As Sabre and others watched, the paramedics carried Victor's father out on a stretcher, placed him in the ambulance, and rushed off with the sirens still screaming.

"He died before they arrived at the hospital," her mother said at the dinner table.

Sabre didn't see Victor again until the funeral. She tried to speak with him, but he wouldn't leave his mother's side. She wanted to do something for him, but she didn't know what to do. Everyone there was crying, except Victor, but the sparkle was gone from his eyes.

Following the service, everyone gathered at the Spanoli's home for lunch. Victor went out in the backyard and she followed him out. "You look sad," she said, "but you don't cry. How come?"

"I'm the man of the family now." Then he ran off to be alone, but not before Sabre saw his wet eyes.

A few days later, Victor came to her house to tell her they

were moving to a place called Chicago where Mrs. Spanoli's family lived. Sabre had never heard of Chicago and had no idea how far away it was. She just knew he wouldn't be next door, and it made her sad.

The following Saturday afternoon he came to say good-bye. He handed her the only three dandelions he could find in his yard. Sabre wanted to tell him how much she would miss him, but the tears filled her eyes and no words came out. She heard Mrs. Spanoli yell at Victor to get in the car. Before Victor left, he said, "Don't worry, Sabre. I'll be back to get you."

She stared at the car as it drove onto the street, with a saxophone sticking out the side. Victor had rolled his window down and played her his last tune. She never saw or heard from him again.

Ron walked over to her, put his arm around her, gave her a good squeeze, and said, "Hey, Sunshine, you still have me. I won't ever leave you." It made her feel better to know she still had her brother. Even though he teased her a lot, he did a lot of really sweet things, too. Whenever she got mad at him, her mom would tell the story about when she came home from the hospital and how Ron would go into the nursery first thing every morning and kiss his baby sister on the cheek. He continued to do that as long as they both lived at home. Even if he had a friend stay the night, he would still go to her, but she didn't get the kiss; instead, she got a flick on the head.

"Sobs? You in there?"

"Sorry, just thinking about someone."

"Is it Ron?"

"It's always Ron." She sighed, took a sip of coffee, and forced a smile.

Bob patted her hand and made a funny face at her. "So, you have the Haley Murdock detention this morning. I hear old Gaylord is doing everything the social worker asks him to do. Tom Gilley said he hasn't missed a drug test, he's taking his parenting and anger-management classes, and he got a job as a loan officer. His methamphetamine, gazelle girlfriend may have been lying about him ever hitting her. You can't blame the guy for being upset with her for using drugs while she was pregnant."

"Yeah, he sure is doing everything by the book, and he's very pleasant. He hasn't ticked anyone off like our perps usually do, either," Sabre said.

"I know this new baby can't go home with him until paternity is established, but what about Alexis? Do you think she'll go home at the next hearing?"

"I don't know. I have a lot of puzzle pieces that don't fit together, but if something doesn't break soon, I won't have any basis for keeping her out of the home. I'd really like to think he'd protect Alexis, but something in my gut tells me otherwise. By the way, what's the story with your client, Jamie's father?"

"Well, as you know, he's in an institution in Atlanta. It's reported he took some bad drugs a few years ago and fried his brain. I spoke to him on the phone, but we couldn't have a coherent conversation. The guy doesn't even know his own name. He thinks he's Mr. Rogers, and he goes around singing, 'It's a beautiful day in the neighborhood.' The damage he did to himself is permanent, so there's no chance of him as a placement for Jamie."

The waitress came back to the table and took their orders. Sabre liked nearly everything on the menu and ordered depending on her mood, but Bob ordered the same thing every time. The waitress didn't bother to ask anymore. Sometimes she would say, "The usual?" Most of the time, she just brought his order out when she brought Sabre's.

While they ate their breakfast, Bob spoke about Corey's progress in school and the new kitten they had acquired. They talked about how the stock market had been dropping and gave each other advice on cases. They discussed the strange things happening at Sabre's office, and they laughed and joked about some of the bizarre things that occur every day at juvenile court.

"I guess we better get to court if we want a parking

spot," Bob said.

"Yup, it's time." They each paid for their own breakfast as they always did, except on their birthdays; then the other one would pick up the check. They left the restaurant and drove to court in their separate cars.

Bob and Sabre went to different courtrooms to take care of their respective cases. By eleven o'clock they were called into Department Four for the Murdock detention hearing on the newborn. It didn't take long. Peggy's attorney, Russ Jensen, appeared on her behalf. It had been three days since the birth of the baby and Peggy had not yet checked into a drug rehabilitation facility like the social worker had encouraged her to do. She assured everyone she would go to a program soon, leaving the judge unimpressed.

Murdock's attorney, on the other hand, presented the court with paperwork on all the programs in which his client had been participating. He hadn't missed a single appointment and continued to test clean. The judge ordered a paternity test for Gaylord and ordered Haley into foster care upon her release from the hospital. He made a few other routine orders, then combined Haley's case with Alexis' and Jamie's jurisdictional hearing for the following week.

Sabre liked appearing in Department Four. She liked the entire staff, the clerk, the court reporter, Judge Cheney and, of course, Mike, the bailiff. Before she left the courtroom, she stopped to talk with Mike to hear the scoop on his daughter's latest accomplishments.

By a quarter past eleven, Sabre had finished her morning calendar. Since she didn't have a trial scheduled for the afternoon, she had the rest of the day to work in her office, a rare occasion.

"Sobs, we lunching today?" Bob asked.

"Sure. Just come by my office when you finish your calendar. We'll go to Pho's."

CHAPTER 9

Detective Carriage discovered the address Sabre provided for Mattie Sturkey belonged to someone named Jerry Fermer. He had been living there for several months. The resident didn't know any Sturkeys or anyone named Mattie. Prior to Fermer, the house was inhabited by Gaylord Murdock. Joe checked out the neighborhood in a five-block radius and ran any similar addresses, but he didn't find anything appearing to house Mattie Sturkey. Detective Carriage decided to go to the school and obtain the address from the school records and perhaps talk to Alexis' and Mattie's teacher.

It started to rain just as Detective Carriage pulled into the elementary school parking lot. He had left in a hurry that morning without his umbrella, so he dashed to the school office. Soaking wet by the time he reached the door, he cursed himself under his breath for not being prepared. He took his badge out of his wet pocket and showed it to the secretary. "Good morning, ma'am. I need to speak with a teacher about a couple of students. Their names are Alexis Murdock and Mattie Sturkey. Alexis is no longer enrolled. Mattie may or may not be."

A big smile crossed the secretary's face. "I remember Alexis, quite a precocious little girl, but Mattie Sturkey is unfamiliar to me. Let me check to see what rooms they were in."

"They both had the same teacher, I believe, and Sturkey is spelled S-t-u-r-k-e-y," Detective Carriage added.

The secretary checked her computer and said, "Alexis' last teacher was Mrs. Wall, but I can't find any records on Mattie Sturkey. Are you sure you're spelling it correctly?"

"Yes, ma'am, turkey with an 'S' on the front."

"I'm sorry, but I can't find that student at all. Perhaps she's registered under a different name, but there's nothing under Sturkey. You can ask Alexis' teacher. She may be able to tell you something."

"Thank you, ma'am. I will."

"Mrs. Wall is in Room A-13." The secretary pointed to a door across the room and continued with the directions. "You go through that door and turn right. When you reach the end of this building, turn right again. You'll be looking at Building A. The room on the corner is number thirteen. You'll have overhang most of the way, so you shouldn't get too wet." She picked up the phone, glanced at his dripping hair and grinned at the puddle he had created. "I'll call her room. She'll be expecting you."

"Thank you, ma'am."

In Room A-13, Detective Carriage saw a slightly overweight, maternal-looking woman with salt-and-pepper hair and a kind face standing near the teacher's desk. She wore a green cotton dress, hitting her about mid-calf, and thick, rubber-soled shoes serving more for comfort than style. She looked like the kind of teacher every fourth grader would love to have.

"Good morning, ma'am. Are you Mrs. Wall?"

"Yes, I am. You must be Detective Carriage. What can I do for you?"

"I need some information on a student you used to have in your classroom and her best friend. The student is Alexis Murdock, and her friend is Mattie Sturkey. Do you remember them?"

She smiled as she responded, "Alexis was only in my classroom for a couple of months, but I remember her well. She's not the kind of student you forget. Have you seen her? Is she okay?"

"No, I haven't seen her, but I have it on good authority she's fine, ma'am. No need to worry. Can you tell me about her?"

"Alexis was the kind of student that makes me love to teach. So inquisitive, she always had to know why and how things worked. Very kind and loving, as well. She enjoyed helping the other students, and was always so well mannered."

"What about her friend Mattie? Is she still in your class?"

"I don't have a student named Mattie. I never have that I can recall."

"Well, this little girl was apparently Alexis' best friend. She sat right next to her in class."

"Alexis sat right here." She walked over to a desk in the front row nearest the window and touched it. "There were boys sitting nearest her. As for her best friend, she didn't seem to have one. Everyone liked Alexis, but no one really got close to her."

"Mattie was deaf. Did you have any deaf students in your class?"

"No, I haven't had a child with a hearing problem for a couple of years now. But Alexis did work with the speech teacher every week. You may want to talk to her."

"Did Alexis have a speech problem?"

"No, she just volunteered to work with her, and since she was such a good student, I let her leave the classroom several times a week to help with the other students."

"Thank you, ma'am. I appreciate all your help."

"My pleasure. I hope everything is going to be okay for Alexis. If you see her, please tell her hello."

"I'll do that, ma'am. Where's the speech teacher's classroom?"

"It's two buildings over." She pointed towards a building that would take him even further away from the parking lot in the torrential rain. "Just a second – let me call to see if Ms. Bilby is in her room before you walk all the way over there."

"One more thing." Detective Carriage stopped and turned. "Did you ever meet her father?"

"Yes, a couple of times, actually. He came to our first parent-teacher conference — a very pleasant man and extremely interested in her progress. He appeared to be very good about follow-up with homework and assigned projects. Mr. Murdock went on a field trip with us once, and he proved to be a tremendous help, very patient with the children. A little boy in his group had ADD and Mr. Murdock was gentle, yet firm, with him. The little boy adored him and responded well. It made the trip much more pleasant for all of us. Other than that, I couldn't tell you much. I know the family, of course. You can't live in Atlanta and not know the Murdocks."

"What about his girlfriend, Peggy Smith? Did you meet her?"

"No. I don't recall Mr. Murdock or Alexis ever mentioning a girlfriend."

"Thanks again, ma'am." He followed her directions to see the speech teacher, hitting only one section where he had to sprint to avoid the downpour.

Ms. Bilby was waiting for him when he arrived. "Hi Detective, how can I help you?"

"I need some information on Alexis Murdock. Do you remember her?"

"Very well. She helped me a lot. She would come to my class a couple of times a week to work with the students. Alexis was especially interested in helping the ones with hearing problems."

"Do you know a student named Mattie Sturkey?"

"I have a first grader named Mattie. In fact, Alexis tutored her more than the others. But her last name isn't Sturkey."

"Could it be a family name or stepparent's name do you think? I know sometimes these children use a different name at home than they use at school."

"If it is, there's no indication of it in her file. We're doing some more testing on her next week, so I just went through her file and the name 'Sturkey' isn't in there anywhere. I pay very close attention to the family history because I'm always looking for anyone who may be able to communicate with the student. It's an odd name, so I'm sure I would've noticed it."

"Do you know if Alexis spent time with Mattie outside your classroom?"

"That's not likely, since Mattie is bused in from another school to work with me. They don't have the resources in her school. About seventy percent of my students come from other schools."

Detective Carriage walked over to a large, pink playhouse with lots of pink accessories. "You have quite a collection here," he commented.

"Yes, the little girls love the Barbie's. Mattie and Alexis spent a lot of time there. It provided a comfortable environment for both of them. They worked hard at communicating with the dolls."

"Is there anything else you can tell me about Alexis?"

"Well, I don't want to diminish her good intentions, because she really liked helping the students, but I think her primary goal was to learn sign language. She'd spend recesses and lunches with me, sometimes helping me with things in the classroom. In exchange, I would teach her something new each time. She learned a lot from Mattie, too. Although she never said, I think she knew someone else with a hearing problem."

"Maybe she just wanted to learn to sign so she could talk to Mattie and the other students," he said.

"I don't think so because when she came to me to help out, she wanted to make sure I knew how to sign before she volunteered. We have a lot of students with speech problems, the majority of which are not due to lack of hearing, but Alexis only wanted to work with the hearing impaired. I'm quite certain she knew someone who was deaf."

"Thank you, ma'am, you've been a big help." He handed her his card. "If you come up with anything else you think I should know, please give me a call."

Detective Carriage hurried to his car through the pouring rain. He had cover for most of the way, but as he approached the parking lot he had about sixty feet without protection. By the time he reached his car, he looked like he'd been for a swim. He drove back to the station to dry out, assess the information he had gathered, and call Attorney Brown to share it with her.

CHAPTER 10

A frazzled Elaine handed Sabre a stack of pink slips as she walked into her office. "It's not even noon yet. What's going on?" Sabre asked, as she thumbed through the slips. "There must be forty messages here."

"Forty-two to be exact," Elaine replied. "Twenty-two are from Crazy Carla; that's five more than she's ever done before, and she did it all before noon. There are seven more from the facility where Carla lives, three from Detective Carriage, and the rest are from people who seem to have something else to do with their time besides call you. I'd suggest you call and check on Carla first. She seems to be having a pretty bad day. They want you to come over there and see if you can calm her down."

"Thanks, Elaine. I'll call right away. Did Detective Carriage leave any details?"

"No, he just thought you'd be very interested to hear what he found out."

Sabre called Carla, but no one could get her to take the phone. Phylis, Carla's caseworker, pleaded with Sabre to come over and talk to her in person.

Sabre called Bob's cell. When he saw her name come up on his caller ID he answered, "Hi, Sobs. What's up?"

"I was trying to catch you before you left court so you didn't drive over here. I won't be able to do lunch. I need to go see Carla. She's been flipping out all morning and they need my help with her."

"Too late. I'm just around the corner from your office, but I don't need to eat. Would you like some company?"

"I'd love it. Thanks."

"I'm pulling up at your back door right now. I'll even drive. Come on out." Bob took a final drag off his cigarette and put it out before Sabre got in the car.

"I really appreciate your going with me." Sabre sighed as she got into Bob's car. "You've met Carla, haven't you?"

"Yeah, I went with you about a year ago when you dropped something off for her; I can't remember what. She acted pretty normal that day, though."

"Carla has been in this assisted living facility for about two years now. She doesn't qualify for hospital care, and physically she's very capable of caring for herself. Most of the time she functions just fine, but something set her off this morning and no one can figure out what. You know, the majority of the time she acts just fine, but sometimes reality is a stretch for her. Her therapist says she's improving."

"I don't put much stock in therapy, as you well know. If I ever end up in the loony bin, make sure they pump me full of good drugs so at least I think I'm happy," Bob said.

Phylis met Sabre at the door. Together they walked to Carla's room. "Carla had breakfast this morning in the dining area and everything seemed okay. In fact, she seemed to be having a better than usual day. She was sitting at a table in the back of the room. All of a sudden she jumped up, knocked over her water glass, and ran across the room. She bumped into a table and almost fell down. People scurried out of her way, but she ran into a woman and her tray went flying. Carla darted out the door and looked up and down the hallway. She flung doors open and looked in rooms as if she were trying to find someone. Then she went back to her room and started searching through her drawers." Phylis stopped speaking just before they reached Carla's room. "Here we are," she said. Before she opened the door she added, "The doctor gave her a sedative, so she's calmer now."

Sabre and Bob followed her into Carla's room, where they saw an attendant sitting in a chair at the foot of her bed and Carla on her twin bed in a fetal position. She lay up against the wall on top of her pillow with her knees in her face and her arms wrapped around her long legs, whimpering like a hurt puppy. The drawers were open on her dresser. Papers and clothes were strewn across the room. On the wall, in big black letters and in Carla's handwriting, read the words, "I'm here. Come find me."

Sabre sat down next to her and cautiously placed her hand on Carla's back, fearful of how she would react. She had never seen her like this. Carla let out a little whimper, but she didn't pull away. Sabre stroked her arm and back, saying, "Carla, it's Sabre. I'm here to help you. It's going to be okay now." She continued to speak to her in the same tone she always used on the phone.

Carla seemed to be comforted by her voice. Her whimpers decreased and she mumbled, "Budfries."

Everyone else looked puzzled, but Sabre knew what she wanted and she began, "Butterflies and green pastures are all around you. In the distance is a sea of golden buttercups. The butterflies are everywhere, dancing on the thick, green grass. Oh, so much color . . ." After about five minutes, the whimpering had ceased and all they could hear was Carla's breathing pattern, the soft sound of slumber.

Sabre continued to sit with her for a few more minutes in silence. She sighed as she stood up and looked around, trying to assess what happened. As she walked around the room, picking up Carla's things and putting them away, she read over and over again what she had written on the wall, but she couldn't make sense of it.

They left the room; only the attendant remained in her chair, keeping an eye on Carla. Phylis, Sabre, and Bob walked in silence until they reached the waiting room at the end of the corridor. Sabre said, "Do you have any idea what she was looking for?"

"No, but it was as if she saw something or someone when she ran from the dining area. I think when she got to her room, she created the mess looking for something to write with, but I'm guessing. None of us can figure what she tried to convey with the message she wrote on the wall. We may be trying to put too much logic into it, but she's never acted like this before. She rants for awhile every day, but for the most part she's not a problem."

"Did she say anything to anyone?" Bob inquired.

"Not really, at least nothing that made any sense. When she ran out of the dining area, she screamed, 'run, run, run' over and over again. She continued screaming as she ran through the hallways looking in rooms. Even after she was sedated, she kept saying it over and over."

A door opened and closed at the opposite end of the hallway. Without a word, Sabre jumped up from her seat and ran towards it, but her high heels slowed her down. Without stopping, she reached down and pulled them off and ran in her stocking feet toward the door. Bob and Phylis glanced at each other with puzzled looks, then ran after her. Bob yelled, "Sabre, what is it?" She didn't stop until she reached the door. She threw it open and surveyed the room until she focused on a man standing near the microwave.

Sabre stood there staring at him as Bob and Phylis rushed through the door, both breathing heavily. The man looked up at the three people all looking at him. He glanced around, as if to see what he had done wrong. He spoke, "What did I do? Am I not supposed to use the microwave?" When no one answered right away, he continued, "They told me this was the staff lounge, and I could eat in here. Am I wrong?"

Phylis said between breaths, "No, you're fine. You're in the right room. Everything is fine."

Sabre, still staring at the tall, blond man about ten feet from her, heard Bob say, "Sabre. Are you okay? What is it?"

"I . . . I'm okay," Sabre said, not taking her eyes off the man. He stood about six feet tall, had prominent cheek bones, and a physique that only comes from working out.

Though mesmerized, Sabre heard Bob's attempt to lighten the situation. "Sabre, he's not a bad looking guy, but chasing him down the hallway is a little much, don't you think?" Bob stepped around Sabre and reached out his hand to the man who appeared to be more than a little confused. "Hi, I'm Bob Clark and this is my twitter-pated friend, Sabre Brown."

The man extended his hand to Bob. "Corbin Steele. I'm new here." He took a step towards Sabre, reached out to shake her hand, and managed to catch her before she hit the floor.

When she came to, the man leaned over her and said, "Can you hear me?"

At first she didn't respond. Instead, she reached up, caressed his face and squeezed his shoulder. "Yes," she muttered, as she tried to stand up.

"Lie still for a few minutes and then we'll help you up. You fainted."

"Are . . . Are you . . ." she asked, unable to finish her question.

"I'm Dr. Corbin Steele. I help out here one day a week. This is my first day." He smiled. "I don't usually have this profound of an effect on beautiful women, but I must say I'm flattered."

As Sabre sat up she felt dizzy. The man cautioned, "Slowly, sit up very slowly."

Her mind grew clearer and she apologized, "I'm so sorry. I guess I acted pretty strange, chasing you down the hall and then fainting."

As if a light bulb came on, she glanced at Bob and then Phylis. "I know what's wrong with Carla. She must have seen him this morning," she said, pointing at Dr. Steele.

"Who is Carla?" the doctor asked.

Phylis spoke up, "She's a guest here. She had an episode this morning. She appeared to have seen someone and went running after them, not unlike what Sabre just did. But Sabre, why would Carla do that? For that matter, why would you?"

"I can explain," Sabre said. She took a drink of water Bob had brought her and breathed deeply. "Where's my briefcase?" Bob handed it to her. Sabre pulled out a photo of her brother Ron, and handed it to the curious onlookers.

"Look familiar?"

Their mouths widened with surprise. Phylis spoke first. "Doctor Steele, he looks just like you. A few years younger, but this could be a picture of you."

Bob moved closer to Sabre and put his arm around her. She knew he understood, more than anyone, what a shock this must've been to her.

Sabre felt validated by the fact everyone else saw the resemblance. Since Ron's disappearance five years ago, she'd seen him so many times in the face of strangers, only to be disappointed. This time, it could've been his double. Still not convinced it wasn't Ron, she knew how to find out. "Doctor Steele, I know this is a strange request, but I'm going to ask anyway. Could I see your right leg, just above the knee? Ron had a birthmark shaped like an hourglass just above the kneecap."

The doctor must have seen the desperation in her eyes. "Okay, first you chase me down the hall and now you want to see my legs." He joked as he lifted his pant leg and showed Sabre. "Sorry, no birthmark."

"No birthmark," she repeated. "I just needed to know. Thanks, and now I'm even more embarrassed."

"Don't be," the doctor said. "It's not every day I get to show such a pretty woman my legs." He sounded sincere in his flattery.

Sabre took a deep breath, exhaled, and explained what had happened to her brother – how he had gone fishing five years ago and had never returned. She felt odd explaining this to his carbon copy. It felt surreal, like she was talking to Ron, yet she knew better. The more she heard him talk, his laugh – all of it confirmed his real identity, but his face made her heart ache.

"Sabre, what does this have to do with Carla?" Phylis asked.

"Carla and Ron dated. In fact, they were quite an item. Although everyone took it hard when he disappeared, it seemed to take the greatest toll on Carla. They'd only been together a few months when he transferred to Dallas. They continued the relationship and managed to see each other at least once a month. Ron's job brought him back here a lot, but at times when it didn't, Carla went to Dallas to see him. She even made plans to move there. She loved him with all her heart. And she had already experienced so many losses in her life. Her father had a fatal heart attack when she was only seven years old. A few years later, her grandparents were bringing her little sister home from a visit at their house and a drunk driver struck their car. All three died in the crash. When Ron disappeared, I think it may have been one loss too many, especially since we weren't sure he was dead. Carla just couldn't let go. For months she'd go to the park and sit on the bench they'd once shared, waiting for his return. She'd arrive there just after dawn and stay all day. She would've stayed there all night if someone didn't go after her. So, every day before dark, I'd go to the park and pick her up and bring her home."

Sabre's mouth felt dry. She reached for her glass of water and drank about half of it. Everyone waited in silence for her to continue. Finally, the doctor asked, "Are you okay?"

"I'm fine," Sabre said. "That continued for months until one day I went to the park and she wasn't there. When Carla realized he wasn't going to return, she lost it. They institutionalized her for several months. When they determined she was harmless, they released her to live with her mother. When her mother died a few years ago, she came here. I would've taken her home with me, but I couldn't give her the attention she needed."

Sabre took a deep breath to keep from hyperventilating. She hated that she couldn't take Carla into her home. "I know Ron loved her, too. He needed someone special to settle him down and I think he found her in Carla. Ron's charm beguiled the women. They swarmed around him, never leaving a shortage of dates on his social calendar, but when he met Carla everything changed. He stopped dating other women and gave all his attention to her. They seemed so happy. They laughed and played like two school kids."

Sabre stopped talking and sat there a minute reminiscing. A heavy silence filled the room until Bob spoke, "So Carla must have seen Dr. Steele and thought he was Ron. And when she ran through the halls looking for him, she yelled his name, 'Ron, Ron,' not 'run, run.'"

"Right." Sabre turned to look at Dr. Steele again. With panic in her voice, she said, "And if she sees you again, she'll have the same reaction. Look how I reacted and I don't have nearly the problems Carla has. She can't see you. She won't understand. It'll devastate her. You have to get out of here." She stopped. "I-I'm sorry. I can't tell you not to work here, but if you had seen what it did to her you'd understand."

Dr. Steele shook his head. "No, you're right. We can't let her see me right now. I'll ask Dr. Hilton to finish the day for me, and then I'll talk to Carla's doctor about this to see what we should do." He turned to Phylis, "Will you please make sure Carla stays in her room for a few minutes? I'll get my things and leave. We'll work something out, but for today, I agree with Sabre. She doesn't need to see me right now."

Phylis left the room to check on Carla. Dr. Steele said goodbye, shook their hands, and turned to leave. Sabre held on to his hand well beyond the appropriate handshake. When she realized it she let go suddenly, but her eyes followed him until the door closed. Bob picked up Sabre's briefcase, put his arm around her waist, and they walked to the car. "I'm frazzled," Sabre said. "I'm sure glad you're driving."

"Want me to take you home so you can rest?"

"No, just take me back to the office. I have a lot to do, and hopefully it'll keep me distracted. I'll be fine once the shock wears off."

After thirty minutes in the office with nothing accomplished, Sabre decided she was wasting her time. She made one last attempt to reach Detective Carriage, leaving him a message to call her back, regardless of the time. Then she packed up and drove home.

Feeling safe and comfortable in her condo, she warmed up a can of tomato soup, toasted a piece of bread, and sat down to a late lunch. She ate about a fourth of the soup and didn't touch her toast. Eating seemed like too much work, so instead, she drew a nice warm bath, lit four aromatherapy candles, and shut off the bright lights. She soaked in the tub until the bubbles dissipated and the water cooled. Then she donned a light pair of sweats and lay down just to rest for a few minutes. The next morning arrived before she awakened.

CHAPTER 11

When Sabre awakened, she thought she'd been dreaming about the man who so resembled her brother that she had insisted he show her his bare leg and prove he wasn't sporting an hourglass-shaped birthmark. It didn't take long for reality to set in and for the pain she experienced the day before to return. She shook it off. Too much work needed to be done to waste another day.

In bright red numbers the digital clock by her bed read 5:10 a.m. She counted on her fingers, "6:10, 7:10, 8:10. Detective Carriage should be in," she said as she dialed the phone.

"It doesn't sound to me like there is a Mattie Sturkey, and the first grader named Mattie doesn't fit into the rest of Alexis' story," he said, after they had chatted for a few moments.

"I'm surprised. Alexis sure sounded like she was talking about a real person. She rattled on for a long time about Mattie. You could see she really missed whoever she was talking about."

"Well, ma'am, let's look at what she's told you. Mattie is her best friend. They went to school together and had the same teacher. Mattie had a hearing problem, and so Alexis wanted to learn to sign in order for them to communicate. They played with Barbie dolls together outside the classroom. Mattie stayed at her house sometimes."

"But Alexis never stayed at hers," Sabre added.

"Perhaps that's because she wasn't real," Carriage said, with a little sarcastic humor.

"Maybe, but when she talked about Mattie her sadness

was real, or she's the best little ten-year-old actress I've ever seen."

"I agree with you. I'm thinking there is someone she knows who can't hear and uses sign language because when she approached the speech teacher she wanted to learn to sign. And that was before she'd ever met the little first grader named Mattie, whom she tutored. Maybe she borrowed her name because of the similarities to her real friend."

"But why would she not tell me about her real friend if there is one? Why would she write her a letter? And why did she send it to her own address?"

"I don't know. I guess you'll have to ask her or read the letter. Perhaps it will give you some clues."

"I'll talk to Alexis, but I'm not going to read her letter. In fact, I'll return it to her and see what she has to say about it. Maybe she'll volunteer some information."

"Have you been able to reach Alexis' grandmother?"

"No, but I'll keep trying."

"Well, if there's anything else I can do for you, ma'am, you be sure to let me know."

"Thanks. I really appreciate all the effort you've made so far. It's above and beyond the call of duty. Perhaps someday I can return the favor, Detective Carriage."

"Well, there is one thing you can do for me right now," he said seriously.

"I'd be glad to. What is it?"

"Please, call me Joe," he said in his strong, southern drawl. Sabre chuckled to herself at the way he said his name . . . Jo-wah. Her brother Ron used to say, "Only in the South is 'Joe' a two-syllable word."

"I'd be pleased, Joe," she said his name with emphasis. "If you wouldn't mind, my name is Sabre. I much prefer it over ma'am."

"Yes, ma'am . . . I mean Sabre. It's a terrible habit I have, but I'll work on it."

Later, as Sabre prepared for court, she tried to figure

out the real deal with Alexis. It helped take her mind off Dr. Steele. Though certain in her mind he wasn't her brother, her heart didn't want to believe it. She missed Ron so much, and she had dreamed so many times of his just showing up somewhere suffering from a case of amnesia. In her fantasy, he'd be living nearby and she'd see him grocery shopping or buying gas for his car or some other normal routine activity. When he saw her, his memory would be jogged by her presence; he'd start to remember everything, and she'd suddenly get her brother and best friend back.

~~~

Sabre's busy morning in court kept her from thinking about anything else. She hustled from one courtroom to another, completing her calendar. She and Bob went to lunch at Pho's since they had missed their chance the day before. Bob seemed to be trying to keep her distracted, but their conversation kept coming back to either Dr. Steele or the Murdock case.

"We have the Murdock/Smith hearing on Monday. Do you know what position you're taking yet?"

"I'm not sure what to do," Sabre said. She explained about Mattie, Alexis' friend, the letter she had written, and what Detective Carriage had discovered.

"So are you going to read the letter?"

"No, I can't. I wouldn't be comfortable with it."

"I'd read the letter."

Sabre thought for a second, but she knew what she had to do. "I'm going to return the letter to her next time I see her. If she wants to tell me what's in it, she will."

"I'd read the letter," Bob repeated.

"Well, it's not as though she's at immediate risk and the answer to her safety lay in the letter. In fact, I'm not sure she's at risk at all, so unless something comes up between now and the hearing on Monday, Alexis may be going home with her father."

They returned to Sabre's office. Bob went in with her. "Where's your file on the Murdock/Smith case? I need to copy your report. I can't find mine."

"You know, they have these little things called a 'hole punch' you can use to punch holes in your papers and then actually attach them inside your folder with an Acco fastener. And then your reports are inside the file when you need them. They work amazingly well. You might want to try it some time," she said, as she handed him her well-organized, color-coded file.

Bob went into the workroom to copy the report. When he returned, he slipped the papers into the empty folder Sabre had given him, thanked Sabre, and left.

Sabre returned her phone calls and checked on Carla. Phylis informed her Carla had improved, but was still pretty shaken up by the "Ron sighting." Sabre left a message for Carla's doctor to call when he arrived. She put a note in her own calendar to visit Carla on Saturday. She tried to catch up on the work piling up on her desk, but concentrating proved difficult at best. She couldn't shake the vision of Dr. Steele's face from her mind.

Suddenly the phones became exceptionally active for a Friday afternoon. Sabre accomplished little else after two cases she had expected to settle fell apart, but it also kept her mind off Dr. Steele. After a few hours of finesse and negotiations, the crises appeared to be over. Sabre picked up the Murdock file, took out the letter, and, without reading it, went to see Alexis.

When Sabre arrived at Jordan Receiving Home, Alexis and Jamie were waiting to see her. She met the children in the interview room. As usual, Alexis shared all of the Jordan gossip. She described the arrival of each new child and the departures and destinations of those leaving. She knew why every child was there and which little ones knew their ABCs. Her knowledge included who got along with whom and who didn't. She told about Billy's bloody nose and Ashley's pierced tongue and green hair, and how Adam, one of the attendants, lost his temper and squeezed a kid's arm and left a bruise. "He's not coming back, though. I think he got fired," Alexis said.

Sabre enjoyed listening to Alexis' stories. Not anxious to broach the subject of the letter, she let her go on talking. When she couldn't avoid it any longer, she removed the letter from her bag. "Alexis," she said, "the letter you sent to Mattie came back to me."

Alexis looked at the letter and glanced down at her feet. With her head still down, she sighed, "Oh."

"The address was incorrect." Sabre handed her the envelope. "I know the letter is open, but I didn't read it. No one has. When mail comes into my office, my secretary opens it and then gives it to me to sort through and read. When I saw it, I put it in your file. I didn't read it because it was a private letter from you to your friend and I didn't have your permission. I apologize for it being opened, but I honestly have not read it."

"Okay," Alexis said. Sabre didn't know whether Alexis believed her or not, but she was glad she hadn't read her personal letter.

"Alexis, why did you mail it to your old address in Atlanta?"

"Because she lived there."

"Who lived there?"

"I did."

"But you said 'she.' Who is 'she'?"

"I did. I lived there. That's all."

"Listen, honey . . ."

"Don't call me that," Alexis snapped. "I told you not to call me that. I'm not 'Honey.' I'm not your honey. I'm not their honey. I'm not anybody's honey," she yelled as she stood up. She wiggled around and twisted her hands as she paced back and forth.

"Alexis, I'm so sorry. I forgot you didn't like to be called that. It's a term I use a lot. I'll try not to use it around you. Are you okay?"

Alexis stared into Sabre's eyes. Her expression screamed for help, but Sabre didn't have a clue what to do for her. Alexis reached up to wipe her face with the back of her hand, but not before Sabre detected a teardrop running down her cheek. Abruptly, like a salamander changing colors with his surroundings, her demeanor changed and she started to chatter.

"Come on Jamie, we need to go now. It's almost suppertime. We need to get back so we don't miss supper." She looked up at Sabre. "Jamie needs to eat so he can stay healthy. We're having macaroni and cheese, fruit, and chips tonight. And we'll have orange sherbet for dessert. I like macaroni and cheese. I hope the fruit is peaches. I like the peaches. Jamie likes them, too. Sometimes they have fruit cocktail. That stuff's nasty." Alexis babbled, slipping more and more into her comfort zone. Sabre knew to stop pushing; she only hoped she hadn't gone too far already.

She walked Sabre and Jamie back to the front desk and rang for the attendant who came right out. Alexis turned to Sabre, her mouth turned up almost in a smile. "Good night, Miss Sabre. Please do come again."

CHAPTER 12

Gaylord Murdock arose early Saturday morning so he could put his things away in his newly rented apartment. It felt good to be out of the hotel and to have his own place. Planning to have Alexis home on Monday, he wanted her room ready for her. There would be no more visiting her at a facility where someone monitored every conversation. The court had ordered supervised visitation, but Monday that should all change. He was sure of it. He knew they had nothing on him and Alexis would come home, maybe even Jamie, too.

He scurried about, readying the apartment for the social worker to evaluate. Although the apartment rented as "furnished," it contained minimal furniture: a sofa and chair in the living room, a little dinette with four chairs in the dining room, and in each bedroom a full-size bed and chest of drawers. The old, unstable furniture felt like a cheap hotel. Gaylord longed for the beautiful antiques he had grown up with, but he could get by in this temporary situation since he didn't plan to stay around long. Once he had Alexis, his attorney said it wouldn't take long to gain custody of Haley, the baby. When he had both of his daughters, he'd leave this awful place. California had been nothing but trouble.

At 10:01 a.m. Marla knocked on his door. Gaylord was pleased she arrived at the scheduled time. On previous meetings, she'd been from ten minutes to an hour late, a habit for which he had little tolerance.

"Good morning, Marla," Gaylord greeted her, as he

opened the door. "Welcome to my humble abode." He smiled, and made a slight bow and a hand gesture indicating she should enter.

Marla returned his smile. "Good morning, Gaylord. How are you this morning?"

"I'm well," he said, "but I'll be even better when I have my babies back home with me. Thanks so much for coming out on a Saturday to evaluate the apartment. I'm sure you have plenty of other things you'd rather be doing today."

"It's not a problem. I'd just be working in my office, playing catch-up as usual."

Marla set her briefcase on the dinette table, opened it up, and took out a notepad to take notes. "Do you mind if I just look around?"

"Not at all. Is there anything you need me to show you? What can I do? Oh, where are my manners? Grandma Murdock is probably turning over in her grave at my lack of southern hospitality. May I get you a cup of coffee or maybe some lemonade?"

"No, thank you. I'm fine."

"I'm sorry, ma'am. I've just never done anything like this before. I don't know what I'm supposed to do, and I want everything to be right so I can get my babies home."

"You're doing fine. Just relax. I'm going to look around, take some notes, and I'll be out of your hair in no time. You're welcome to stay here or follow along. It doesn't matter to me."

"Thank you," he said, a little relieved. Marla chuckled. Gaylord thought she acted a little giddy around him. He watched as she looked around the combined living room and the dining area. "I know there isn't much in here, only the furnishings that came with the apartment, no pictures on the walls, no television or stereo. I didn't bring much across country with me. I plan to get some pictures to decorate the walls, but I'm waiting for Alexis to help. I don't see a need for a television, though. People spend too much time in front of the TV. I'd rather we spent our time

81

together as a family."

Gaylord followed Marla as she entered the master bedroom. It had the same sparse furnishings with no decorations or wall coverings. Gaylord had cleaned the room before she came and covered the bed with a blanket. He had made Alexis' room, however, look homier. He'd covered the bed with a pale pink bedspread and propped her floppy, brown, stuffed puppy between two pillows. The many hours of cuddling this once fluffy ball of fur had created mats from head to toe. Marla walked over to the bed and picked him up. The fur was so matted around the eyes just a hint of dark brown came through, but his little black, plastic nose sat prominently on his endearing face. The leather patches on the bottom of his feet indicated his worth. When Marla hugged him he flopped around her neck, appearing to hug back.

"That's Dogwog," Gaylord said. "Alexis has had him since she was about two years old. She saw it in a store one day and fell in love with it. She wouldn't let go when we tried to put it back on the shelf. She didn't cry; she just held on real tight, and she looked so cute we didn't have the heart to tell her no. She has slept with him ever since. I know she misses having him with her now, but she feared losing him at Jordan. The social worker who brought her in told her to leave him behind because sometimes things get lost there."

Gaylord watched Marla carry Dogwog with her as she continued around the room, opening and closing doors and drawers. Three little dresses, two pink and one green, with the tags still on them hung in the closet. "Did you just buy these?"

"I picked them up yesterday afternoon. I thought it would be a nice surprise for her when she came home. Pink is Alexis' favorite color so I bought her two pink ones. Do you think she'll like them?"

"They're lovely. I'm sure she'll be pleased."

Marla opened the chest of drawers containing Alexis'

things: her socks in pairs and hooked together at the top with the tip of one sock folded over the other, four pairs of underwear, and some undershirts carefully folded. Marla picked up a photo from the top of the chest of drawers.

"That handsome, well-dressed couple are my parents on their twenty-fifth wedding anniversary. They renewed their vows in the white gazebo in our backyard. Alexis loves that photo. She's very close to her grandparents," Gaylord said.

"Nice looking couple. Where are they now?"

"They're in Atlanta. They wouldn't live anywhere else."

"They're not traveling or anything?"

"No, I don't think so. Why do you ask?"

"Well, I've left them several messages, but I haven't heard back from them. I thought maybe they were out of town. When did you last speak to them?"

"Just a couple of days ago."

"Do they know what's going on here?"

"No, I haven't told them, and if possible, I'd just as soon they didn't know. When I know how things are going to work out, I'll tell them everything. Otherwise, they'll just worry."

"I understand," Marla said.

Gaylord, frustrated with the whole process and unsure if she meant she wouldn't say anything to his parents or if she was just placating him, forced a smile.

Next to the photo lay Alexis' bright pink scrapbook with the words, "Alexis Murdock, My Pride and Joy." Gaylord's attorney had taken the book to show Marla, so she must have been familiar with the contents. Nevertheless, she picked it up and thumbed through the pages, glancing at Alexis' photos and awards over the years.

"I started the album the day I learned of Elizabeth's pregnancy. We were so excited," Gaylord said, thinking back to when Alexis was young. "Alexis has always been a very good girl, even as a baby. She didn't cry or fuss much, and she's sharp as a tack. We tease each other a lot, and she often gets the best of me. I miss her so much. It sure will be nice to have her home."

"I understand," she said.

"Do you really? Do you have any idea what I'm going through? What Alexis is going through? We haven't been apart, even for one night, since her mother disappeared. This can't be easy on her. And it's killing me."

Marla looked at him and nodded her head. She continued her inspection of the house. Gaylord had made sure there was nothing there that might be dangerous for a ten-year-old. He'd stocked the bathroom with ample toiletries, and the kitchen had plenty of food in the refrigerator and cabinets, as his attorney had instructed him to do. He had only a few dishes and minimum silverware in the cupboard and drawers, but a stack of paper plates and plasticware provided a temporary solution.

When Marla had completed her tour, she said, "That's it. I'm finished here."

"How did I do? Is everything alright?"

"I don't see any major problems with your home, but your attorney will receive a copy of the report with my recommendations prior to the next hearing." She thanked Murdock for his time and left.

Murdock felt comfortable the evaluation had gone well, but he wouldn't relax until he had both of his girls home. He had tried to be patient, but he couldn't understand why they were still not with him. Counting on his visit with Alexis today to be his last supervised contact, he left forty-five minutes early for a ten-minute drive to see her.

Kathy, one of the attendants, recognized him when he walked in. "Good afternoon, Mr. Murdock. How are you today?" He knew his cordial and polite manner made him a favorite at Jordan Receiving Home. He had witnessed several attacks on attendants from intoxicated or high parents. He didn't fit the usual mold; he even dressed and smelled better than the rest.

"Just fine, Kathy," he responded after a quick glance at her nametag without her noticing. He had acquired this trait as a teenager by watching his Uncle Steve, who used it to hit on waitresses and store employees. Murdock had perfected it in college and in the many sales jobs thereafter. "How about you? Are you having a good day?"

The technique worked on Kathy; she appeared pleased he remembered her name. "Yes, everything's going well today. I'm glad they decided to let you see Jamie. He needs to see you. His mother doesn't come here often, and as far as Jamie's concerned, you're his father. Please wait in Room Four, and I'll go get the children."

When Kathy, Alexis, and Jamie walked into the room, Murdock picked Jamie up and swung him around. Jamie giggled with delight. Alexis walked over to her father, smiled, and gave him a hug. "Hello, Father," she said.

"Hi, sweetheart. How are you?"

"Fine."

"What did you do today?"

"We had a project to do for Thanksgiving. We made turkeys out of paper plates and we got to paint the tails. Trevor spilled some paint on the floor, and some of the kids stepped in it and tracked it all over. The teacher got real mad so we had to put the paint away and use construction paper to finish the turkeys. Some of them turned out real good, though. I got done early so I got to help some of the little ones finish theirs." Alexis continued on about the events of the day.

Gaylord turned to Kathy, who remained in the room, but had stood back by the wall. "Is there any way you can give us a little privacy? I'm not going to hurt my children," he said.

"I'm sorry, Mr. Murdock, but the court order is for supervised visitation, which means you're not to be left alone, not even for a moment. Even your conversation is supposed to be monitored. It makes no sense to me. I certainly don't believe you're any threat to your children, but I could lose my job if I don't follow the rules. I'm really sorry."

"Don't worry about it. I wouldn't want you to lose your job. I shouldn't have even asked." He smiled at her and opened the sliding glass door leading to the grassy square. The sun was shining and the clear sky a beautiful shade of blue, the seventy-four degree temperature inviting. "Do you mind if we go outside? It's really a nice day."

"Good idea," Kathy responded. "We could all use some fresh air."

Mr. Murdock, Alexis, and Jamie walked out into the square. Jamie ran to the sandbox. Kathy lagged behind, seemingly giving them a little privacy.

Alexis and her father kept chatting about everyday things, such as her schoolwork, the disasters and scandals at Jordan, and Jamie's behavior. As soon as Murdock thought Kathy out of earshot, he lowered his voice and said to Alexis, "Are you sure you're doing okay here?"

"Yes, I'm fine. Everything's really okay," she answered.

"Have they been asking you a lot of questions?"

"No, not many."

"Remember, the Murdocks don't talk to strangers," he said. "Family must stick together. It's only family you can really trust. Do you understand?"

"They don't seem like strangers, Father. Some of them are really nice to me."

"I know, sweetheart, but they aren't family. Sometimes people aren't what they seem. Just be careful."

As Kathy moved closer, Gaylord spoke up. "It shouldn't be long now, sweetheart. I know you're anxious, but you'll just have to be patient until Monday. The judge will likely send you home then."

He turned to Kathy and said, "I know I'm not supposed to talk about when she'll come home, but she keeps asking, and it's hard to see her so sad."

Kathy looked at Alexis. As the tears welled up in her eyes, Alexis turned to Jamie and tossed him a ball in the sandbox.

Murdock continued, "She kept asking over and over when she could come home. She hasn't been away from me since her mother left us. I know it's hard on her, and although I didn't want to get her hopes up, I'm quite certain the judge will send her home on Monday. Sometimes, I just don't know what to say. I hope I didn't do the wrong thing."

"I'm sure she'll be fine. Kids bounce back pretty fast, and she's exceptional."

"Thanks, Kathy. I'm trying so hard to be a good father. I know I've made mistakes, and if I had made better choices, we wouldn't be in this situation, but I didn't know Peggy used drugs until she was already pregnant with my child."

Gaylord could see Kathy was pleased he confided in her. "I don't really know much about the case, other than the allegations of domestic violence. I know Peggy used drugs because Haley was born positive. I also know you tested clean on all your drug screens because they make sure we have those records here for visitation purposes."

"That's all true, except I've never hurt Peggy. I would never hurt her. When I came home that day, I could see she was high, and I got really upset. She put the children at risk, and who knows what damage she caused Haley. We argued, she came at me with a soup ladle, and when I tried to stop her, she fell and hit her head on the coffee table. You can ask Alexis."

"No need; I believe you. I can't imagine your hurting anyone."

Murdock reached down and gently picked up Kathy's hand, placing his other hand on top, cupping it between his. "How very sweet of you. It's nice to know someone believes in me. This process has been very hard, and I have no one I can talk to about it. Thanks for listening."

Kathy's eyes fluttered when he touched her hand. Murdock saw her reaction and gazed into her eyes. She kept eye contact until she started to blush and turned away. Tongue-tied, she managed to blurt something out sounding more like a grunt than a word. "Sure."

Murdock smiled, showing his beautiful, white teeth, and Kathy sighed. She suddenly let go of his hand. Upon release, she took a deep breath and regained her composure. Murdock had charmed her, and he knew it. He saw her look at the clock. "Looks like it's time to go," he said. "I don't want you getting in trouble for extending my visit beyond the allotted time."

"Thank you," Kathy responded meekly.

When they reached the lobby, Murdock hugged both Jamie and Alexis and said his goodbyes. He stood there and watched them go through the door. Kathy turned toward him just before she closed the door, the surprise evident on her face when she saw him still watching them. She turned back, but before she did, Murdock smiled and winked.

CHAPTER 13

Sunday morning, although awake, Sabre wasn't anxious to leave her soft, comfortable bed. She lay there, taking in the early morning sun streaming through her bedroom windows; it cast a yellow glow over the room. A ray of sunshine hit upon a corner of a metal picture frame on her dresser, sending off a sparkle that seemed to make Ron speak from his photo. "I'm here with you," Sabre's mind heard him say. She smiled.

Sabre reached into her nightstand drawer and retrieved her little red notebook. She read through her list as she always did, and added an entry to the end, followed by the date. She'd begun dating each entry at about age twelve, so she'd be able to look back and see how long it took to accomplish each dream. It also put things like *Marry Victor Spanoli* in perspective. After all, she'd wanted to marry Victor. By the time she reached the ripe old age of twelve, she could see how silly it was.

Skydive, she wrote. Sabre had been thinking about it a long time, but she wasn't sure if she had the nerve. Last night, as she looked through some Christmas boxes, she came across a card from her friend Nancy, flying through the air, holding a banner that read, "Joy to the World." Looking at the card, Sabre had decided the time had come. Now it was written in the book; she had to do it. She'd made a commitment . . . a commitment to Ron's memory.

Sabre meandered downstairs, made herself a pot of coffee, and poured it into her favorite mug, a gift from Ron. On the side of the mug, it read, "Know how you can be proud of me all the time? Lower your expectations." Still in her pajamas, she took her coffee out on the veranda and sat down. She admired the beautiful magnolia tree and the dark green grass covering the hillside in front of her condo. She lingered there for as long as she dared and then went upstairs to clean up and start her day.

The work at the office could wait, so she drove to the bay and took a nice, long walk. Reflecting on the events of the past week, she thought about what she had to accomplish today. The most pressing thing was to prepare for this week's hearings. Still conflicted about the Murdock case, she planned to take another stab at reaching Ruby Sterling.

Sabre walked from one end of the bay to the other and back again, watching the seagulls flying overhead. One swooped down and grabbed a piece of chicken off a hot grill. People yelled and swung at him as off it flew. By this time of the year, most of the tourists were gone, leaving the beaches and the boardwalk for the locals. The smell of the salty air and the aroma from the few remaining barbeques filled her nostrils. It all had such a calming effect on her that she walked six miles before she realized it and decided she needed to get to her office.

Generally going to the office on Sunday was a treat because no one else showed up, allowing her to work without interruption. Today she halfway hoped Dave or Jack had decided to work. When she arrived, the parking lot and alley were empty, so no one was working upstairs, either.

She began with her cases for the morning calendar. Elaine had pulled each file and put the appropriate, colored hearing form in the front for her. She picked up the Stevens case and read the report. She represented John Stevens, a kid in the Marine Corps, who allegedly shook his eight-month-old baby so hard it caused brain damage. The baby also had a fractured femur and broken ribs. Stevens, still denying the allegations, agreed to submit on the report. He participated in all the programs recommended by the social worker, and had moved out of the home. The maternal grandmother had flown out from North Carolina to stay with the mother and help with the baby. Sabre was pleased the case had settled. She knew it would have been a tough trial with little chance of winning.

Sabre worked through the other nine cases, leaving the Murdock file for last. At five o'clock, darkness setting in, she counted the time difference on her fingers. It would be eight o'clock in Atlanta. She picked up the phone to call Ruby Sterling, but stopped when she heard a faint knock on her front door. Sabre walked quietly down the hallway and peeped through the peephole. She could just barely see the little figure standing there. When she opened the door, Alexis strutted in. Sabre glanced around outside for a car or an adult who might be with her, but saw none.

"Alexis, how did you get here?"

"I walked," she said proudly.

"Does anyone know where you are?"

"Nope."

"What are you doing here? Not that I'm not glad to see you; I am. But why did you sneak out and walk all the way over here? And how did you find your way?"

"I watched when we went by your office last week. Remember, on our way to McDonald's?"

"And you remembered?"

"Yeah. It wasn't hard. I just watched the buildings and stuff."

"So why did you come here?"

"I wanted to see you."

Sabre reached down and put a hand on each arm and looked directly into Alexis' eyes. "Are you all right? What's the matter?"

"Nothing, really. I just wanted to see you." She shrugged.

"I need to call Jordan and let them know you're with me."

"Will they make me go back?"

"Did something happen there? Did someone hurt you?"

"No. Everything's fine. I like living there. I just don't want to go back yet."

"Alexis, I need to let them know you're okay. I'm sure they have people out looking for you. They may have even called the police. We don't want people spending their time trying to find you when you're safe with me. I'll call Marla and let her know, and you can stay with me until you're ready to go back. Okay?"

"Okay." She nodded.

Sabre called Marla on her cell phone. "Marla, it's Sabre."

"Sabre, I was just about to call you. Alexis is missing from Jordan Receiving Home."

"Marla, it's okay. She's with me. She snuck out and came to my office."

Marla sighed. "Thank God. I was so worried. You sure she's okay?"

"Yes, she's fine."

"Why did she do it, do you know?"

"Not yet, but I'm going to keep her with me for awhile and see what I can find out. Will you let them know at Jordan?"

"Sure. I'm just glad she's with you and she's safe. Something must have happened to make her sneak out. She's not one to break the rules. I hope someone hasn't hurt her there."

"I don't think that's it, but I'll see what I can learn. See you in court tomorrow." Sabre hung up the phone and turned to Alexis.

"I'm sorry," Alexis said. "I didn't mean to scare anyone."

"I know you didn't. It's okay, but next time just call me and I'll come get you. Alright?"

"You will?"

"Of course I will. You have my cell number so you can reach me anytime."

With her brow wrinkled, Alexis looked at her advocate. The wrinkle started to melt and she took a step toward Sabre and gave her a hug. They remained clenched for a minute before Alexis let go.

"Listen, Alexis, since you're here, maybe you could help me with some things in the office."

"Sure, what can I do?" Her voice brightened.

"Lots of things; I need these papers shredded, pencils sharpened, and copies made." Alexis took directions well and asked questions when she didn't understand something. At first, she worked without saying much, but after a little while she seemed to relax and started chattering.

Sabre worked and tried to listen at the same time as Alexis spoke, ". . . and then Joey got his foot caught between the bars on the chair and he couldn't get it out. They tried everything, but he was stuck. They had to get maintenance to come and take the chair apart so he could get out. Joey thought he would have to walk around the rest of his life with a chair on his foot. He wouldn't even be able to get dressed. How would he put his pants on?" They chuckled.

After Alexis described Joey's predicament, her voice grew quieter. "My father came to see me today. He said I'd be going home tomorrow. Am I? Am I going back to live with him?"

Sabre laid her pen down, walked over to Alexis, and knelt down so they met eye to eye. "When we go to court tomorrow, the judge will decide whether or not you'll return to your father. I'll make a recommendation to the court and so will Marla. The judge will listen to the reasons why you should or should not go home and then she'll make the decision. What would you like me to recommend to the court? Do you want to go home?"

Alexis lowered her head and responded in a whisper, "No."

"Alexis, why don't you want to go home?"

"I just don't," she said. After a few seconds of silence she added in a louder voice, "I like it at Jordan. It's fun there. And what about Jamie? Will Jamie stay at Jordan?"

"I think so, at least for now. Later, he may be able to go live with you and your father if everything checks out okay."

"No, Jamie is safe where he is and I need to stay at Jordan with him. He needs me."

"Did you tell your father you don't want to go home?"

Alexis spoke emphatically, "No. And you can't tell him, either. Just make the judge leave me where I am."

"Alexis, I can't just tell the judge to not send you home. I need a reason. I need your help here. Remember, I can't tell anyone what you say, unless you tell me it's okay. So maybe if you shared with me what you're afraid of, I can figure out a way to help you."

The tears started to well up in Alexis' eyes as she pleaded, "Please, Miss Sabre, just let me stay at Jordan . . . with Jamie."

Sabre took the fragile little girl in her arms and held her, not sure what to do. She didn't want the children separated, and she didn't know if Alexis was afraid to go home or if she just didn't want to leave Jamie. Sabre needed more information, something explaining Alexis' reluctance to return, something to give her a reason for a continuance.

They sat for a long time in silence, with Alexis in Sabre's lap and Sabre's arms wrapped around her. Their embrace was interrupted by a knock at the front door. Sabre loosened her grip and stood up, "You stay here until I see who it is. It's probably someone from Jordan checking on you. Just wait here."

Sabre walked down the short corridor into the reception area, and looked through the peephole. Just as she did, the mail slot opened and something flew at her. It hit her in the stomach, swirled around, and bright red color came zooming toward her head. Sabre screamed.

She dodged and ducked, trying to avoid contact, but it seemed to keep coming at her. She saw some white on its back and chest amidst the red blur. It appeared about six inches long with a long, narrow wingspan reaching at least a foot. At first, she thought it was some kind of strange bird. When she realized it was a bat, her fear escalated and Sabre panicked.

Screaming and twirling around the room, she crashed into Elaine's desk, knocking over the desk lamp when her foot caught in the cord. Weaving and bobbing, she tried to avoid the missile streaking at her, until the bat dug its claws into the collar of her blouse. Sabre swung at it over and over again, her hands flaying around as she tried to remove the bat from her body. The bat, close to her throat, made her gasp for air. When it finally let loose, she tried to run, but the light cord wrapped around her foot threw her off balance. Sabre felt herself falling, and fought to untangle her foot and regain her balance, but the floor came at her quickly. She reached out to hold on to the desk. Her hand slipped across the top and her head hit the corner, knocking her out.

Alexis ran into the room just in time to see Sabre twirl and fall and the bat free itself from her blouse. She knelt down by Sabre and started to shake her, "Wake up. Wake up," Alexis said, but Sabre didn't move. The bat flew around and around the light near the ceiling. Scared, Alexis ran back into Sabre's office and slammed the door behind her.

She stood by the door trying to figure out what to do. She knew she needed to call someone, but she didn't know who. If she called 911 the cops might come and take her to jail for running away. "What do I do? Who can I call?" she said aloud. "Marla. I'll call Marla." She reached for the phone.

"M-M-Marla, Sabre's hurt."

"Alexis? Is that you?"

"Y-yes,"

"Where are you?"

"S-Sabre's office."

"Is anyone else there?"

"No," she whimpered.

"Are you hurt?"

"No."

"You said Sabre was hurt. Do you know how bad she is?"

"I think she's d-d-dead." Alexis began to cry. "I can't get her to wake up."

"I'm coming right over. I'm on my cell phone so I'm going to keep talking to you until I get there, but I'm going to pick up the other phone and call and get Sabre some help. So you may hear me talking on the other line. Just hold on, okay?"

"Okay."

Marla kept the cell phone to her ear and picked up her landline. She called 911 and told them what little information she had. She explained she'd be there shortly, and if they got there before her, to not frighten Alexis. She hung up the phone and climbed in her car. She could hear Alexis breathing on the other end. "I'm leaving right now. The ambulance may arrive before I do. You just keep me informed and I'll tell you what to do, okay?"

"Okay."

Marla continued speaking to Alexis as she drove to Sabre's office, but all she could determine was something had come in and flown at Sabre, Sabre lay injured on the floor in the other room, and Alexis was in Sabre's office with the door closed.

The police and the ambulance arrived before Marla did. With some work and encouragement from Marla on the phone, they convinced Alexis to unlatch the back door. She refused to go to the front door because "the flying mouse" might be in there. Shortly after Marla arrived, the paramedics carried Sabre out on a stretcher, alive but unconscious. The bat had been captured. Other than that, she obtained little information. Marla remained there while they took Alexis' statement, then she and Alexis drove to the hospital and waited for Sabre to awaken.

CHAPTER 14

A haze of pure white surrounded Sabre. Unrecognizable voices bounced off the fog as the room spun. She struggled to focus, blinking her eyes and straining until the fog finally dissipated and she saw a familiar face staring down at her.

"Ron," she murmured. She reached up for the figure in front of her, but her arms seemed to be glued to the bed. They wouldn't move. "I'm dead," she whispered, and the darkness came again.

She struggled for the light, needing to see Ron again. Although she tried to open her eyes, her eyelids felt too heavy to move. Sabre concentrated on focusing, putting every bit of energy she could muster into opening them. As she summoned the strength from within, she could see some light streaming through. She continued to concentrate on getting her eyes open until she saw Ron's face.

"Good morning," he said.

Sabre tried to respond, but nothing came out. Her mouth felt like cotton. She wanted to ask for water, but no words came. Ron's concerned face became clearer, his body leaning over Sabre's, clad in blue scrubs.

She heard the voice again, coming from Ron, but it didn't sound like him. Ron's voice was strong and resonant, yet soft and comforting, unlike this ordinary voice. She struggled to stay conscious, to keep her eyes open.

"Sabre, can you hear me?"

"*Uh...huh.*"

"You're in the hospital."

Sabre responded with another guttural sound. Still confused, her mind raced with crazy thoughts about why she was in the hospital and what Ron was doing there. Was she dead? Was this heaven? Limbo perhaps. Would she remain in this state of flux and confusion for all eternity? She heard the voice again. "Sabre, I'm Dr. Steele. We met the other day when you visited Carla. Remember me?"

Things started to make sense to Sabre, though she didn't know whether to be happy or sad. She thought Ron had returned, but only Dr. Steele stood before her. At least she was alive. She nodded her head, "*Hm...mm.*" Her mouth dry, she scanned the area, looking for water. Dr. Steele reached for a glass and put the straw to her mouth.

"Just a sip," he said.

The water felt good in her arid mouth. She swirled it around. Licking her dry lips she said, "Why am I here?"

"You had an accident. You fell and hit your head, but you're going to be okay."

Sabre tried to remember what had happened, but her head hurt. She could only remember Alexis had been with her. "Alexis?" She was afraid to hear the answer.

"I don't know who Alexis is, but no one else was hurt, just you. To be sure, I'll have someone check on her for you. You'll be able to have visitors in a little while, but for now, you need to rest. I'll be back in a few hours to check on you."

The sedative Sabre took made her sleep for most of the morning. As soon as she woke up, she called Marla to check on Alexis. Just as Sabre hung up, they delivered lunch to her room.

"Just set it right there, thank you," she said.

Sabre sat up and pulled her tray towards her, although she didn't feel very hungry. She worried about getting her work done, and her head pounded.

Bob walked in and saw Sabre sitting up in her bed, with her untouched chicken breast, green beans, and orange Jell-O in front of her. "Hey Sobs. Boy, some people will just do anything for a little attention."

Her face lit up. "Hi."

Bob stepped up to her bed. "How you feeling?"

"Well, if you could just lift the eighteen-wheeler off my head, I think I'd be okay."

"You're in a hospital. Maybe you could have it surgically removed."

Sabre chuckled. "Did you just come from juvey?"

"Yes, I covered your cases. I stopped by your office early this morning and picked up your files. As usual, your notes were great. So, I only had to continue a few cases."

"What would I do without you?"

"Just completely fall apart, I imagine," Bob responded. "By the way, I settled the Stevens case."

"What do you mean, you settled? I thought I had it all worked out. What happened?"

"Donna, the 'I'm-an-idiot-minor's counsel,' happened. She wasn't sure she wanted the baby placed with the mother."

"For gosh sakes, the grandmother moved in with her. There's no way she would let any harm come to her grandbaby."

"Yeah, well, Donna nearly had the social worker convinced. She almost went sideways on us until County Counsel put some pressure on her. Anyway, it's done now."

"How did the rest of the cases go?"

"I did everything except Jackson, Billings, and Murdock. They all had to be continued. I wrote the hearing dates on your forms in your files. I hope I didn't mess up your calendar too much."

"It'll be fine. Whatever dates they are, I'll be there," she said. "Do you have a trial this afternoon?"

"No, why?"

"I have the Curry trial. I just need you to get another date. My client is whacko. You'll love her. She's the one I told you about who calls at two or three in the morning and screams and cusses on the voice mail expecting someone to pick up the phone. It's nice when she's in custody, because I don't get those phone calls."

"No worries. I already had the pleasure. I met with her this morning in the interview room. She yelled at me, and when I didn't get riled, it made her angrier. Mike offered to take her out of there, but I didn't care. After trying to calm her and put her at ease, to absolutely no avail, I just told her what I needed to tell her and left. When we did the hearing, she started yelling at Judge Cheney because she wanted her kids out of foster care and back with her and her crack-dealing boyfriend. The judge couldn't get her to stop yelling and cussing, so she sent her back to lock-up."

"So, you did the case this morning?"

"Yup, we just got a new trial date, and it made Mike happy because he could put her on the early bus back to County Jail."

"Thanks, Bob. You're an angel."

"No problem. I enjoyed dealing with Madam Curry. It spiced up my morning."

"Do you remember what the date is for Murdock?"

"Yes, as a matter of fact, I do. It's set over to next Monday. Gilley wanted an earlier date, but then his calendar conflicted with the court, so you got a week."

"Good, I need the extra time."

"How is Alexis? Have you heard?"

"I spoke with Marla this morning. She said the incident shook Alexis up pretty good, but she's okay. She received such a good reception back at Jordan for being brave and helping me, she didn't get much flak for running away. She's meeting with the psychologist today to help deal with it all. I'm more concerned about why she ran away in the first place. Alexis told me last night she didn't want to go home, but she wouldn't say why and she didn't want her father to know."

"You'd think she'd be anxious to go home. Do you suppose it's because she doesn't want to leave Jamie behind?"

"That's part of it, I'm sure. But I don't think she knew Jamie wouldn't be going home with her, at least not until after she said she didn't want to go home. I guess it's possible someone else told her, or she just assumed it. No, I think it's more than that."

"I don't know. Murdock sure appears to be a decent guy. If he is in fact snowing everyone, he definitely plays the game well. Most of those derelicts can't keep up the front this long. They usually crack within the first few weeks if they're faking. He's either really good at it, or he's genuine."

"I agree. He's quite the southern gentleman. Maybe he's for real."

"By the way, have you heard any more from Atlanta?"

"No, but I'm going to try to reach the maternal grandmother again. I haven't heard from Detective Carriage in a while, so I think I'll call him this afternoon."

"So what happened last night? I heard something about a bat. Was it a bat or a bird?"

"It was definitely a bat. Someone knocked on the door. Before I could even look out the peephole, they stuck it through the mail slot. The dang thing came right at me, and it scared the dickens out of me. I screamed and tried to get away from it, but it just kept coming at me and then it got caught in my blouse and I couldn't get it out. I somehow knocked the lamp off Elaine's desk and got my foot tangled in the cord. I must've hit my head on the desk when I fell. I don't remember anything more until I woke up this morning. I thought I had died. Everything looked foggy and I thought I saw Ron standing by me, but as it turned out, it was just the infamous Dr. Steele."

"That must have been eerie. He was on duty when you came in last night. I'm not sure he ever went home. He was very helpful this morning. He even spoke with me personally when I called to check on you."

"He's been very kind, but it sure is uncomfortable

being around him. I don't want to say anything to him because he's been so nice. He came back in this morning to check on me and said I could go home tomorrow. I tried to convince him to release me today, but he wouldn't. He wanted to keep an eye on me another day just to be safe."

"Well, I'm sure he won't keep you here any longer than he has to. They need the beds." Bob paused for a moment. "Do you have any idea who did the bat thing?"

"Not a clue."

"Got any jealous wives looking for you?"

"My life should be so exciting." Sabre chuckled. "It was obviously intentional, though. What I'm not sure of is whether someone played some kind of sick prank or if it was malicious, and if they intended it for me or someone else in the office."

"Well, we do make our share of enemies in this business, but it could be a random act of idiocy. Have you spoken to the police?"

"Yes, a detective came by this morning and took my statement."

"Did you tell him about the other strange things you've been experiencing at the office? It's just too coincidental, so many things happening at your office and only when you're there alone. It seems someone is, at the very least, trying to scare you – probably some sick client, or a parent of a child you represented that you ticked off somewhere along the line."

"Yes, I told him. He encouraged me to stay away from my office at night, especially if I'm alone."

"That's good advice. I don't want you there anymore, either."

"But it's going to be so hard to get everything done. Everyone else always leaves so early."

"The guy upstairs – Casey, what's his name – works later than most. You could check with him and leave when he does. I'm sure he'd be glad to keep an eye on you."

"Yeah, he'll think I'm coming on to him. He's been

trying to convince me to go out with him for a year."

"So take advantage of it. He'll be wetting all over himself just to be your hero. The rest of the time you can take the work home and do it. Or, if he's not there and you really need to be at the office, I'll go hang out with you. Just promise me you won't be there alone."

"Yeah."

"Promise me."

"Okay. I'll be careful."

Bob shook his head from side to side. "That's not good enough. Will you do as I ask? Not be at the office alone?"

"Yeah, yeah, but I'm not going to get indebted to Casey. I'll make sure Jack's around when I'm there. It's all a little too weird."

"So, what else did the doctor say this morning?"

"He said his time would've been split between Carla's facility and the hospital, but now he's spending more time here because of Carla."

"I mean about you, goofball. What did he say about your condition?"

"He said I have a concussion, but I don't appear to have anything permanent except maybe a small scar here where I got the stitches," Sabre said, pointing to the bandage on the side of her forehead.

"Well, I better get going and let you rest."

"Okay, and thanks again for covering my cases," Sabre paused, "and for hanging out all night in the waiting room. Marla told me."

"Where else would I be when my 'little snookums' is lying in a hospital bed?" He reached over and kissed her on the forehead. "Get some rest."

"You, too."

After Bob left, Sabre called her office and gave Elaine a short list of people she could tell about her hospital stay if they happened to call. Among those was Joe Carriage.

"By the way," Elaine said, "Ruby Sterling called this morning."

"She did? What did she say? Did she say when to call back?"

"Whoa, she just called a few minutes ago. You can probably reach her right now." Elaine gave Ruby's number to Sabre before reading her phone messages to her. Sabre wrote down the phone number of two other clients who had to be called right away.

"The rest can wait until tomorrow when I'm back in the office," Sabre said, as if there was no question of her release or her ability to start right back to work. She finished with Elaine and then dialed the number for Ruby Sterling, hopeful she would gain some insight into the Murdock case.

The phone rang five times. Sabre, about to hang up, heard "Hello."

"Good afternoon. This is Attorney Sabre Brown from California returning your call. Are you Ruby Sterling?"

"Yes, I am," Ruby said sharply.

"Mrs. Sterling, I represent your granddaughter, Alexis Murdock. How are you today?"

"Alexis is just a child. Why would she possibly need an attorney?"

"She's not in any trouble. We're just trying to keep her safe, and I could sure use your help with that."

"Has something happened to her? Is she hurt?"

"No, she's fine," Sabre explained. "I need to know some things about Alexis and her father, Gaylord Murdock." No response. "When did you last see Alexis?"

"About five years ago."

"And Mr. Murdock?"

"The same."

"What can you tell me about Gaylord?"

"Nothing."

The pain pill Sabre had taken earlier had worn off, making Mrs. Sterling's abrupt demeanor difficult to deal with. Sabre's head pounded and her mind wasn't clear or sharp. She wished she had waited until she had returned to the office to make this call.

"How well do you know Mr. Murdock or his family?" Sabre tried again.

"Not well."

"Mrs. Sterling, I'm sure you want your granddaughter to be safe. If so, I really need your help."

Ruby's voice softened a little. "I'd like to help, but I can't. I'd better go now."

"Wait." Sabre raised her voice, trying to keep her on the line. "What about your daughter, Elizabeth? Maybe you can fill in some blanks there."

"Sorry. I can't help you. Goodbye." She hung up the phone.

Sabre, frustrated at herself for not handling the situation with more finesse, had reached another dead end. Her head ached, but reluctant to take more drugs, she tried to sleep.

She had been sleeping about ten minutes when the phone rang. She answered it and heard the southern accent she had become so comfortable with. "Sabre, Joe Carriage here. Are you okay?"

"Yes, I'm fine. Thanks for asking."

"What happened to you? I'm sorry, ma'am. That was rude of me. Sometimes my job gets ahead of my manners. You don't have to answer the question."

She responded by saying, "Sabre."

"Sabre?" he replied, puzzled.

"Yes, it's Sabre, not ma'am. Remember?"

"I'm sorry, *Sabre*," he said. "Why don't I just hang up and call again? I'll start over and get it right."

She laughed, "No need, and I don't mind telling you what happened." She recounted the events that had taken place in her office, including the information about Alexis running away and the reason she'd given for doing it. Detective Carriage didn't say a word while Sabre spoke. At one point, Sabre, unsure if he was still there, stopped and asked, "Joe?"

"I'm listening."

When she finished the story, he asked, "What kind of bat?"

Not quite the reaction or question Sabre expected, she said. "The scary kind. Who cares?"

"What color was it?"

"It was red – a big, red, scary bat!"

"Did it have some white on it?"

"Yeah, I think so. I can't be certain. Why?"

"Different kinds of bats inhabit different parts of the country. I've done a little research on them."

"Why would anyone do research on bats?"

"I have strange hobbies," he said. "Do you mind if I call the police officer handling your case? I may even be of some help to him."

"No, go ahead." Sabre took the detective's business card out of the drawer next to her bed, and gave Joe the name and number on the card. "He should be able to give you the information you need."

"Thanks, *Sabre*," he said. "By the way, what happened at the hearing this morning?"

"We continued it until next Monday."

"Great. So we have another week."

We? Sabre found it odd Detective Carriage took such possession of this case, but she wasn't about to decline any favors. Grateful for any help she could get, especially in Atlanta, she needed to keep him in the loop.

"I finally spoke with Ruby Sterling," Sabre continued, "for what it's worth. She wouldn't tell me anything. She's a nut I don't think I can crack, and I'm not sure she could help us even if she wanted to. I'm not convinced she even knows anything."

"Don't give up on her. I believe she has more information than you may think."

"Why do you say that?"

"Just a hunch. Listen, I know it's none of my business, but I don't think it's a good idea for you to be working in your office alone at night."

"I've been hearing that a lot today." She laughed.

"Well, just be careful, okay?"

As she hung up, Dr. Steele entered her room. "Are you getting any rest?" he examined her head and eyes.

"It seems like I've been in bed for a week. May I please go home?"

"Maybe tomorrow."

"Tomorrow? What's wrong with today? I'm feeling fine."

"Is your head still hurting?"

"A little," she lied.

"A little or a lot?"

"Okay, a lot, but I can hurt at home as well as here."

Sabre studied the doctor as he examined her. She still saw her brother, although she had spotted some major differences. Ron always stood tall and walked like he meant it; Dr. Steele had a shuffle, as if he couldn't quite raise his feet off the ground. Although Dr. Steele had a pleasant smile, she never saw the little smirk occupying such a part of Ron's personality. She felt sad. What would Ron be like if he were still around?

Sabre, so absorbed in her scrutiny of the doctor, started when he spoke. "You're making good progress. You should be able to leave in the morning, but I want you here one more night and I want you to make an appointment with my office to come in on Wednesday."

"Whatever you say; you're the doctor."

"Yes, I am," he asserted, quashing any notion he may be someone else. "Try to rest. I'll see you in the morning." He walked out the door. Sabre watched him leave and observed his every move. His shoulders drooped, not straight and tall like Ron's. The door closed. Sabre conjured up an image of her brother, some of which had started to fade, but grew clearer now. At least she got that much from Dr. Steele. Sabre laid back, closed her eyes, and tried to rest, hoping the hammer would stop swinging in her head.

CHAPTER 15

J oe Carriage's shift ended at 4:30 p.m. Before leaving, he walked down the hallway to the records room, checked in with the clerk, and looked through the old files to determine if the Sterling case could have been misfiled. He double-checked the log-in sheet to see if the file had been removed by anyone else. Joe had logged the file back in on October 25th at 3:24 p.m. and had personally delivered the file to the record room. Nothing indicated anyone else had checked the file out.

After nearly two hours, he gave up the search and went back to his office. He picked up the notepad where he had written the name, Gregory Nelson, the detective whose number Sabre had provided.

When Joe reached Nelson, he introduced himself and explained he was helping Sabre on a juvenile case. "Do you think there is a connection?" Nelson queried.

"Perhaps, but I don't have anything to substantiate it. If I come across anything I'll certainly let you know. I'm curious about the bat. Can you tell me what kind it is, or at least what it looks like?"

"Actually, we just got the report back from forensics. They had some expert examine it. Let me see, it says . . . . You know what, I'll fax it to you and you can read it yourself."

"Thanks." Joe gave Nelson his fax number, thanked him for his help, and hung up. The fax arrived within moments. Joe still marveled at how quickly things could move across the country. Most people his age functioned comfortably in the tech world, but Joe, raised on a farm, didn't take technology for granted, a southern boy through and through. His idea of fast was a tractor at full throttle.

He read the faxed report, but he already knew what it would say. Only a few species of bats were red in color.

The flying mammal is a member of the Chiroptera Order. It is commonly called a "Red Bat" because of the color of its fur. It is 11.2 cm. in length and weighs 13.4 grams. It is bright red in color, indicating it is a male. (Unlike other bats, the male red bats are a different color than their female counterparts, who are more of a dull red.) Its back and breast are frosted white in color, and there is a whitish patch on each shoulder.

The Red Bat flies at speeds up to 60 km. per hour. It is one of the fastest bats in North America. They seem to be attracted to the light. They have been observed around streetlights at night and are often reported as a "red blur." The Red Bat lives east of the Rockies, across southern Canada and most of the Eastern United States. It is highly unusual to find one in California. Contrary to popular belief, they do not attack humans, but because of their extremely fast speeds, it could appear as such, particularly in close quarters. The head resembles a mouse, but it has smaller eyes and a larger mouth full of teeth, therefore much fiercer looking than a mouse.

Joe stopped reading. The report made him think about his friend, Steve Parker, and the case he had been working on when Joe first joined the Atlanta Police force. It still hurt to think about Steve. They had known each other since grade school, and he was the reason Joe had joined the police force. They ran track together all through high school and had continued to run together several times a week afterward. Steve had always known he would be a cop. It was as much a part of him as the blood in his veins. His passion grew stronger every day he spent on the force. His sole mission in life, to make the world a better place to live, ended prematurely; his life was taken from him on his way home from work one night by a hit-and-run driver. They never found the person who ran him off the road and into the lake. He left behind a three-year-old boy and a pregnant wife.

Prior to his death, Steve had been working on a case that puzzled him. Joe needed to see the puzzle, so he drove to see Sally Parker, Steve's widow. She greeted him with a big hug and invited him in. "Joe, it's been way too long. How have you been?"

"Good, and you?"

"Things are okay. Little Steven is in the third grade now. He's doing really well. He can't seem to get enough sports. He's playing soccer, baseball, and basketball. He just goes from one sport to another. Steve would've been proud." She paused a moment. "Ella Mae is in gymnastics. It's so fun to watch those little ones tumble and roll. She takes it all very seriously. She has to wear certain clothes when she goes. She calls it her uniform, like her big brother's. So, Joe, when are you going to start raising a family?"

"I don't know. I can't seem to find anyone who's willing to put up with me, much less bear my children." Joe smirked.

"You need to slow down long enough to let one of those young women catch up with you."

"Maybe someday." He winked.

"You said on the phone you wanted to look through some of Steve's old notes. I hope you know what you're looking for, because it's not going to be easy to find anything. As you know, he wasn't the most organized person around, but I managed to put his papers and old notebooks in plastic bins so they're all in one spot."

She walked towards Steve's old office, Joe following her. "They're all in here," she said, as she walked into the room. Joe looked around, thinking about the many times he had been in this room with his friend. Not much had changed. Steve's desk still sat in the corner, with the computer on it and the same eight-by-ten photo of Steve and Sally in Hawaii on their honeymoon. Except for the new computer and the color of the walls, the room hadn't changed.

"I have the bins stacked in here," Sally said, as she opened the closet door. "There are quite a few of them, so it may take you awhile. Just make yourself at home, and take as long as you need."

"Thanks, Sally."

"Can I get you a cup of coffee, coke, or some water, maybe?"

"No, thanks. I'm fine. I just finished a huge cup of coffee."

"Just yell if you need anything." Sally smiled and left the room.

Joe pulled the four fifteen-quart, clear containers out of the closet and stacked them near Steve's big black office chair Sally had bought for their second anniversary. Joe had helped her get Steve out of the house for the surprise delivery.

Joe placed the first container on the corner of the desk, sat down in Steve's comfortable chair, and started looking through the mishmash of loose papers, yellow notepads, and little bound notebooks. Some of the notebooks were dated. Some not. Some notepads even had case names written on them, but most didn't. It wouldn't be an easy task. The few materials with dates on the outside really helped Joe's search, which he limited to the time just prior to Steve's death. He had to thumb through many of the notes to find dates. He set aside everything except what Steve had written his last year. The process took Joe over an hour. He ended up with one plastic container about three quarters full.

He put the other three containers back in the closet and sat down to read. Just then, Sally stuck her head in the door. "Would you like to join us for supper?"

"No, thanks. I'm fine. I really want to get through this."

"Okay." Sally smiled. "I remember the many times, in the early years, when Steve would work right through supper. After little Steven arrived, though, he made an effort to be at the table – like a family – whenever he could." She left Joe to his research, but returned with a plate of food. Joe surmised she had done the same thing many times for Steve. She set the plate down on the desk. "You gotta eat."

"Thanks," he said.

She left the room and Joe resumed his reading, taking an occasional bite from his plate. He spent the next couple of hours going through the notes, remembering conversations they had had about the cases. It didn't matter much what they were doing – playing basketball, running, or whatever – Steve talked nonstop about his work. Except for his family, nothing else appeared important to him, his work always at the forefront of his mind.

A little over halfway through the box, Joe found an entry containing a date about one month prior to his death and at the top of the sheet the name, "Sterling." He flipped quickly to the last entry Steve ever wrote. It read, "Not a bird . . . a RED BAT."

CHAPTER 16

Flower bouquets of all shapes and sizes filled Sabre's room. There were mixed flower arrangements, three different colors of roses – red, pink, and a beautiful salmon color – and a colossal bouquet of fully opened, yellow gladiolas. "Wow! You think you have enough flowers?" Bob exclaimed.

"Aren't they beautiful? Everyone has been so thoughtful."

"Yeah, and only a few people know your whereabouts. Can you imagine if the word got out? You would have to get a bigger room just for the flowers. Everyone loves you, Sobs."

"I don't know about that. I obviously have my share of enemies, or I wouldn't be here."

Bob walked around the room reading the cards and commenting. When he stopped at the three-foot gladiola extravaganza, he asked, "Who are these from?"

"I don't know. There's no card, but whoever sent them knows my favorite flower and color, or they just got lucky with their selection. The card must have been lost between the flower shop and the hospital. I wish I knew who to thank for them."

"Or you have a secret admirer," Bob said. She knew the mysteriousness made him uncomfortable. Bob sighed, "Look, Sabre, too many strange things have happened, and the bat incident has put it over the top. I don't want you to be alone. If I had it my way, I wouldn't even let you out in public, but I know I can't stop you. I know you'll be cautious, but I also know you won't hide from the world. I'm just worried about you and so damn frustrated I can't help you find this cowardly son-of-a-bitch."

"I know. I've represented hundreds of clients, especially minors whose parents might be unhappy with me. Heck, all the attorneys at juvenile court have; it comes with the territory. But I'll be careful, and I already promised you I wouldn't be at the office alone. You know I won't break a promise to you."

"I know, but I plan to stick close to you."

"Geez, if you stick any closer, we'll have to wear the same clothes."

Bob smiled, "Come on Sobs, you need to leave this 'sick' place before you catch something you can't get rid of."

"I'm ready."

Bob carted the flowers to the car. While he was gone, Sabre caught a glimpse of herself in the mirror. She looked like she had been beaten. Scratches occupied a good portion of her face, a bandage covered the right side of her forehead, and the bruising on her right eye had darkened. In spite of how she looked, she felt fortunate and anxious to return to work.

When Bob returned, he tried to convince her to go home, but she insisted he take her back to the office.

"I won't work long," she said. "I just need to go through my phone messages, return a couple of calls, and pick up my files to take home. Besides, my car's still there. I'll need to drive it home."

"All right," he acquiesced. "But I'm staying at the office with you, and I'm following you home. I'm not leaving until I know you're safe."

"You worry too much," Sabre said. "So how'd court go today?"

"Piece of cake. I'm the king of juvenile court. There's nothing there I can't handle."

"You are the king," she said. "You have earned the title.

You're the best attorney juvenile court has ever seen, except for me, of course. You know the law, you're personable, and the judges, the clerks, and the bailiffs all love and respect you. You're an excellent trial attorney and you have an incredible, although somewhat twisted, sense of humor. I think my cases were in capable hands."

"Thanks, but it's no fun without my queen." He smiled. Sabre's skills complemented Bob's. Where he excelled in the courtroom, she negotiated her way through. She was organized. He was not. They both enjoyed the work, and they loved to pull harmless pranks on unsuspecting people. Together on a case, they became almost unbeatable. Even if they lost, they entertained the court.

When they arrived at the office, Elaine and Jack greeted her. Sabre handed the red bouquet of roses to Elaine and said, "Here, put these on your desk."

"Thanks, they're beautiful." She smiled. "Your mail and messages from yesterday are on your desk, and here are the rest of the messages from this morning. There have only been about six messages from Crazy Carla in the past two days. Have you been talking with her?"

"Yes, I spoke with her several times yesterday and again this morning. I figured it was something I could do while I lay around."

She took the messages, thanked Elaine, and she and Bob walked back to Sabre's office. "If you still insist on sticking around, you can use David's office to make phone calls or whatever."

"Thanks, I will. Just do what you need to do. I don't have court this afternoon, and since your trial continued, we're both free." Bob placed the bouquet of gladiolas on Sabre's desk and went into David's empty office to work.

Sabre sat down at her desk and read through her messages. She spotted one from Ruby Sterling. It read, "Please do not call me at home." She had left a different number and indicated she'd be there until about 3:30 p.m. Sabre looked at the clock; it read 12:23 p.m. With the time difference in Atlanta, she had about seven minutes to reach her. She picked up the phone and dialed, hoping Ruby hadn't left early.

A female voice answered the phone. When Sabre identified herself, she put Ruby on the line.

"Hello, Mrs. Sterling. Are you okay?" Concern colored Sabre's voice.

"Yes, I'm fine. I need to talk to you, but I couldn't talk from home. I need to know how my granddaughter is." Mrs. Sterling's voice cracked. "Where's Alexis now? Is she safe?"

"She's fine. She's in a receiving home. It's a temporary placement where children stay while they're waiting for the courts to decide their placement."

"Can people get in to see her?"

"Not without approval from the court, and then the visitation is supervised. The only ones who can see her are the psychologist, the social worker, her father, and me, of course."

"Can anyone go with her father on a visit?" Before Sabre could answer, Mrs. Sterling asked another. "Can he take her out of there?"

"No, he can't take her out of there and he can't bring anyone with him on the visit. Why? Is Alexis in some kind of danger? Will her father hurt her?"

"Yes, Alexis is always in danger, but not from her father. He won't hurt her. He loves her with all his being, but he may not be able to protect her."

Mrs. Sterling took a deep breath. Silence ensued, and Sabre waited.

"Before I tell you anything more," Mrs. Sterling continued, "I need your word you won't tell anyone. What I have to say may help protect Alexis. That's the only reason I'm telling you. But if you talk, it could get her killed. Do you understand?"

"I understand. I promise you, whatever you tell me, I will use it only to protect her."

"Another thing, don't call me at my house. If you need

to reach me, call this number. They may have the house bugged. I don't trust them."

"Who is 'them'?"

"I don't know who they are, but they've been driving by again and sitting in their cars in front of my house." She lowered her voice, as if afraid someone might hear her.

"How long have they been doing that? And what do you mean 'again'?"

"They came a few years ago, when Elizabeth disappeared. And now they're back."

"Are you sure it's the same guys?"

"No, I haven't seen them up close, but the pattern's the same. They drive up, they stop, and they just sit there watching my house. They're not trying to be discreet. In fact, they go out of their way to make sure I see them. Sometimes one of them will get out of the car and lean up against it and just stand there facing my house."

"Have you called the police?"

"No, I can't. They may be in on it. You can't trust the Atlanta Police Department. Please don't tell them anything I tell you."

"Okay, Mrs. Sterling, I won't, but why don't you start at the beginning. You said they came there before when Elizabeth disappeared. What can you tell me about that?" Sabre didn't know if this woman was delusional or really being stalked. She sounded genuine and truly frightened.

"Elizabeth is my daughter, you know. She is such a beautiful girl and real smart. She finally had what she deserved – a real good life with a loving husband and our precious little Alexis. Then all of a sudden she was gone, and these guys came to my house threatening me before I even knew she was gone."

"What do you mean? You didn't know your daughter was missing when they came to your house?"

"No, that's how I found out."

"Why don't you tell me what led up to Elizabeth's disappearance."

"Ok, let me back up a little," Mrs. Sterling said. "Elizabeth and Gaylord lived here in Atlanta after they got married. With them so close, I saw them almost every day, and Alexis and I became the best of buddies. Then, when Alexis was about four years old, they moved to Dallas on a temporary assignment through Gaylord's work. They lived there for about a year and then they came back to Atlanta. They were only back about a month when . . . ." Mrs. Sterling's voice started to break up. She paused for a moment.

"I'm sorry," Sabre said. "I know this is difficult."

"I'm okay." She took a deep breath. "Elizabeth would bring Alexis to my house every morning when she went to the gym. It was our special time together. We enjoyed getting reacquainted. She had grown and matured so much in the year they'd been gone. Every morning when they'd come by, Elizabeth would knock on the door and I could hear Alexis calling, 'Grandma, it's me.' I'd open the door and let Alexis in. Elizabeth would give me a quick kiss on the cheek and take off for the gym."

Mrs. Sterling paused again. "One morning I heard the knock – only it was much louder – and I didn't hear Alexis. So I opened the door expecting to see Elizabeth, but she wasn't there. Instead, two burly looking guys with tattoos stood there with my granddaughter. One of them was huge. He must've been six-foot, five. He wore a t-shirt, and I could see the muscles bulging out all over the place. His arms were as big around as most people's waists. He had a large, blue-and-green tattoo across his arm that read, 'Mama tried.'

"Well, they pushed the door open so hard it nearly knocked me down. I grabbed Alexis and held her in my arms. She trembled with fright, and her arms wrapped so tightly around my neck I could hardly breathe. She kept her eyes shut, and she buried her head in my chest so she didn't have to look at them. She lay there in silence, too afraid to speak or even move. They must've scared her real bad."

Sabre waited again while Mrs. Sterling composed herself.

"Then, one of the guys pulled out a gun and held the tip of the cold, steel barrel on the back of Alexis' head. She squeezed me even tighter. He looked at me with eyes void of any emotion. It wasn't his lack of concern about frightening a little girl and an old lady to death, but rather that he showed no emotion at all. There was nothing in his eyes, like he was dead inside. Up until then, he hadn't said a word. The other goon told us what to do. When the big guy spoke, his words cut through my heart like ice, and I knew he wouldn't hesitate to pull the trigger if I gave him a reason.

"He said, 'Here's what you're going to do. When we leave here, you're not going to tell a soul anything about this visit. You're not going to try to find your daughter, Elizabeth.'

"I interrupted him and asked what they had done to her, but he pushed the gun tighter on Alexis' head and told me to shut up and just listen. Then he said, 'The only thing you'll tell the cops is your daughter dropped the kid off this morning and never came to pick her up. You'll call her father after a few hours and let him know Elizabeth didn't come back from the gym. And then you'll stay away from the kid.'

"When I asked him why I couldn't see Alexis, he said, 'Lady, it doesn't matter why. These are the rules. I make 'em. You follow 'em. Now let me tell you one more time.' He stuck out his thumb on his left hand as if he was counting and said, 'You never saw us.' Then he raised his index finger and said, 'Your daughter dropped the kid off and never came back to pick her up.' He raised the middle finger and said, 'You call her husband and report it.' On the fourth finger he said, 'And then stay away from the kid. You got it?'

"I was too scared to speak, but I nodded my head. It

felt like some bad gangster movie. I stood there holding my baby, who clutched me with all her might, and I looked into the eyes of this cold, calculating man. I remember those big fingers in front of my face and the gun stuck against Alexis' head. I tried to listen to the words and hoped he wouldn't hurt us.

"He moved his face right in front of mine, and his cold eyes penetrated my soul, and he said in almost a whisper, 'We'll be watching your every move. If you don't do exactly as I say, you'll live the rest of your life knowing you tortured and killed this little girl.' Then he pulled the gun away, they moved toward the door to leave, and he told me not to bother to go to the police because he had them in his pocket."

Sabre listened intently, barely believing what she heard. When Ruby stopped talking, Sabre asked, "Then what did you do?"

"I did exactly as he told me to, nothing. I tried to comfort Alexis. I sat there with her in my arms and rocked her for at least an hour. I tried to get her to eat, but she wouldn't. I thought about calling the police, but I was too afraid of what they would do. I tried calling Elizabeth's cell phone, but the big guy answered it. I recognized the voice. Before I ever said anything, he said in a very reprimanding tone, 'Now, Mrs. Sterling, what did I tell you?' I heard him kind of chuckle and I hung up. I waited for a few hours, called Gaylord, and told him I was concerned because Elizabeth hadn't come back for Alexis, just as the goon told me to do. I told him she hadn't called or anything and I couldn't reach her on her cell. We both knew she wouldn't ever do that unless something was seriously wrong."

"How did Gaylord react?"

"He was beside himself. He called the police, who said they couldn't do anything until she was missing for twenty-four hours. So he called his father, who has a lot of influence in this town. They had an investigation going immediately once old-man Murdock got involved."

"Did the police come to your house?"

"Yes, these two cops came – one young, one quite a bit older with gray hair. They had already been to the gym, and no one there had seen Elizabeth that morning. I was supposedly the last person who had seen her, so they came to me. The young guy asked most of the questions and he took a lot of notes. I felt so nervous I could hardly talk. They asked Alexis a few questions, but she wouldn't say a word, and they had no reason to press it because they didn't know she had seen anything."

"What did you tell them?"

"I just told them Elizabeth had dropped Alexis off and left like she always did. They asked me questions about her demeanor, and if she'd said anything else. But I just told them she acted normal. The younger one kept asking me things. He tried to be sensitive and still do his job, but the older guy told him to let up, just the same. I was grateful. I didn't want to slip and say something. I thought at the time the older cop was concerned about upsetting me."

"What do you mean, 'at the time'?"

"Well, later on, I went down to the police station. I decided to tell them what I knew. I figured the goon lied about having the police in his pocket and they could protect Alexis. When I pulled into the parking lot, I saw the gray-haired cop standing by a car talking to someone inside. At first I wasn't sure it was the same cop who had been at my house earlier, so I drove up closer and sure enough it was. I thought, 'This is good; I caught him before he left.' He was the one I wanted to talk to anyway because he'd been so nice to me." Ruby paused to take a breath.

"So did you stop and talk to him?"

"No, because when I got close enough to see his face real good, I could see the big goon who had been at my house earlier sitting in the car. The really big goon."

"Are you sure?"

"I'm sure. He filled the whole space in the driver's seat and I could see the tattoo, 'Mama tried,' on his arm sticking out the window. He reached over with his other hand and gave the cop an envelope full of money."

"How do you know it had money in it?"

"Because the cop took the money, fanned it out, stuck it back into the envelope, and put it in his pocket."

"So what did you do then?"

"I drove out of the parking lot and went home. I was so afraid they might have seen me, but apparently they hadn't, because the cops came back to my house a few times and asked more questions. The gray-haired one always treated me real nice. They both did, but I figured he'd act different if he'd seen me. I always told them the same thing. Once the young cop came by himself, but I didn't know who to trust, so I didn't say anything. I was too afraid of what they would do to Alexis if I told."

"Did Gaylord know about any of this?"

"Not from me. They may have threatened him, too. I don't know. But if they did, they made a believer out of him, because he never said a word. Nor have I ever told a soul, until now. I sure hope I'm not making a mistake trusting you."

"All I want is the same thing you do, Mrs. Sterling, for your granddaughter to be safe. I'll do whatever I can to make that happen."

"I hope so. I don't care what happens to me. My daughter is gone and I don't get to share in Alexis' life anymore. I don't know if I'll get a chance to see either of them ever again. It's all I live for – that possibility. I'd gladly give up my life to have Alexis safe and unafraid."

"It's not going to come to that. And we're going to make sure Alexis is protected."

When Sabre hung up the phone, she wondered just how she would be able to keep her promise. She looked up and saw Bob standing in her doorway. "You're pale as a ghost. What's up?" he asked.

The knots tightened in Sabre's stomach as she shared the details with Bob in hopes he could help her form a plan.

CHAPTER 17

The dawn awakened Sabre long before the alarm rang out. She opened her eyes, looked around, and let out a lingering sigh. Her own bed, her own home, and the need for routine and normalcy overpowered her.

Sabre propped up in the bed, reached into her nightstand, and removed her little red notebook. She read through her goals. Her last entry read, *Skydive.* Certain she could live without any more excitement right now, she thought it best to put it on hold for a little while. She read on, *Learn another language.* She made a mental note to check on some schools in Mexico where she could immerse herself in the culture.

Reading through the rest of the list, she hoped to implant the items into her subconscious. She had read somewhere, if you could transfer your dreams to your subconscious, they had to come true; your mind wouldn't let you *not* accomplish them. So, every day she read through her list. She chuckled again when she saw *Marry Victor Spanoli.* She had crossed it off her list, but it remained the only entry in red ink, so it always jumped out at her. At six years old, red ink seemed appropriate. She wondered about the "subconscious thing." If that entry implanted in her subconscious, she feared she may never marry – not that she was looking. She liked living alone, but maybe someday.

Sabre felt good this morning, except for a slight headache. She stepped out of bed with a smile on her face and headed downstairs to make her coffee, thinking she needed to buy one of those coffee pots where she could set the timer and wake up to the smell of coffee brewing in the mornings. On the way down the steps, she noticed her little brown bear sitting on the wrong step. He always sat on the second-to-the-top step, but this morning he sat on the fourth step from the top. For a split second she felt uneasy, but dismissed it thinking she must have moved him when she vacuumed. She placed him back where he belonged and went downstairs and brewed her coffee.

Sabre picked out one of her preferred mugs, threw a piece of wheat bread in the toaster, and walked into the living room. The sun streamed in through the sliding glass door, making her aware the blinds were slightly open. Fear welled up inside her. She would never have left the blinds like that. Hurrying across the floor, she checked the slider and found it locked. Moving first to the front door and then the back, she checked the other locks, all locked. "I'm way too jumpy. Bob must've left it open last night when he came by here."

The phone rang, startling her. She picked it up, but no one answered. She hung it up. Concerned, she ran upstairs to get dressed. The phone rang again. She picked it up and snapped, "Hello."

"What's the matter with you this morning? You get up on the wrong side of the bed?" Bob asked.

"I'm sorry. The phone rang a second ago and no one answered. I thought it was someone goofing around," she fibbed.

"Sorry, I'm the culprit. I called on my cell and I could hear you, but apparently you couldn't hear me. I kept saying hello, but you didn't answer." He heard her sigh. "You okay?"

"Yeah, just a little jumpy; I'll tell you about it later. I'll be leaving here in about fifteen minutes for court. Did you call about something special?"

"No, just to check on you. See you in a bit."

Sabre finished getting ready and drove to the

courthouse. She pulled into a parking space and sat for a moment, collecting her thoughts. Her head spinning, she thought about everything that had happened: the bat, the conversation with Mrs. Sterling, the stuffed bear in the wrong spot, and her open curtain. "Ahhh....!" She jumped, startled by the knock on her window.

"Hey, it's just me," Bob said. "You okay?"

"I'm fine," she said, as she exited the car.

"Sorry, Sobs. I didn't mean to frighten you."

"It's okay, just lots of things making me jumpy these days. I noticed one of my stuffed animals sitting on the wrong step this morning and I don't recall moving him, and my window blind was partially open. Do you think maybe you moved the blind last night when you checked the house?"

"I don't recall moving the blinds, but I certainly could have. I did look around pretty carefully. What else could it be? It's not likely someone came in your house just to move a bear and mess up a curtain."

"You're right. Just too much going on, and it has me a nervous wreck," she said, dismissing the concern. She changed the subject. "I haven't been able to get the conversation I had with Ruby Sterling out of my head. How terrified they must've been. I don't know what to do with the information. What good does it do me? How am I going to protect Alexis? If I tell anyone, it might be her death sentence. I just don't know what to do."

Bob put his arm around Sabre's shoulder and gave her a hug as they walked towards the courthouse. "Let's think about this. For starters, you need to keep Alexis safe. She's probably better off at Jordan Receiving Home than she would be anywhere else right now. Agreed?"

"Agreed," Sabre replied.

"Okay, talk to Marla. Don't tell her what you know because she'll have to write it up in a report. Just tell her you have some reason to believe Alexis could be put in harm's way. She'll trust you and beef up security the best she can."

"Good idea," Sabre responded. Not thinking clearly, and with her head still aching, she appreciated Bob's help.

"Then you call Detective Carriage and see if he has found the Sterling file yet. Maybe there's a clue in there."

"Do you think I should tell Detective Carriage what I know?"

"Can you trust him?"

"I don't know. He's been very helpful, providing me with information he has found. He followed up on Mattie for me and has kept me informed on everything. Well, as far as I know, everything. I do have to admit I wondered in the beginning why he seemed so anxious to help me. And Ruby did tell me the thugs said they had the police in their pocket."

"Do you think he is somehow involved with all this?"

"I just don't know. He could be. In my gut I don't think so, but I'm just not willing to take the risk. What if I'm wrong?"

"Good reasoning. See, you are thinking logically. So, get whatever information you can from Carriage and we'll take it from there. We still have five days before the hearing. In the meantime, I don't want you at the office by yourself, and I think you should stay with us for a few days."

"Do you think there's a connection between this case and all the crazy stuff happening to me?" Sabre grimaced.

"Perhaps, in which case, even the slightest thing we've been writing off to coincidence may be a part of some diabolical scheme."

"No, that's just too crazy." Sabre tried once again to dismiss it all. "Look, I'll be fine. I promise not to be at the office alone, but I'm not staying with you and your family. Besides, if someone is after me, it's only going to put all of you in danger as well. In fact, are you sure you want to hang around with me? You never know," Sabre said in a spooky voice.

"You joke, but I think we need to take this seriously.

Look, I have a friend, JP, who's a private investigator. You met him just a couple of months ago at Corey's school play, remember? Tall, nice-looking guy, very intense?"

"Yeah, the one who reminded me of the movie star, what's his name . . . Robert Urich."

"He's the one."

"So, what about him?"

"Well, I'm sure you could stay with him for a little while. I'll give him a call and make the arrangements."

"Bob, I'm not leaving my home. You're overreacting. I'll be fine." Sabre had made up her mind. "Let's finish up here." They walked into the courthouse and went to work.

With Sabre's head bandaged, the scratches, and her black eye, word of the incident didn't take long to spread around the courthouse. Everywhere she went she had to explain what had happened. She shared with Judge Cheney, Mike, and the court clerks in Department Four what had really occurred. The rest of the questions were answered with silly responses – things like "wild date" or "got to fix that trapeze." Bob made up an elaborate story about some guy on stilts. The stories kept changing from one courtroom to the other. Some people kept pushing the issue. When they did, the stories just became more preposterous.

Bob and Sabre completed their morning calendars and walked out of the courthouse together. "Wreaking havoc in the courthouse about your accident was fun," Bob said.

"Yeah, it broke up the monotony for sure, but I started to run out of clever things to say. You, on the other hand, seemed to improve as the morning went on. And the story you and Mike cooked up together–about the whips and chains and leather – please! I should be so lucky."

"Mike really got into it. I think he had that little social worker going for awhile." Bob laughed. "So, what's up, Sobs? Time for lunch?"

"Yup. Pho's?"

"Sure, it's close and I have a trial this afternoon. How

about you?"

"No, but I have a doctor's appointment at three o'clock. I plan to stop and see Carla on the way. She's worried about me. I think she just needs to see I'm okay. Also, her therapist asked me to stop in sometime between one and three today. He wanted to talk to me."

After lunch, Sabre drove to see Carla. Things had been pretty bad for Carla since her encounter with Dr. Steele, whom she believed to be Ron. She had suffered a relapse, and didn't seem to be gaining any ground. During Sabre's visit, Carla mostly sat and stared at the walls. Sabre held her hand and talked to her until time for her appointment with the therapist.

Dr. Vincent, a rather plain looking, fifty-five-year-old man, stood about five-feet, ten inches tall. He had a stocky build and a full head of bushy, brown hair, with very little grey sprinkled throughout. On his rather large nose, appearing to have been broken several times, sat a pair of "Buddy Holly" glasses. He was a gentle, soft-spoken man and was well respected in the community. His credentials from Stanford and Notre Dame permitted him to work wherever he wanted. Fortunately for Carla, he chose to work with patients in her facility, and he seemed quite pleased with the progress Carla had made prior to this recent setback with Dr. Steele.

Sabre walked into his office and extended her hand, "Good afternoon, Dr. Vincent."

"Hi, Sabre. Thanks for taking the time to meet with me." He looked up and his gaze went to the bandage on her forehead. "What happened to you?"

"Long story," she said as she sat down in front of his desk. "What can I do for you, Doctor?"

Dr. Vincent, appearing impressed with her direct manner, got right to the point. "Well, you're aware of the situation we have here with Carla and Dr. Steele. So far, we've averted any further problems. Dr. Hilton has been gracious enough to continue to help out in Dr. Steele's stead, but he can't for very long. We need Dr. Steele to come back to work. Although, I'm concerned about the trauma it will cause Carla. Dr. Steele is an excellent doctor and it's difficult to find doctors of his caliber, but he agrees we can't risk the damage to Carla. I think I may have a solution, one very beneficial to Carla."

Sabre listened, hoping he wasn't going to suggest Carla be moved. She knew it would devastate Carla. "What are you proposing, Doctor?"

"Well, we don't know how long it'll take, but Dr. Hilton is willing to fill in for as long as he can and Dr. Steele has agreed to work with us. But I'll need your help also."

"I'll do whatever I can," Sabre said.

"Here's what I propose. I believe we can help Carla deal with reality by bringing Dr. Steele into therapy with her. I'll make sure she's fully prepared beforehand. As she gets to know him, she'll see lots of similarities, but she'll also begin to see the differences. I don't think it'll take too long before he can fill his role as doctor. Once he's back here working, it'll help her even further to realize he's not Ron. The first sessions will be rough on her, though, and I'd like you to be there for her. She trusts you and draws strength from you. I think it'll help her to see reality through your behavior."

"You really think so?"

"I do. Carla was pretty well-grounded before this happened. Oh, she had a way to go, but this is the last big piece we need to deal with. I think it may be a blessing in disguise. She may even be able to build on it and restore some peace of mind. I wouldn't suggest it if I didn't think it would be helpful. As much as I respect Dr. Steele, we can always hire another doctor. There's only one Carla. More importantly, if we don't deal with this and she happens to meet him on a street somewhere, we could lose her."

"So when do we start?"

"I need a little time to prepare her. I'll have to see how it goes. My guess is we should be ready in a week or so. I want to start as quickly as we can, but I want to make sure she's ready. By the way, do you have a photo of Ron I could borrow for a little while?"

Sabre reached in her briefcase and pulled out a photo. Without speaking, she handed it to Dr. Vincent. "Wow! They do look alike, don't they?"

"I thought so." Sabre stood up to leave. "You'll let me know, then, when you want to begin?"

"Yes, we'll be in touch. Thanks for your help . . . and for the photo."

"Thank you, Doctor. I only want what's best for Carla."

"Me, too, and we're going to do whatever we can."

Sabre had just enough time to drive to her appointment with Dr. Steele. Seeing him still felt strange, but it was getting easier. Just as Dr. Vincent had hoped to accomplish with Carla, Sabre now saw more differences and fewer similarities.

Dr. Steele greeted her with a smile when she walked in. "Hi, Sabre, how's the head?"

"I think it's a little better today, but I've had some awful headaches since I left the hospital."

"Let me have a look." He examined the gash on her head, changed the bandage, looked into her eyes, and asked a lot of questions.

He had an exceptional bedside manner, easy to trust and talk with. She suddenly felt very comfortable in his presence, but was her comfort zone about Ron or Dr. Steele? She tried to separate the two.

Her thoughts were interrupted by another question, "Have you had any blurred vision or been seeing any spots?"

"No."

"Good. You're going to be fine. Just let me know if you have any of the symptoms we talked about or if the headaches don't go away in a few days." His manner was so "not Ron" that for a moment she could see Dr. Steele. He said, "Go ahead and get dressed."

TERESA BURRELL

Her brow wrinkled, "I am dressed. That was my head you examined."

He chuckled. "Just a little doctor humor." Ron had returned, always the tease. If Sabre couldn't separate Ron and Dr. Steele, how would Carla?

"I went to see Carla and Dr. Vincent today. He said you're willing to help Carla through this crisis. That's really nice of you."

"Yeah, well, I'm a nice guy," he said, the sides of his mouth turning up in just the slightest of smiles. His dead-pan look returned. "I just hope it works for her. Dr. Vincent asked me to read her file, to become familiar with her behavior and her history. He's really concerned about what might happen to her if she accidentally runs into me. She already had a glimpse, nearly setting her over the edge . . . and look at your reaction."

Sabre, still a little embarrassed said, "I'm so sorry about that. I must've looked pretty ridiculous chasing you down the hall, barging into the room and then, the kicker – fainting."

"Hey, don't be silly." He smiled. "I'm used to it. It happens to me three, four times a day. It must be my dashing good looks and my charming personality."

Sabre forced a smile. She wanted him to stop joking, to be serious. She didn't like it when she saw Ron in him. She wanted to see Dr. Steele. When he teased, it just made her tense and confused. She'd have to overcome this, or she'd never be able to help Carla. "Well, I appreciate your willingness to help. I'm sorry for any inconvenience it's causing you with your work at the facility."

"Don't worry. Dr. Hilton understands and is willing to help out. And there are others who can pitch in temporarily. I have plenty of doctor friends who owe me favors."

"I'm sorry you have to call them in for this."

"Don't be. I can't think of a better cause." For just a second, there was silence. Dr. Steele had a blank look as he studied her face. Suddenly, he stopped staring, stood up, closed his file, and said, "Make an appointment to come back in a week. I want to check the wound."

Sabre arose to leave. "Thank you, Dr. Steele."

"Corbin. The name's Corbin. My father is Dr. Steele."

CHAPTER 18

Joe picked up the notepad he had obtained from Steve's house. He opened it up to the page that read in big letters, "STERLING," underlined twice, the way Steve often wrote the case name on which he was working. He read through the notes. As usual, Steve had left a few pages at the beginning he had titled "Suspects." He would always write down names as he came across them and later go back and fill in the reasons why he thought they may or may not be involved as he proceeded with his investigation. The rest of his notes read like a diary, which made it easy to follow and included a lot of detail. He used to tell Joe to write everything down. "You never know when some little thing will trigger something. The thing appearing to be the most irrelevant often turns out to be the key to what you're looking for."

Joe read through the "Suspects" section with the usual suspects listed. There were friends and family members, including Gaylord Murdock and Ruby Sterling.

> *Ruby Sterling: Nervous old lady. Not likely involved, but may know more than she's telling.*
>
> *Gaylord Murdock: Nothing pointing to him – no abuse, no history, his whereabouts well accounted for. Could've hired it done. Has the means but no obvious motive.*
>
> *Elizabeth Sterling: Could've run off with another man, but no evidence of it. Not likely she'd leave without the kid. No one saw her at the gym*

that morning. Her mother the last one to report seeing her.

Amongst the notes he read:

> *July 9: Bill anxious to put this to bed, not sure why. I'm following up by myself tomorrow.*

Then a lot more entries about people he had talked to, mostly dead ends.

> *July 14: Bill seems upset about the time I've spent on this case.*
> *July 17: Bill spoke to contact claiming to be friend of Elizabeth's. He says she left with another man and doesn't want to be found. Bill wants to close case. He says we have more important cases to spend our time on. I don't like the smell.*
> *July 19: Went alone to the gym and discovered a locker with a few of Elizabeth's belongings–change of clothes, hair brush, toothbrush, toothpaste, workout journal, and a small folded piece of paper inside journal with a poem.*

Joe continued to read what Steve had written:

> *Just a poem? A riddle, perhaps? What does it mean? Maybe nothing.*

Steve had written the words on the notepad, along with the note itself tucked inside. It read:

> *Color, a pretty, bright red*
> *In the darkness, toward the light;*
> *Circling, circling the head*
> *Blinding speed, causing sheer fright.*

The hand-written letters were flawless. Joe held the note up and stretched his arm out to distance it from his face. At just an arm's length, he could swear it had been typed. With his own handwriting so bad, he marveled at how someone could write so perfectly. As he pulled the note closer, again reassuring himself it had been hand written, he noticed an indentation across the bottom edge of the paper. Joe picked up a pencil, turned it sideways, and shaded across the indentation, revealing a telephone number. He wrote the number down and continued to read through Steve's notes.

Steve ran into a lot of dead ends, but still continued to follow up on a few items. He had scheduled an appointment for July 20th to see someone who called himself "John Doe." On July 21st, the only entry in his notepad read, *Dirty Cop???*

Joe picked up the phone and called the number he'd lifted off the paper in Steve's notepad, only to find it disconnected. He decided to call Howard Martin, an FBI agent from Dallas, whose life Joe had saved on a case a few years back. He was so appreciative of Joe he told him repeatedly to call if he ever needed anything. They had little contact afterward except that every year, without exception, Joe received a birthday card.

Joe spun his rolodex to the M's, found "Martin, Howard," and dialed the number. They exchanged pleasantries and took a few minutes to catch up. Then, Howard made the offer, "So, is there something I can do for you, Joe?"

"Yes, as a matter of fact. I have an old phone number from about five years ago. It's disconnected now, but I need to know who it belonged to back then. Can you run it for me? The phone company is so frustrating, and I don't want it going through Atlanta PD."

"No explanation necessary. Anything else?"

Joe, hesitant to bring up Davis, knew it would be difficult to find out much about him locally without causing a lot of suspicion. "There is one more thing."

"Name it."

"Will you see what you can find out about William Davis? He's been with our department for about thirty years. I don't want to be asking too many questions here."

"I understand. I'll try to have something for you by tomorrow morning. Is that soon enough?"

"That would be great. Thanks, Howard."

"Anytime," Howard said. "I mean it. Thanks to you, I'm alive. That incident in Atlanta was my last undercover job. My face had been out there too long, and I have two little boys who need their father. I'm just not willing to risk it anymore." Before he hung up, he inquired, "Joe, are you in any danger?"

"Not as far as I know, at least not yet. I'm still working on a hunch."

"Okay, but be careful. It's dangerous when your enemy is close."

Joe hung up the phone and went down to records to see if the Sterling file had turned up, but it hadn't. He needed to find out what Steve referred to when he wrote "dirty cop." He surmised it was Bill, his partner, although it could've been anyone. He thought it a good place to start, but he had to be careful. Questioning another cop's loyalty could get you ostracized quickly. He didn't know Bill very well, although he seemed nice enough. He always smiled and greeted him when their paths crossed. Joe had spoken to him just a few weeks back when he had first looked at the Sterling file.

Joe approached his desk and stood there as Bill finished a phone call. "Hi, Carriage. What can I do for you?" Bill motioned toward the chair, "Have a seat."

Joe sat down. "Remember a few weeks ago I asked you about the Sterling case?"

"Yeah, you still messing with that?"

"Yeah. I'm trying to help the kid's attorney. Social Services removed the child from Murdock and now it's looking like they're going to return her, but there've been some strange things happening to her attorney."

"And what does it have to do with the Sterling case?"

"Probably nothing, but I'd feel terrible if something happened to her and it turned out I could've done something about it."

"She's an attorney, Carriage. I'm sure she has upset a lot of 'bad guys.' Attorneys are just like us, always at risk of someone coming after us when they don't like what we do or where we're sticking our nose." Suddenly it sounded more like a threat than advice. His voice softened a little, "Look, Joe, I realize she's dealing with the husband of a woman who disappeared a few years back, but nothing ever implicated Murdock. I think the guy is clean."

"You're probably right. The kind of work Sabre Brown does ticks off a lot of people. It could be anyone. By the way, Sally Parker said to tell you hello."

"Oh, when did you see Sally?"

"I had dinner at her house a few nights ago."

"Do you see her often?"

"No. Actually, it's been quite awhile," Joe answered, not volunteering any more information and looking to see if Bill would question his motives.

"So why now?" Bill probed.

"I decided to pick up Steve's notes on the Sterling case to see if there's anything in there that might help me out."

"So, did you find anything?"

"I haven't had a chance to read them yet," Joe lied. "I'm going to go through them when I get home this evening. Steve always put his thoughts and concerns in his notes – stuff he didn't write in the reports. He also made a lot of crazy remarks, so it ought to at least be entertaining reading." Joe paused. "What do you remember about Ruby Sterling, Elizabeth's mother?"

"Not too much. Why do you ask?"

"I tried to make an appointment to see her, but she wouldn't talk to me. She said she had nothing to say to the

Atlanta PD."

"She probably blames us for not finding her daughter. Loved ones need someone to blame when there is no perp, and it usually falls on us, but anything she says isn't going to be credible anyway."

"Why's that?"

"Well, I don't know if she went kind of crazy when they couldn't find Elizabeth or if she was like that before, but I think she's a few ants short of a picnic, myself."

"Why, what did she do?"

"Her story kept changing. First she didn't want to talk about it. Then she did, but she didn't know anything. She couldn't remember if Elizabeth had dropped the kid off or if she had picked her up herself. Every interview with her was an experience."

"Do you think she was involved in any way?"

"No, she's just nuts."

Joe stood up and extended his hand to shake Bill's. "Thanks for your help. I appreciate it. I know you and Steve were tight."

"Yes, indeed," Bill responded. In a tone sounding like a concerned parent, Bill said, "A little word of advice, kid. Stick to the cases you're paid for. There's not enough time to save the world."

If this hadn't been a case in which Steve had been involved, he might have heeded the advice. However, it had been Steve's case – one of his last cases – and somehow he felt obligated to help out. It also gave him a little piece of Steve back. Something about this case nagged at him. Maybe Steve's death wasn't an accident. If, in fact, there were dirty cops involved, then there could've been a cover-up of his accident as well. He wouldn't stop until he had the answer.

Joe looked at the stack of files on his desk, the phone calls he had to return, and the reports he still had to write. It would be at least three hours before he could eat dinner. He walked to the vending machine and bought a package of

Oreo cookies and a soda.

Seven o'clock arrived before Joe finished what he needed to and felt comfortable leaving. Though not anxious to go home, he had nowhere else to go. Since his girlfriend, Jennifer, had left him, his social life had dwindled. Other than his workout every morning, he didn't do much outside of work.

He had to admit that even when Jennifer had been around, he spent most of his time being a cop, but at least when he went home at night, he had someone to talk to. Joe would work too many hours and then go home and spend the next couple of hours re-living his day with Jennifer. He hadn't been a very good listener, either. Her crisis at the Art Museum didn't seem as important to him as locking up the scum bags walking the streets of Atlanta. Joe knew he was too absorbed in his work to make a relationship work, but he hadn't realized it until it was too late to fix the damage.

Joe pulled into the drive-through at Burger King and bought a Whopper, fries, and a soda. He tried not to eat so much fast food, but there was nothing to fix at home. If he stopped at the grocery store and then cooked dinner, it would be yet another hour before he ate. He picked up his food and drove out of town.

The closer he came to his home, the lighter the traffic became and the faster he drove. Joe could feel the pavement on the two-lane highway below him speeding past under the dark sky with just a sliver of a moon, the only other light coming from his headlights. He gained on the SUV in front of him. The taillights came closer and closer. He moved into the left lane to pass, but the SUV went with him. The son-of-a-bitch came right at him. Joe swerved. He heard a loud crash, metal against metal, ringing in his head as he felt the impact. His car hit the gravel on the side of the road. He turned the wheel and managed to straighten it out. He pulled the car back onto the highway, but the SUV drove at him again. This time

Joe's car started to roll and the noise grew louder, clang after clang. He turned the wheel, but everything was spinning. He lost control as he saw ground, then sky, and felt his body hit the door. French fries hit him in the head as they flew by, and a splash of soda felt cold against his face. Suddenly, it all stopped.

Joe raised his head and looked around. His face felt wet. He thought it was his soda until he saw blood all around him...his blood, everything red, his arm, his shirt. It felt like someone was pouring water on the right side of his head. He touched his head with his right hand, and brought it back covered in blood. What the hell? He tried to focus, looking at the blood, at the car, outside the window, but only darkness lurked before him, except for one dim headlight.

He had to get out of the car and he needed help. He tried to move his legs, but excruciating pain and a wedged leg wouldn't allow him to budge. He reached for the phone on his belt, pushed the call button, and the face lit up a bright pink. He wiped it on his shirt, but only made it bloodier. His fingers hit the numbers 9-1-1. "This is Detective Joe Carriage. Someone just tried to kill me. They ran me off the road with a black Ford Bronco."

"What is your location, Joe?" the dispatcher asked.

"I'm north of town, just past the old Jefferson Plantation."

"Are you hurt?"

"Yes, I'm bleeding, and I'm stuck in the car. I need help," Joe said, just before his phone went dead.

CHAPTER 19

Sirens screeched and lights flashed all around Joe. He heard banging and shouting, "Joe, hang in there. We'll get you out." Joe tried to sort out the chaos. He remembered the accident, the blood. He heard a horn honking. It was deafening. He managed to lift his head from the steering wheel and turn towards the window. When he did, the honking stopped. Men in uniform stood all around and a familiar voice said, "Joe, the door is stuck, but we'll get you out. Just sit still. Don't move."

Joe smiled at the sight of his partner, Brett, who nodded his head in response. He struggled to hold his head up off the horn, but it hurt when he moved. The men worked arduously, until Joe felt a gust of cool air hit his face. He heard a loud screech, more banging, and clanging as they pried the door open. "My poor car," Joe moaned.

"Sorry, buddy," Brett said. "It's you we need to take care of." Joe nodded his head. Brett spoke again, "Can you move your legs?"

"Not far. I'm pretty jammed in here."

"Okay, just sit still," he commanded.

The officers forced open the passenger door and worked from both sides. Within minutes they had him out of the car. The paramedics had a stretcher ready for Joe, but he refused. He had to see if he could walk. He stepped down one foot at a time; at least his legs functioned. He felt stiff, his ribs and head pounded, and the bleeding wouldn't stop. They encouraged him to lie down, but he wouldn't. He reached back in the car and retrieved his backpack. He pulled out Steve's notepad and tucked it in his jacket pocket. Someone yelled, "Get him on the stretcher."

Two paramedics and three police officers walked over to Joe. "Come on, man. You're bleeding all over the place. Let us take you in and get you checked," one of the officers said.

Joe acquiesced and sat down on the stretcher. They put his feet up and he laid his head down on the pillow. Brett stood near his head, trying to comfort him. Joe clutched the notepad inside his jacket with his left hand, and with his right he reached up and grasped Brett's shoulder, pulling him close to his face. He whispered in his ear, "Meet me at the hospital. I need to give you something."

Before Brett could respond, the paramedics raised Joe up, placed him in the back of the ambulance, and started to work on him.

Lights flashing and siren blaring, the ambulance sped off with Brett close behind. When they arrived, Brett jumped out and met Joe as they removed Joe from the ambulance. "You're going to be okay, man," Brett said as he ran alongside the stretcher.

"I know," Joe said. He reached inside his pocket, pulled out the notepad, and slipped it to Brett. "Here, take this and don't let anyone know you have it, especially anyone in the department. Put it somewhere it can't be found. It may be the reason I'm here."

"Sure thing, buddy."

"And here," Joe said as he stuck his keys in Brett's hand. "Stop at my house and pick me up a change of clothes. Okay?"

"You bet."

By the time Brett returned to the hospital, Joe had been x-rayed, stitched up, and had taken care of the paperwork. "Hi, buddy. How you feeling?"

"Not too bad, considering." Joe folded his receipt and put it in his pocket. He turned to Brett and said, "Let's get out of here." As they walked out, Joe asked, "How'd you do? Did you stash it away?"

"Sure did. I'll show you where it is later," Brett said. "I brought your clothes. They're in the car. You going to the department to clean up?"

"No. I'm going to stop at the gym and shower there. There are some things I need to do before I go into the office."

"Joe, what's going on?"

"I don't want to involve you," Joe said.

"I'm already involved. Whatever this is, it doesn't sound like you should be doing it alone." Brett paused. "I hate to add to your troubles, but someone broke into your house and tore it apart. What were they looking for? The notepad?"

"I think so." Joe sighed. "How bad is my house?"

"It didn't appear, from first glance, anything was missing. Your television and stereo were still there. Mostly it's a mess. They didn't take time to break things up much."

"Well, I guess that's something."

"Joe, I'm concerned about you. First, you're run off the road, and now your house is ransacked. Do you know who's after you?"

"I have a pretty good idea."

"So, what can I do to help?"

"I appreciate it, Brett, but I don't want to put you at risk. I'll tell you this much. I think it's inside the department."

"A cop?" Brett's right eyebrow curled up. "Are you sure?"

"No, I'm not certain yet, but if it is a cop I don't know if he's acting alone or what. I just don't want you caught up in the middle of this."

"I'm your partner. If it's a cop after you, I'm already suspect just by virtue of being your partner. So it's better if I know what to watch out for," Brett said.

"You're right, Brett. I'm sorry."

"Don't be sorry. Let's just get this guy, or guys, or gals, or whomever. So what's the story?"

On the way to the gym, Joe gave him the *Reader's Digest* version and told him he would fill him in on the details after he cleaned up. "Okay," Brett said. "Just be careful. Go on in. I'm going to get us some sandwiches from Daria's Deli, and I'll meet you back here. We can go in one car from there."

"Okay. See you in a bit." Joe hobbled off. He felt stiff and the medication was wearing off. He didn't exactly know where to go from here, but he was glad he had some help.

Joe took a shower and scrubbed the blood out of his hair, trying to avoid the bandage. He felt better. Brett returned with the sandwiches, and they ate them in the car as Brett drove.

"So where do we start?" Brett asked.

"I'm pretty certain Bill Davis, Steve's old partner, is the one after me. He thinks there's a lot more on that notepad than there really is. I think Steve got too close."

"So we start with Bill. We need to check into his background and his associations. It may be difficult to find out what he engaged in five years ago, though."

"And we can't do it through the department because we don't know who all is involved," Joe said. He and Brett were both well aware of the consequences when someone turned on a fellow officer. You better be one hundred percent sure or you better not nose around, especially with one of the 'good old boys.' Bill had been with the department for over thirty years and everyone liked him. He wasn't an overly zealous cop, easy to work with, and considered trustworthy. If they started asking questions and turned out to be wrong, they'd never be able to work in Atlanta again. "We can use the notepad as bait. He still needs to get his hands on it because he isn't certain what's in it," Joe suggested.

"That's too dangerous, Joe. He's already tried to kill

you once. What's to keep him from completing the job?"

"You got a better idea?"

"Let's see what we can find out about Bill for starters."

When Joe returned to the office, instead of a greeting of sympathy for his accident, he met with discontent. No one asked him what happened or inquired about his well-being; instead, they hardly spoke to him.

He got one of the clerks to confide in him. The rumor going around the office was that Joe falsely accused another cop of something. The clerk didn't know the identity of the cop, and no one seemed to care.

Bill was way ahead of him. He knew if he started a rumor about Joe, it would ruin any opportunity he had to get information. He wouldn't dare ask questions about anyone within the department.

After work, Brett called Joe and they met in a state park, where no one would see them. "I'm sorry, man, about what's going on at the department. I hope you realize why I let them think we weren't working together."

"No need to apologize. I trust you. You're in a difficult situation. If you side with me, you will be ostracized, too, and nothing will be gained from that. So, just let everyone think you're unhappy having me as a partner. You'll still be suspect for awhile, but you may hear something that'll help," Joe said.

"Well, one thing for sure, it's got to be Davis. It was pretty clever of him to start the rumors."

"Yeah, it really ties our hands. Any ideas where to go from here?"

"I say we hit the streets and find out what's out there. They always know the bad cops before we do."

"Good idea. And," Joe said, "thanks for sticking by me."

"I know you'd do the same for me. So, let's get to it."

They spent the rest of the evening trying to find out anything and everything they could about Bill Davis. Most of their investigation led to dead ends, until they came across "Action Jackson" dressed in a cheap, navy blue pinstripe suit, a pink, ruffled shirt, three heavy gold chains, and a top hat, and carrying an oak cane with an enormous fake emerald on the tip. After some cajoling, a little cash, and the "good cop, bad cop" routine Brett and Joe played so well, they burrowed some information out of him.

"So what do you know about Bill Davis that we don't know?" Joe asked.

"His money goes back to the streets."

"Drugs?"

"No, he wouldn't touch that stuff. No, he's a gambling man."

"Poker?"

"Nope. He's the worst kind – bets on sports, especially the races. He really likes the ponies, and he bets heavy on them. A few years ago he got in way over his head with the creditors, both the banks and the street sharks. He was about to file bankruptcy, which was the least of his worries. The word was out he was a dead man if he didn't come up with the money for the sharks. Then suddenly he was cleared for more loans, and he kept his house and all."

"Did he win big on the ponies or something?" Joe asked.

"Nope. That's the kind of event 'Action Jackson' would know about," he said with conviction. "I know every big bet and big win that goes down. It's my job to know. No, he found another way to clear his debt and he's still walking, so some kind of deal was cut."

"You said a few years ago. Do you know when it happened?"

"Five, six years, maybe," Jackson responded.

"And you have no idea how he got the money, or how he paid his debts?"

"Nope, and don't care much, either. It's my job to know what bets go down and who wins and who loses. If the 'marks' find another way to pay their debts, it's their business. That's about all I know." Jackson clicked his heels, did a little soft shoe, tipped his hat, turned, and strolled away. Every thirty feet or so, he did his little dance again until he vanished out of sight.

Brett started after him, but Joe stopped him, "Let him go. He doesn't know anything else. Even if he did, he won't talk any more once he starts dancing."

Joe and Brett drove back to Joe's house to pick up a few things. Brett had convinced him to stay at his house at least for the night. Joe shook his head and sighed when he walked into the shambles someone had made of his home. He turned chairs back on their feet as he walked through. He walked over to his answering machine and discovered three new messages.

He hit the button to play them. "Call your mother. She needs to know her baby is okay." Joe smiled and shook his head. The second message was a computer sales pitch; Joe hit the erase key. The third was his FBI friend who said, "This is Howie from Dallas. I tried your cell phone, but got no answer. Please call me first chance you get."

Joe checked to see when the call came in. The machine said, "Friday, 9:13 a.m." He looked at his watch and murmured, "It's too late to call him now."

"Who's that?" Brett asked.

"A friend of mine, FBI Agent Howie Martin. I think I may have told you about him. Back in my rookie days, I stumbled into a mess and ended up saving his life. He feels like he owes me, so he was more than glad to help me out when I called. I found a phone number in Steve's stuff on the Sterling-Murdock case. He's checking it out for me. It may be nothing, but he's going to see who it belonged to back then. He's also going to see what he can find out about Bill Davis for me. He knows not to call me at the office. I'll call him first thing in the morning."

CHAPTER 20

After Sabre met with Bob at Clara's Kitchen for their usual Thursday morning *tête-à-tête*, she went to court, completed her morning calendar, and afterwards, drove to see Alexis at Jordan Receiving Home. She hadn't seen her since the incident with the bat. Alexis smiled when she saw Sabre and greeted her with her usual, "Good afternoon, Miss Sabre."

"Hello, Alexis. You look lovely, as usual." Alexis always looked so tidy and well dressed, though the Jordan staff told her Alexis was quite the little athlete. When she played, she played hard and got as dirty as the rest of them, but she always insisted on appearing "proper" when she "received visitors."

Alexis appeared to be happy to see Sabre. Although she started right in with her chatter about the staff members and the other children, she acted a little more subdued than usual. Sabre put her arm around her; the little girl felt fragile. "I'm so sorry about the incident at my office with the bat. But you know what?"

"What?"

"You were so brave. I'm so proud of you. Who knows how long I would've lain there before someone found me, if you hadn't taken charge and called for the help I needed." She gave Alexis a little squeeze. She felt Alexis stand up a little taller, and watched her face light up.

"Thank you," Alexis said. With a devilish little smirk she added, "Does this mean you're not mad at me anymore for leaving Jordan without permission?"

"Of course I'm not mad at you. You just scared me because you could've been hurt. There are lots of scary things out there."

"I know," Alexis responded.

"Please promise me you'll never do it again. Okay?"

"Okay. Next time I'll call you and you can come pick me up," she said with confidence.

"Deal," Sabre said, reaching her hand out. Alexis took it in hers and shook on it.

Alexis' mood seemed to lighten and her exuberance returned as they continued with their visit. She reported all of the Jordan Receiving Home gossip. She knew about every staff member and each and every minor in the Home, what they did and didn't do, down to the smallest detail.

Sabre visited with her for awhile before she broached the subject of her mother's disappearance. "Alexis, I need to ask you some things that may be painful for you, but I really need to know. Do you think you can help me?"

"Probably."

"Do you remember the day your mom disappeared?"

"Nope," she said quickly. Then she added, "I just remember she used to play with me and read to me a lot. And then one day she wasn't there anymore."

Alexis looked so sad. Maybe she didn't remember anything about that day. So, Sabre let it drop and finished her visit, with Alexis continuing her account of the Jordan Receiving Home news. As she listened, Sabre continued to be amazed at the intelligence and maturity of the ten-year-old girl.

When Sabre got into her car to leave, she felt the car leaning to one side. She stepped out, walked around to the back. The rear tire on the passenger side was flat. Sabre, frustrated, hated inconveniences. She much preferred to deal with a major crisis, for which she had an abundance of patience. Little things like this annoyed her. She removed her cell phone from her bag and dialed the number for the Auto Club. They informed her the wait would be about forty-five minutes. Sabre walked over to a bench at a bus stop about twenty feet from her car, sat down, and called Bob.

"I'm close," he said. "I'll be right there."

Within ten minutes, Bob arrived. He parked two car lengths behind Sabre's car on the same side of the street and walked to where she waited. "Thanks for coming," Sabre said.

"No problem. I was driving back to my office from court when you called. I had just stopped to buy a pack of cigarettes at my little corner store." Bob took a drag off his cigarette as he walked over to the car to look at the tire. "Aren't these new tires?"

"Yeah, I got them about a month ago. Remember? You were with me when I first went to look for them. I went back the next day and bought them."

"You must've picked up a nail or something."

"Yeah, that's what I thought."

Bob looked at the tire, feeling it with both hands, the cigarette hanging from his mouth, smoke seeping out. "I don't see or feel anything, but that doesn't mean much. They'll check it when they get here." Bob took another drag off the cigarette, dropped it on the ground, and stepped on it. Sabre cocked her head, raised her eyebrow, and frowned at Bob. He reached down, picked up the cigarette butt, and carried it with him as they walked back to the bench.

The tow truck took close to an hour before it arrived. The driver, a thin wiry man with mechanic's hands, stepped out of the truck. He checked Sabre's card and did the necessary paperwork. He put air in the tire and checked for leaks. "I don't see anything wrong with the tire. It could've been a slow leak, but I don't feel any air coming out anywhere."

"So I can drive on it okay?"

"Oh, yeah. It's fine. I'd take it back in where you bought it and have it checked, but it looks to me as though someone let the air out."

Sabre's heart lurched. She looked at Bob and caught a glimpse of the worrisome look on his face. "Probably some kid walking by, who just decided to have some fun at someone else's expense," she said, in an attempt to reassure herself.

It may have convinced the tow truck driver, but Bob didn't look satisfied, and neither was she. "I don't like it," Bob said. "There are just too many strange things happening to you."

"But nothing that can't be explained. It's not as if someone has shot at me or mugged me."

"No, but they may as well if they're going to scare you or annoy you to death."

"We don't even know for sure about the tire. I'll have it checked tomorrow." Sabre dismissed any thought of sabotage. She signed the paperwork, thanked the tow truck driver, and said, "Come on, Bob. Let's get out of here."

"Where are we going?"

"I need to go to the office for a little while, and then I'm going home."

"Are you sure you won't reconsider going to JP's place to stay?"

"No. I'll be fine," Sabre said, still refusing to be run out of her home. "Thanks so much for coming by to wait with me." She gave Bob a little hug and asked, "Where are you going now?"

"Back to my office. I'll be there for a couple of hours. Just call me if you need me." Bob walked with Sabre to the driver's side of her car. She got in and started the engine. The window open, Bob put his hand on the door, tapped with his finger, and said, "Lock your doors." She hit the lock button, the click sounding especially loud.

Sabre drove off, anxious to get to the office. She had wasted too much time today, and she already lagged in her work due to the hospital stay.

Elaine and Jack were still at the office when she arrived. She spoke with them briefly before going into her office. She had a multitude of phone calls to return and cases to prepare for court, so she buried herself in her files and tried to forget about everything else. When she came across a fax from the Atlanta Police Department, she called to Elaine, "What's this?"

"Oh, that came the other day. I thought you already saw it. It's the mystery page–page eight–from Peggy Smith's file. Remember, we couldn't read the one we had? This one is much clearer."

"Good, I must have missed it before. Thanks."

"I'm sorry. I thought you'd already seen it."

"Don't worry about it. It's not a problem," Sabre said.

"Okay. I'm about to leave. Is there anything you need before I go?"

"No thanks. You have a good evening. See you tomorrow."

Sabre dialed the number for Detective Carriage's office. His voice mail answered. She left a message for him to call her at home that night or in the early morning. She tried his cell phone, but it went directly to voice mail. "That's odd." She made a mental note to call his office in the morning. After putting the form inside the Murdock/Smith file, she placed it in the stack of things she planned to work on the next day, and resumed work on the cases she'd been neglecting because of her concentration on the Murdock case.

She had worked for almost another hour when Jack, the attorney in the front office, stopped in her doorway. "You ready to go, kid? Bob made me promise to chase you out when I leave. He doesn't want you staying here alone and I agree. I told Elaine the same thing; I don't want her here alone, either. That bat thing may have been a sick prank, but we don't know. If it was meant for someone in this office, it may or may not have been you."

"True, although you have to agree I'm the most likely suspect. You don't create too many enemies with your trust and estates practice, and anyone who knows David knows he's never here, especially on the weekends."

"True enough, but until we know more, we need to be careful."

"You're right. Let me just grab a few things and I'll be out of here," she said. "And, Jack . . . thanks for looking out for me."

He smiled at her with a paternal kind of smile. "Hey, I've grown fond of you, kid. I certainly don't want any harm coming your way. Besides, you've brought some life back into this office, all bubbly and enthusiastic. You keep us in stitches with your weird stories and crazy remarks."

"Thanks, I kind of like you too."

Sabre gathered up her files. Jack walked her to her car. He checked her tires. No indication of a leak. As she pulled out of the alley, she noticed a car across the street pull away from the curb and maneuver into the lane behind her. She drove straight for about three blocks and turned right. The car did the same. She made two more turns before she drove onto the freeway, continuously glancing in her rear view mirror; the car remained behind her. Sabre, alert but not scared, knew the majority of traffic was headed toward the freeway this time of night. Though the rush hour traffic had subsided a bit, the highway remained crowded, requiring some maneuvering to merge over to the middle lane. The car merged over as well. It stayed behind her for a couple of miles. Sabre, uncertain at this point if it was even the same car, decided to take the next exit off the freeway to see if the car would follow her. She changed lanes. The car did the same. Her heart beat faster. She checked her doors; they were locked. She checked her phone. It worked. Trying not to panic, she decided if the car followed her off the freeway, she would go straight to the police department. She could call them on the way and alert them. *Thank God for cell phones.*

Sabre saw the sign for the next off ramp. With her blinker on, she eased off. Glancing in the rear view mirror, she saw the blinker flash on the car behind her. Someone was after her, and she had already exited off the freeway. Too late to change now. Her heart pounded as she watched the car follow her. When she reached the street, she turned right. She picked up her cell phone to dial, glanced in her mirror again, and saw the car make a left-hand turn. Sabre took a long, deep breath, made a u-turn, and drove back onto the freeway. When she reached for her water bottle she felt herself tremble. She took another deep breath and tried to calm down. She had frightened herself again, jumping at every little thing. She knew she had to get it under control. Maybe that was the plan; maybe someone was trying to keep her in constant fear. *No, this is silly. I have to take my power back. I'm imagining things and making myself paranoid. That's it. I'm going home to have a nice cup of hot tea and forget about everything.*

CHAPTER 21

Sabre drove to the office, looking forward to a full day to catch up on her work. Bob arrived about five minutes later, carrying two large cups of coffee.

"Good morning, Sobs." He smiled as he handed her one of the cups. "I thought you might want to start your day with a mocha – decaf, light on the coffee, extra chocolate, no whipped cream or foam – just the way you like it."

"Thanks." She took the coffee and sipped it. "It's perfect and still nice and hot. You must've read my mind." She took another drink of coffee. "So what are you doing here so bright and early this morning?"

"I knew you didn't have court and neither did I, so I thought I'd just come by to see you."

"Oh, fess up. You knew I'd be in early, and you weren't sure Jack would be here so you stopped by just in case."

"Well, that was my plan initially, but I called and Jack said you were on your way, so I decided to bring you some coffee anyway," he confessed. Bob looked at his watch. "May I use David's office for a minute? I need to make a phone call."

"Sure. Help yourself."

Sabre picked up the Murdock/Smith file and pulled out the fax she had received the day before. She read through it, not really expecting to find anything significant, when suddenly she let out a yelp. Bob dashed into her office.

"What's the matter?"

Jack ran in right behind him, "Are you okay?"

"I'm sorry. I'm fine, just startled by something I read."

Jack went back to his office, but Bob remained. "What is it, Sobs?"

"Peggy Smith has another child. I can't quite make out the name, but it looks like a girl. I wonder where she is."

Sabre reached for the phone and dialed the direct line for Detective Carriage's office. He answered it on the first ring. "Joe Carriage."

"Joe, it's Sabre Brown."

"Sabre, I'm glad you called. I planned to call you when I got in this morning, but I got tied up. You know how it is."

"No problem," she said. "Joe, I got the page you faxed me yesterday on Peggy Smith's family history. It looks like Peggy has another child, a little girl. Do you know anything about her?"

"Just a minute; let me grab it." He found the file in the stack on his desk. "Here it is." He paused. "She's five years old, just turned five in September. It says she's living with her mother, but you're telling me she's not there?"

"No, this is the first I've heard of her. Can you make out her name?"

"It looks like Honey . . . Honey Stone."

"Honey? Are you sure it's Honey?"

"Yes, why?"

"Alexis always becomes upset when you call her 'honey.' She says things like, 'I'm not Honey' or 'Don't call me Honey.'" Sabre paused for a minute. "The letter Alexis wrote to Mattie, I saw the greeting. It read, 'Dear Honey.' I wonder if she was writing to her. And where is she? Where is Honey?"

"I don't know. I'll see what I can find out about her and call you back in a few."

Sabre hung up the phone and turned to Bob. "Did you get that?"

"Yeah. So Peggy's little girl is named Honey and right now no one knows where she is."

"Right." Sabre reached for the phone again.

"You calling Marla?"

"Yes. I'm sure she must know."

"But if she does, why haven't we seen it in any of the reports?"

"Good point." Then she murmured, "I should've read her letter."

"Sobs, I need to run to my office to pick something up. I'll be right back, okay?"

"Sure. See you in a bit." Sabre dialed Marla's number and left a message for her to call back.

Bob left her office, returning about ten minutes later with the Murdock/Smith file. Sabre was just hanging up the phone with Marla. "So what did you find out?"

"Marla didn't know anything about Honey Stone. She's looking into it right now, and she's beating herself up for missing it."

"That poor woman. She works so hard, but there's never enough time to do everything she needs to do," Bob said. He liked Marla too, and that said a lot. Bob had little respect for most of the social workers, but Marla was different – diligent and reasonable at the same time – a combination Bob found lacking in most of the others. "What about Carriage? Has he called back yet?"

"No," Sabre responded. "What's this?" she asked, as Bob lay a piece of paper in front of her.

"It's the letter Alexis wrote to her friend."

Wrinkles formed across Sabre's forehead and her eyes frowned at him. "Where did you get this? And what does it say?"

"How should I know? I haven't read it. I copied it the day I copied your Murdock report. You said you weren't going to read it, and I thought if I made a copy then you'd have it if you ever needed it."

"You're so smart. I probably should've done that, but it didn't seem right."

"Well, you're not as twisted as I am, or as jaded." He smiled at Sabre. "But keep working juvenile and it won't take long. You'll be just like me."

Sabre picked up the letter and looked up at Bob again. She still felt uncomfortable reading Alexis' private letter. Bob spoke, "Just read the damn thing, or I will."

"Okay, okay. I'll read it." She commenced reading it to herself, then started over, and read aloud so Bob could hear it too.

> Dear Honey,
>
> I'm sorry I didn't teach you your ABCs. It's all my fault.
>
> I'm not living with father and Peggy any more. There are lots of people here. You would be safe here with me.
>
> We have a new baby sister. Her name is Haley Murdock, like my last name. But she's real pretty like you and she can hear real good, just like Jamie.
>
> I miss you. I love you.
>
> XXOO
>
> Alexis
>
> P.S. I asked God to bring you this letter. I hope you get it. And I hope you're not too hot.

Sabre marveled at how well she wrote. Alexis was a precocious little girl. Sabre surmised everything she had written had been given a lot of thought; now she just needed to figure out what it meant.

The phone rang. It was Detective Carriage. "Hi, Joe, what did you find out?"

"Well, Honey is Peggy's daughter all right. The best I can tell, she last lived with Peggy and Gaylord. She apparently hasn't started school yet. She should've, though, based on her age. Sabre, here's the kicker."

"What's that?"

"She's deaf. Peggy's boyfriend beat her when she was two years old and caused her to lose her hearing. The son-of-a-bitch is sitting in prison, but that doesn't help Honey,"

Joe growled.

Some of the pieces started coming together for Sabre, but the puzzle was still far from complete. She read the letter to Joe. "For some reason, Alexis must be calling Honey 'Mattie.' She's never mentioned Honey. In fact, none of them have, as far as I know. Why wouldn't she just call her Honey? Why did she say she was her friend and not her sister? She always calls Jamie her brother."

"I don't know. I checked to see if a missing person's report had been filed on her. There wasn't, at least not in Atlanta, but I'm expanding the search. I also have someone checking to see if a death certificate has been filed."

"I've tried not to think of that possibility. I better be careful when I talk with Alexis." Sabre cringed. If she's not alive it could explain why no one talked about her. It might just be too painful.

"There's obviously a lot we don't know. I'll investigate further, and you'll be the first to know if I come up with anything."

"Thanks for everything, Joe. I really appreciate it."

Sabre thought she should tell him what she had learned from Ruby Sterling. Before she could, Joe spoke up, "Sabre, there are some other things I need to share with you, but right now I have to run. Just do me a favor."

"Sure, what?"

"Be careful. Don't take any chances, okay?" he said, his voice tense.

"Okay, but you're scaring me. Is there something I should know?"

"I don't really know a whole lot yet. It may be nothing and it may not even affect you. Just be cautious, okay?"

"Sure thing."

"By the way, my cell phone is working again if you need to reach me."

"Thanks, what was wrong with it?"

"Long story. Tell you next time." She heard the dial tone.

Sabre hung up the phone and shared the conversation with Bob, except the last part about being careful. It would only make Bob more nervous, and he already drove Sabre crazy with his concern for her safety.

"So what's next?"

"I need to call Marla, give her the latest bit of information, and see if she has learned anything new. I'm sure she'll be talking with Peggy and Gaylord very soon to see what they have to say," Sabre said. She drew a deep breath, "I need to talk with Alexis." She didn't cherish the thought of broaching this subject, but she wanted to talk with her before Gaylord or Peggy did, in case they were hiding something.

"Well, if you don't need me, I'm taking off. I'm meeting with a client in twenty minutes," Bob said.

"Go ahead. I'm fine. I'm going to hang out here for a few hours, do some work, and see what turns up. Then I'm going to pay a visit to Alexis. I'd like to take her out of Jordan for awhile, but ever since I spoke with her grandmother, I'm afraid to. I guess I'll just speak with her there."

"Okay, Schweetie," Bob said in his Humphrey Bogart voice, as he gave her a hug.

Sabre walked him to the door and thanked him again for coming by, for the coffee, and for the letter. She walked back to her desk and called Marla. She left her a message letting her know the latest from Atlanta. For the next couple of hours, she buried herself in work, trying not to think about her visit with Alexis and hoping she'd have more information before she went.

On her way to Jordan Receiving Home, she received a call from Marla. "There doesn't seem to be a missing child report filed anywhere on Honey Stone," she told Sabre. "Our department hasn't found any death certificates yet, either, but that process takes a little longer."

"Have you questioned either Peggy or Gaylord yet?"

"No, but it's my next step. I had planned to do it

earlier, but a new case came in with pretty severe injuries to a three-year-old. A little boy got in the cookie jar without permission, so his stepmother punished him by holding his hands over a gas burner on the stove. His hands had first- and second-degree burns," Marla spit out the words with contempt. "No matter how long I do this job, I'm still sickened by the horrible things these parents do."

"Geez, what's the matter with people? She should be hanged."

"Careful, Sabre, she may turn out to be your client."

"Good point," Sabre said. "Well, I'm on my way to see Alexis. I'll let you know if I find out anything I can share with you."

"Thanks. We'll get to the bottom of this."

Sabre arrived at Jordan just as Alexis finished up an art project. Alexis told the attendant she needed to clean up first before she saw her attorney, but the attendant convinced her it was okay not changing her clothes. Alexis had red, brown, and yellow paint on her pink shirt and on her frayed pant leg. Although she had washed her hands and face, she had a little spot of paint on her upper arm and on her neck. For the first time, Sabre saw her looking like a regular kid.

"I'm sorry, Miss Sabre. I didn't have a chance to clean up properly. Our art project went later than I thought, and they made me come out without cleaning up. I did wash up, but I wanted to change my clothes, too. I didn't want to keep you waiting, either. I know your time is important. You see my dilemma?"

Sabre turned her face to hide her expression, amazed and amused at Alexis' vocabulary and mannerisms. She sounded like a little southern belle someone had set at the wrong speed. Alexis didn't have a strong southern accent, and she spoke so much faster than anyone else Sabre had ever met from the south, but her attention to etiquette was southern to the core. "Yes, I do see your dilemma. And thanks for being so considerate of my time. By the way, you look just fine. You really don't need to dress up on my account. If I didn't have to, I certainly wouldn't wear these monkey suits and high heels. I'd much prefer wearing jeans and a t-shirt."

As they spoke, Kathy, the attendant, brought Jamie out. Alexis took his hand and led him back to the interview room. The sliding glass door to the patio was closed because clouds filled the sky, making it chillier than usual. Jamie seemed to be more at ease, not as needy. Instead of clinging to Alexis, he went straight to the toys. Alexis seemed comfortable with his newfound independence.

Sabre let Alexis tell her all the latest Jordan gossip before she brought up the subject of Honey. First, she reminded Alexis of the confidentiality rule. She tried to think of a delicate way to bring it up, but decided there wasn't one. "Alexis, tell me about Honey," Sabre said. "Honey Stone."

Alexis' face turned pale and her eyes grew wide in astonishment. Then, just as quickly, she composed herself and said, "I don't know what you're talking about."

"Do you know where she is?"

"I don't know what you're talking about," Alexis said again, this time her voice quivering, tears welling in her eyes, speaking almost in a whisper.

A little voice came from the corner of the room. Jamie sat holding a doll and speaking to it. "Honey gone," he said. "Honey gone."

Alexis' eyes grew even wider at Jamie's remarks. She took a deep breath and her little body convulsed. Sabre couldn't stand the pain in her fragile little face. She moved next to Alexis on the sofa, pulled her close to her, and whispered, "I'm sorry. I'm sorry for upsetting you. I'm sorry for whatever you have seen or suffered through. I don't mean to add to your pain." She sat there rocking her while Alexis snuggled up into her arms exposing the little girl hidden deep inside. She didn't say a word as Sabre comforted her. "It's okay," Sabre said. "When you're ready."

CHAPTER 22

Sabre walked into Marla's office to see the frazzled social worker on the phone, another line ringing, and a co-worker standing in her doorway vying for her attention, her desk in its usual state of disarray.

Marla put the first caller on hold, clicked over to the other line, and said, "Please hold on; I need to talk to you. I'll just be a minute." She went back to the first line, motioned with her head toward a chair, and mouthed to Sabre, "Have a seat." She finished up the conversation on the first line. Before she picked up the second line, she turned to the worker in the doorway, "What can I do for you?" she asked in her frenzied state.

"The Bartlett file? Do you have it?"

Marla dug through some things on her desk, pulled out a file, handed it to the social worker, and picked up the second line and said, "What did you find out?" She waited for a response. "What about surrounding states?" Another pause. "Okay, please fax me what you have. And thanks, I appreciate it." She hung up the phone, took a deep breath, and turned to Sabre.

"Looks like your day is going well," Sabre said.

"It's been like this since I arrived this morning," Marla said, taking another deep breath. "That call was about Honey Stone. No missing person reports have been filed on her, either in Georgia or anywhere near there."

"So, she is missing?"

"Not according to Peggy and Gaylord, but sometimes a relative will file something when the parents don't, so I checked." The phone rang. She picked it up and said, "Marla Morton." She paused while the person on the other end of the phone spoke. "Set it for Monday afternoon. I can't do it today." She paused. "Fine. Bye." She turned to Sabre, "Sorry, it's just one of those days."

"I understand. So what are Peggy and Gaylord saying about all this?"

"Peggy said Honey is with a cousin who lives near Atlanta."

"Have you talked to the cousin?"

"No. According to Peggy, they went camping and they can't be reached by phone right now. She gave me a phone number for their home, but it's disconnected."

"So does Peggy ever check on Honey? And why is she with the cousin?"

"Same questions I asked. Peggy said she spoke with Honey yesterday and she was fine. She says the cousin calls her occasionally to check in with her."

"She said she spoke with Honey?"

"Yes, that's what she said."

"But Honey is deaf. She couldn't have had much of a conversation with her on the phone."

"I asked about that. She then said the cousin talked for her."

"That's odd," Sabre said.

"The whole conversation with Peggy was odd. She fidgeted the whole time and I caught her in some obvious lies. She gave me the cousin's name – Adelle Thompson – when I pressed her, but she continued to refer to her as 'my cousin' instead of Adelle. She said she left Honey there because it made it easier on her. She said Honey has stayed there on and off since her birth. Apparently, whenever Peggy fell on hard times, this cousin would help out and take Honey in."

"When did Peggy last see Honey?"

"Just before they left for California. They dropped her off and left that night or the next day."

"Did you talk to Gaylord?"

"Yes, he has the same story, pretty much. But according to him, Honey lived mostly with the cousin and she only came to their house once in a while. He said Adelle brought her over to stay a few days with her mother before they left for California. The day before they left, Peggy returned her to Adelle. He said they spoke with the cousin every few days, or at least once a week. Of course, he didn't know what's been going on since he and Peggy split up."

"Did he sound nervous like Peggy?"

"No, he was very cool and unconcerned. He didn't see anything out of the ordinary."

"Did you ask why they've never mentioned Honey before?"

"Yes, I did. Gaylord kind of shrugged his shoulders, said he hardly knew the girl, and it wasn't any secret. He didn't know why Peggy hasn't mentioned her, except she's not real close to Honey. He said Honey is more like a niece or a cousin to her than a daughter. And, from what he's seen and heard, Adelle pretty much raised her."

"What about Peggy? Did you ask her why she has never mentioned Honey before?"

"I sure did. She just said, 'I dunno. It just never came up.' I couldn't get anything else out of her."

"So where do we go from here?"

"You've been working with a detective in Atlanta on this case, right?"

"Yeah. Joe Carriage."

"Do you think you could ask him to see what he can find out about Adelle Thompson? I have a request into Human Services, but it could take awhile. I can't really 'red flag' it because there's no indication she's missing or anything. She's probably with the cousin, but I'd sure like to know before the hearing on Monday."

"Sure. I'll call Joe and see what he can do. I'm sure he'll help if he can," Sabre said. "Now, I better get out of here so you can get something done." Sabre rose to leave. The phone rang again. She waited a minute to see if it had anything to do with her case. Marla answered the phone, spoke for a second, and then shook her head at Sabre. As Sabre walked out the door, she heard Marla dealing with yet another crisis.

She got into her car and plugged her ear phone into her cell so she could talk and drive at the same time. She'd shut the ringer off while in Marla's office. She had two missed calls and three messages waiting, two of them from Joe. She dialed his number.

"Joe Carriage."

"Hi, Joe. How are you this afternoon?"

He didn't answer her question. "Sabre, I'm glad you called. There are some things happening here you need to know about, but first let me give you the information I have on Honey Stone."

"Okay—"

"We've found no trace of any reports filed indicating this child is missing. There's no death certificate filed on her. It seems Honey lived, at least part of the time, with some relative of Peggy's. We don't have a name yet, but . . ."

"We have a name: Adelle Thompson. Peggy says she's a cousin, but she couldn't articulate the actual lineage. She supposedly lives outside of Atlanta. Peggy said she's camping right now, but she had a story so riddled with holes we really have no idea. We were hoping you could follow up for us. We just want someone to see this little girl so we know she's safe."

"I'll do it right now. Let me call my partner; we'll get an address, and I'll call you back shortly."

"Sure thing. I'm headed back to my office. You can call me there or on the cell."

"Is someone else at your office with you? You shouldn't be alone there."

"Yes. Jack's there working, but thanks for your concern."

CHAPTER 23

With just a sliver of daylight, Joe and Brett looked for the number on the mailboxes. The houses, not well marked in the area, made it difficult to find Adelle Thompson's house. They turned into what appeared to be the correct dirt driveway, with a trailer set back about two hundred feet from the highway. They drove past a pickup and an old Chevy coupe with more rust on it than paint. The Chevy had two missing tires and a broken windshield. The pickup didn't appear to be operable, either. Junk littered the yard. A large German shepherd, tied to a sagging clothesline post, barked angrily at the approaching strangers. The only thing inviting was a swing hanging from a huge, old oak tree just to the left of the trailer.

Joe and Brett stepped out of the car and walked to the door, kicking beer cans and bottles out of their way. Joe knocked. A wiry, skinny woman, who stretched to less than five feet tall, with a black eye and missing teeth, answered the door. "Are you Adelle Thompson?"

A man yelled out from somewhere in the trailer, "Who the hell's at the door, Adelle?"

She yelled back, "I don't know yet. I'm a askin'." She turned back and said in a slurred voice, "I'm Adelle. Who are you?"

In spite of the big wad of gum in her mouth and a screen door between them, Joe could smell alcohol on her breath. He held his badge up so she could see it, "Detective Carriage, Atlanta PD, and my partner, Brett Wood. We need to ask you a few questions. May we come in?"

"Sure, why not?" Adelle said as she opened the screen door, still chomping on her gum. "Who else is here, ma'am?" Brett inquired.

"Just my ol' man. He's layin' down, not feelin' too good, if you know what I mean," she said.

They stepped from the front door into the kitchen-living room area. Leftovers from several meals and dirty dishes covered the counter and the kitchen table. Empty Styrofoam containers and paper bags from fast food restaurants, half-empty coffee cups and ashtrays full of cigarette butts decorated the room. Dirty dishes soaked in a dark gray tub of scummy, stinky dishwater in the sink. Joe couldn't decide which smelled worse – the dishwater and rotting food, or the cigarette smoke and alcohol permeating the air.

The small living room contained a sofa and coffee table, a recliner, and a fifty-inch television, leaving little space to walk. Boxes and junk were crammed in the corners and piled waist high. A pizza box with one dried-up piece of pizza still inside sat on the coffee table with six empty beer cans and two full ashtrays. A half-eaten piece of bread with peanut butter and jelly lay face down on the coffee table next to a box of Marlboro Lights and a cigarette lighter with a naked woman on the casing.

Adelle stumbled as she kicked aside the trash on the floor to make a pathway to the sofa. She grabbed a blanket, a pillow, and a pair of men's dirty underwear off the sofa to clear a spot for the detectives to sit. As she picked up the items, an empty beer can rolled onto the floor and a piece of pizza fell from the blanket. She made no attempt to pick them up; she just threw everything down on the recliner and sat on top of them.

"Have a seat," she said, as she motioned toward the sofa. Joe sat down on the edge of it across from Adelle. She turned and looked back at Brett, "There's room for you, too, dearie."

Brett was too uncomfortable to sit anywhere, and he

wanted to be positioned where he could see down the hallway. He could hear someone snoring, but he didn't know who else might be in there. "No, thank you, ma'am. I've been sitting all day," Brett said, cringing.

Adelle took the wad of gum out of her mouth and stuck it on the side of the ashtray. She reached for the pack of Marlboro Lights, and popped a cigarette in her mouth. "Mind if I smoke?" Before anyone could answer, she lit up. "What are you here for? Is someone complainin' about our mutt again? He ain't done nuttin' wrong. He's been tied up for weeks, ever since he bit the mailman," she slurred.

"No, ma'am. We're not here about your dog." Joe said. "You have a cousin named Peggy Smith, correct?"

"What's that woman up to now?"

"Actually, we need some information on her daughter, Honey. Is she living here with you?"

"No, she ain't here no more."

"Do you know where she is?"

"She was wit' Peggy last I knew."

"When did you last see her?" Joe asked.

"Couple months ago, I guess."

"Where?"

"At Peggy's boyfriend's house in Atlanta," Adelle said. "She lived wit' us a couple of years, you know. We had her more than Peggy did. Then 'bout a year ago, Peggy started seeing her again. Honey would get real excited when Peggy came around, but Peggy never paid her no attention. Oh, she'd act all gushy over her, givin' her kisses and stuff when she'd first see her, but then she'd just kind of ignore her. I still don't know why, but that kid loves her mother. She wanted to see her real bad. So we started takin' her over there every few weeks to spend a few days. Peggy's boyfriend had a little girl who hit it off real well with Honey. Her name was Alex, or Alexie, or somethin' like that."

"Alexis?"

"That's it . . . Alexis. She even tried to learn sign

language so she could talk better with Honey. She's a sweet little gal, that one. She's the one who took care of Honey when she stayed there. God knows Peggy couldn't do it."

"Why's that?" Joe replied.

"You kiddin'? She's drugged out of her mind half the time. I tried to get her to stop that stuff. Been tellin' her for years. I would say, 'Peggy, yer killin' yerself with that junk. If ya want to get a little high, have yerself a few beers. A few beers never hurt nobody, but that other stuff, ya can't be doin' that.' But she wouldn't listen to me. She wouldn't listen to nobody."

"You said you would take Honey to visit her mother. The last time you saw her, were you taking her for a visit?"

"Yup. I took her over there to spend a couple of days. She was supposed to be comin' back, but Peggy came by late one night and said she was keepin' her. She said they were movin' to California and Honey was goin' with 'em."

"Did she have Honey with her when she came by?" Joe asked.

"Nope. I think her boyfriend, Murdock, was in the car, but he didn't come in."

"Did you actually see Murdock in the car?"

"I saw someone in the car. It was definitely a man and it looked like him, but I couldn't be certain. It was too dark. But who else would it be?"

"So, he stayed in the car and Peggy came in?"

"Yeah, she just ran in and told us she was takin' our Honey to California, and then she left, actin' all crazy like."

"What do you mean?"

"I don't know. All anxious and jittery, probably comin' down from somethin' she'd done."

"Have you spoken to Honey or Peggy since?"

"Nope, not a word. I didn't even get to say good-bye to her." Through tears, Adelle asked, "Ain't Honey with Peggy?"

"I haven't seen Peggy," Joe said. "I was asked to come by here and get some information." Joe stood up. "Do you mind if we look around a bit, ma'am?"

"Go ahead. I ain't got nuttin' to hide."

"I'd like to ask your husband a few questions also."

"I expect he's asleep by now. If'n he is, you ain't gettin' him awake for nuttin'. That man could sleep through a bomb goin' off."

Joe and Brett followed Adelle back to the bedroom, looking around for any signs of Honey. The door to a small bedroom on the left side of the hallway hung halfway off the hinges, and the room was piled with junk. Joe stepped inside, but he could only go about a foot and a half because no floor space remained open to walk. "That was Honey's room when she lived here. Now we just use it for storage," Adelle said. "Of course, I'll clean it up when she comes back."

In a room at the end of the hall a heavy-set, unshaven man lay face down across the bed. Adelle shook him, saying, "Harry, wake up." He just lay there. Except for the snoring, they would have thought him dead. "Harry," she screeched in her shrill voice. "Harry, wake up. Some cops want to talk to you." He stopped snoring for a minute, but he still didn't move. She yelled again, still nothing. Adelle grabbed his shirt, shaking as hard as she could, still screaming at him to wake up. He moved a little and moaned, then turned over and within seconds started snoring again.

With little room to maneuver in the small room, Joe felt claustrophobic. "It's all right, ma'am," he said. "It doesn't look like he'd have much to say anyway." Brett started to walk back down the hallway first. Joe stepped back and let Adelle go next, keeping an eye on his back.

"You've been most helpful, ma'am. We sure appreciate it." He handed her a card and said, "Please call me if you hear from either Peggy or Honey. Would you?"

"Sure. Is she okay? Honey, I mean. Is there somethin' wrong? They better not hurt her. I've been worried sick ever since they left – Peggy with her drugs and her fancy boyfriend with his gamblin'. Who knows what might happen to those kids."

"Are you talking about Gaylord Murdock? Is he a gambler?"

"Yeah, that Murdock guy. Comin' from all that money and everything. Peggy thought she had herself a good catch with that one, as far as the money goes and such, but he ain't got no money. His folks do, but he ain't got none 'cause he spends it all gamblin'."

"How do you know?"

"Peggy told me. She said he's gettin' worse and worse. He's all mixed up with some thugs in Atlanta. I think that's why they went to California. I think he's hidin' out, if you ask me."

"Is there anything else you can tell me about Gaylord?"

"Nope, I only saw him a couple of times. He always acts real proper and such, like he's too good for us. I didn't like him much. He made me uncomfortable, but it never bothered Harry. He always says, 'He ain't no different than us, pees with his pecker just like any other man.' Anyway, we never spent no time with them, never socialized or nothin' like that. He was too good for that."

"Thanks again, ma'am. You be sure and call us now if you think of anything else we should know." Joe looked at her black eye, no doubt in his mind where it came from. "And you be careful, ma'am. Take care of yourself, you hear?"

"I will," she said, but Joe knew nothing would change.

CHAPTER 24

Sabre sat at her big oak desk, trying to focus on her tasks at hand. She grabbed the phone every time it rang in hopes it would be Joe with news he had found Honey Stone. Her mind refused to entertain any possibility other than that Peggy's cousin, Adelle, had her. Her knotted gut, on the other hand, was painfully aware of the possibilities. The phone rang again.

"Sabre, it's Joe. I just left Adelle Thompson's."

"Did you see Honey?"

"I'm afraid not. She's not there. According to Adelle, she's still with Peggy."

Sabre's heart sank. She imagined the worst. Silence followed while she tried to catch her breath. "Sabre, are you okay?"

"Yes," she said, her voice quaking. She took another deep breath. "So Peggy says she's with Adelle and Adelle says she's with Peggy. Did Adelle seem credible?"

"It's hard to say. She was pretty drunk. Her old man had passed out already, and she had a fairly fresh black eye I expect came from him. I don't think she hurt the little girl, but he may have done something to the kid. My gut feeling, though, is she told the truth." Joe filled Sabre in on the details. "One more thing: Adelle said Gaylord is a gambler and he's mixed up with some heavyweights. Do you know anything about that?"

"No, it's news to me."

"Well, Adelle didn't like Gaylord much. I think his social status made her feel inferior. That may or may not have been intentional on his part, but she did feel put down. It could be she's exaggerating what she heard from Peggy about the gambling. I'll see what I can find out. Maybe the social worker could talk to Peggy about it as well."

"I'm sure Marla would be happy to."

Sabre thought about what she had learned from Ruby Sterling and wondered if Elizabeth's disappearance had anything to do with Gaylord's gambling. She thought again about telling Joe, but was too afraid for Ruby and Alexis if he weren't clean. The more he helped her, the more she questioned his intentions. Yet, he seemed so sincere.

Sabre's thoughts were interrupted when Joe spoke again, "Sabre, there are some other things you need to know, for your own safety as well as Alexis'. There may not be a connection, but there have been too many coincidences for my liking." Joe paused for a second, trying to figure out where to start. "I haven't been totally honest with you. I told you my only interest in helping you was to protect Alexis, but the truth is I have my own agenda. I had an interest in helping you right from the beginning because of my friend, Steve."

"Who's Steve?"

"Steve Parker was my best friend through grade school and high school. He's the reason I became a cop. He and his partner, Bill Davis, worked on the Elizabeth Sterling-Murdock case. He didn't finish the case because he died in a car accident. When you wanted information on Elizabeth, I thought it might be a way for me to help Steve. He would've done the same for me. I guess I should've told you from the beginning, but it just didn't seem important then."

"And now it does?"

"Well, there are still a lot of unanswered questions, but I think my investigation of this case is ruffling some feathers. And if it is, I'm concerned it could lead to you and to Alexis. Here's what happened — I went to go see Steve's wife, and look through his records to see if I could find anything on the Sterling-Murdock case. I knew Steve would have taken his own personal case notes. I remembered Steve telling me about a riddle he had come across. It drove him crazy trying to figure it out. He wasn't sure at the time if it had any bearing on the case, but he was determined to solve it and find out. Steve drove himself to solve any puzzle. It's one of the things that made him an excellent cop.

"Anyway, I recall his obsession with the puzzle he had found. He agonized over what it might mean. He would call and try to use me as a sounding board. I was so busy at the time, I got frustrated with him, but he kept hounding me. I knew he wouldn't let up until he had it figured out." Joe sighed. "He attacked this with a vengeance. He kept hitting me with bits and pieces, trying different angles to solve it. The night of his accident, he called and left a message saying he had figured it out. He said he would tell me when we met for coffee the next morning. But I never saw him again, because he was killed about twenty minutes later."

"I'm so sorry, Joe. I had no idea. What does it have to do with Alexis or me?"

"Well, a few other things have happened since I read Steve's notes. Several entries on his notepad indicated there might be some bad blood in the department. If it's true, Steve's death may not have been an accident. So, I put out some feelers and shortly thereafter someone broke into my house."

"And you think they were after his notes?"

"I'm pretty certain of it, but I can't prove it," Joe said. "That same evening, someone ran my car off the road. They tried to kill me, much like Steve was killed. I think whoever did it probably figured if I didn't die from the accident, I would certainly heed the warning."

"But you didn't?"

"No. Now I need to find out if Steve was murdered. If it's within the department, that's even worse."

"Do you have any idea who it is?"

"I have a pretty good idea, but I can't prove it. I think it's Bill Davis, Steve's partner. They investigated the case together, but Bill seemed real anxious to close it quickly."

Sabre thought about the information she had heard from Ruby. She was still torn between telling and keeping her word until Joe said, "If something doesn't break soon, I won't be able to continue to work there. The word is already out I suspect a cop of being dirty, and that's a cardinal sin in the department, not to mention the fact he tried to kill me once. It's likely it'll happen again."

Though difficult for Sabre to break her word, she believed Joe, and she saw no alternative. She had to trust he would protect Ruby and Alexis. "Joe, I might be able to help."

"I doubt it, but I appreciate the offer."

"No, I mean I have some information that might be of use to you."

"What is it?"

"First, you have to promise you'll protect the people involved."

"Absolutely."

Sabre told him about her conversation with Ruby. She reiterated the threats made against Ruby if she told anyone and about Ruby going to the police, only to see Steve's partner with one of the thugs. She gave Joe the description of the cop, as Ruby had given it to her. It matched Bill Davis.

"Sabre, you are my guardian angel! You may have saved my life, kid. I promise I'll do everything within my power to make sure Ruby is safe. We now have the missing link. This gives us enough to go to Internal Affairs. They'll obtain the information from Ruby, and they'll protect her. Internal Affairs is relentless when it comes to cleaning up the department. This will probably re-open Steve's accident as well. IA will want to know if there's any connection, and I bet they'll find one."

"Well, you're welcome. I hope it helps," Sabre said, hoping her trust had been correctly placed.

"You did the right thing. You won't be sorry," Joe said.

"I hope not," Sabre said, as she hung up the phone. "I surely hope not."

Sabre phoned Marla to let her know Honey was not with Adelle. "Oh, my God," Marla said. "Where is she?"

Sabre knew her question was rhetorical, but she answered anyway. "I don't know."

"I'll see what I can find out from Peggy and Gaylord. I'll let you know."

~~~

Marla took Wayne, a senior associate, with her to question Peggy and Gaylord. She didn't really want to be alone with either of them, and she wanted a witness in case one of them said something incriminating. She decided to drop in to catch them as unaware as she could.

Marla knocked on Peggy's door. Peggy opened it before her knuckles hit the door the second time. The look on Peggy's face indicated her disappointment. "Oh," she said. "What's up?"

"We need to talk to you. Can we come in?"

"Actually, I was just leaving," Peggy said, obviously lying.

"This won't take long," Marla said, as she stepped inside. Turning to her associate, she said, "Peggy, this is Wayne, my supervisor."

"Hello," Peggy said, but turned anxiously toward the door so she didn't see Wayne extend his hand to shake hers.

"Nice to meet you," he said, putting his hand back down by his side.

Peggy paced in short, rapid trips around the room, twisting her hands and puffing on a cigarette. Every few seconds, she looked at her watch and then the door. Marla guessed she was about to score some drugs, but decided not to question her on it yet. She figured Peggy's anxious state might help her obtain the information she needed. Her drug deal could be dealt with later.

"Peggy, please sit down for a minute. We have a few questions we need to ask you." Marla said to her in a gentle but commanding tone.

Peggy sat down at the table and Marla and Wayne joined her. Her cigarette almost gone, Peggy reached over and put it out in the ashtray. Marla spoke, "Peggy, we need to ask you one more time. Where is your daughter, Honey?"

"I told you. She's with my cousin."

"Your cousin, Adelle Thompson?"

"Yes, that's right."

"Peggy, the police in Atlanta have spoken with Adelle. Honey's not there. Adelle said you had her – that you came by and told her you were taking her with you to California."

"No, she's lying. She's not with me. You can see she's not with me." Peggy reached for her pack of cigarettes and lit one up. She stood up and started pacing again. "She's lying."

"Why would she lie about it?"

"Because she hates me. She just wants to get me in trouble." She took a long drag on her cigarette, sucking it deep into her lungs. "She wanted to adopt Honey, but I wouldn't let her. Honey always liked me better than she did Adelle, and she hates me for it." The smoke came out of her mouth and nose as she spoke. She was becoming more and more anxious.

Someone knocked on the door and Peggy rushed to answer it. She spoke for a moment with the man at the door and then stepped partly outside, blocking the door so the social workers couldn't see them. Wayne stood up and walked toward the door. When he did Peggy said, "No, she's not home. Come back later. She should be back in about an hour." She closed the door, turned, and said, "Someone looking for my roommate."

"Right," Wayne said.

"Peggy, if you want to have Haley and Jamie back in your custody, you have to clean up," Marla said.

"I'm clean, honest. I haven't used in a long time. I've been clean for weeks. I swear."

"Then why aren't you drug testing?"

"I've been trying to, but they had my number messed up. The paper had me down as a four and then when I got there they said I was a five, and so I went on the wrong day."

"No, Peggy, the paper said you were a five. You need to go on the days they're testing fives."

"I did. I went on Monday, but they closed early. They were supposed to be open until eight o'clock and I got there at five minutes to eight and they wouldn't let me in. They'd already locked the door."

"Why did you wait until so late to go?"

"Because I didn't have a way to get there. I had to hitch a ride, and by the time they got me there the doors were locked."

"Why didn't you use the bus tokens I gave you to get to your testing?"

"I didn't have any more. I used two of them to go see Jamie and Haley, and then I must've left them on the bus, 'cause I couldn't find the rest of them when I got home."

It was no use. She had an excuse for everything. Marla let it go. She and Wayne continued to question Peggy about Honey, but she kept denying any knowledge of Honey's whereabouts. Marla and Wayne finally gave up and left.

Once outside, Wayne shook his head and said, "Isn't it amazing how stupid druggies think the rest of us are? At least we interrupted her 'score' for a few hours."

"Do you think she knows where Honey is?"

"Well, she's either the world's worst mother, or she knows where she is."

"Or both."

"Good point," Wayne responded. "She never once gave

any indication of concern the child might be missing. She never suggested we ask the police to help find her. Instead, it was all about what Adelle was trying to do to her."

"Anyway, we can consider her officially missing now and the police will investigate. Let's swing by and see if we can catch Murdock. Then I'll go back to the office, write up the report, and fax it to Atlanta so they can begin their investigation."

Darkness had set in by the time they reached Gaylord's apartment. "Good evening," he said. "Come on in. What can I do for you?"

Gaylord, well mannered, polite, and cheerful was much easier to deal with than Peggy. Marla really hoped he wasn't involved in any way. "We'd like to ask you a few questions."

"Sure, what about?" He motioned to the sofa. "Have a seat. Can I get you some coffee or anything?"

"No, I'm fine," Wayne said.

"Me, too," Marla added. "Gaylord, you remember Wayne? I believe you met him at my office early on."

"Yes, and we've spoken several times on the phone, also."

Marla spoke, "Gaylord, we need some more information about Peggy's daughter, Honey Stone. The police went to see Peggy's cousin, Adelle, this afternoon. Honey's not with her."

Gaylord's voice went up a notch and his brow wrinkled with concern. "What do you mean? She's not with her? She has to be with her. Peggy took her back there the day before we left to come here."

"Adelle said Peggy came by her house and told her she was taking Honey with her to California."

"That doesn't make any sense. Why would she say that?"

"I don't know. Did you go with her?"

"No, I had too much to do. Peggy went by herself."

"Are you sure she took her to Adelle's?"

"She said she did, and she had nowhere else to take her." Murdock thought for a second, "Oh my God, poor Honey. Where do you suppose she is?"

"We don't know."

"Do you think Adelle or her husband . . . what's his name? Harry? . . . may have done something to Honey?" Gaylord suggested.

"Why do you ask?"

"I hate to put people down, but they had some real problems. I only saw Adelle a few times, and Harry only once, but every time Adelle came around she looked like she'd been beaten up. I'm sure he knocked her around. She always had some excuse for the cuts and bruises. As far as I know, he never hit Honey, but like I said, I didn't see much of any of them."

"So the last time you saw Honey was at your house the day before you left to come to California?"

"Correct."

"Was Peggy high when she left with Honey?"

"No, she didn't seem to be. She hadn't been using for months prior to then. She stayed clean from the time she became pregnant with Haley until recently when she started using again. I thought it was the stress from the pregnancy getting to her." His brow wrinkled. "Does Peggy know Honey isn't with Adelle?"

"Yes, we just spoke with her."

"Peggy must be beside herself," Murdock said. He sat, shaking his head in disbelief. "I'm sorry; I can't even imagine what it would be like to not know where your little girl is. If I didn't know Alexis' whereabouts, I don't know what I'd do. Thank God she's safe. Every day I pray for her to come back home with me, but at least I know where she is."

CHAPTER 25

Sabre agreed to meet with the detective investigating the whereabouts of Honey Stone. She walked into the police station and checked with the desk clerk. A policeman came out and greeted her, "Good morning, Miss Brown. Thanks for coming by," he said, as he shook her hand. "Gregory Nelson."

"Nice to meet you. I'm glad to help," she responded. Something about him looked familiar, but she couldn't place him.

He caught her staring at him. "You don't remember me, do you?"

"No, I'm sorry. Do I know you?"

"I handled the bat incident. By the way, how's your head?"

"Much better. Thanks for asking." She gave him a warm, appreciative smile.

Nelson asked Sabre a few questions indicating his familiarity with the facts of the case. Marla had written her report and provided it to Nelson the night before.

"You seem to know about as much as I do about this case. What do you need from me?"

"Actually, I need to know about Alexis. What's she saying about what happened to Honey?"

"I don't know. She hasn't even acknowledged Honey's existence. I tried bringing the subject up yesterday, but it really upset her, so I let it go."

"Do you think she'll talk to me?"

"I doubt it."

"Do you think she knows something we don't?"

"I think she knows a lot we don't." Sabre shared what she knew about Alexis' imaginary friend, Mattie, and how Sabre now believed it to be Honey. "There must be some reason why no one in the family has mentioned her."

"And why Alexis felt it necessary to create an imaginary friend so she could talk about her," Nelson added. "I'm going to have to talk with her. She may know something that'll lead us to Honey and possibly save her life."

"I know. Just be gentle with her. She's a lot more fragile than she tries to act."

"I will. I promise," Nelson said.

Sabre believed him; his voice was warm when he spoke Honey's name. His brows wrinkled and empathy emanated from his face, as he looked at the photograph of his own family sitting on his desk.

Sabre left the police department and drove to the facility for the third session with Carla, Dr. Vincent, and Dr. Steele, hoping it would be easier than the first two. The sessions drained everyone, especially Carla. During the first one, Carla had clung to Dr. Steele the full hour, afraid to let go for fear he would disappear. At the end of the session, Carla had to be physically removed from him and taken back to her room. Sabre stayed with her for two hours until Carla finally fell asleep.

The second session went a little better. At least it appeared easier for Dr. Steele, since Carla didn't wrap herself around him for the whole time. She stayed very near him, though, and she never took her eyes off him.

Dr. Steele and Dr. Vincent were already in the room when Sabre walked in wearing blue jeans, a gray sweat shirt, and tennis shoes, her hair pulled back in a ponytail. It was Saturday, and she didn't dress up on her day off. Besides, she knew Carla would be more comfortable if she came in street clothes.

"Good afternoon," she said.

"Hello, Sabre. Thanks for joining us," Dr. Vincent said. Dr. Steele nodded his head and smiled.

"My pleasure," she said. "I'm not late, am I? I rushed to get here."

"Nope, you're right on time. Carla's on her way," Dr. Vincent responded. He turned to Dr. Steele, "Corbin, I know it's difficult to put much physical space between you and Carla, but try to walk around as much as you can. Let her see your walk."

After the last session, Sabre and the two doctors had met and made a list of the similarities and differences between Ron and Dr. Steele. They hoped to emphasize the things more "Steele-ish" so Carla would see the doctor rather than Ron. One of the most obvious to Sabre was Dr. Steele's walk. Another difference was that Ron almost never stopped smiling and joking. Dr. Steele, on the other hand, acted more serious.

Phylis brought Carla into the room. Her eyes lit up as she saw Dr. Steele, and she dashed toward him. "Carla, you remember Dr. Steele," Dr. Vincent said.

Dr. Steele walked toward her with his hand extended to shake hers, trying to act natural and hoping to avoid another bear hug from Carla. Carla stopped for a second and looked at him, her eyes following his movements, his expression, appearing to drink in the very essence of him. Her expression, quizzical for a few seconds, changed to sheer joy as she neared. She reached for his hand and then pulled him into a hug, mumbling stuff in his ear that apparently made no sense to him. After some coaxing from Dr. Vincent, Carla let go.

To Sabre, the session seemed much like the first two, but in their recap after Carla left, Dr. Vincent seemed encouraged. Although he couldn't be certain what Carla was thinking, there seemed to have been several times when she had questioned Dr. Steele's behavior. Dr. Vincent also pointed out that Carla had left with less resistance. "I believe, with a couple more sessions, Dr. Steele will be able to resume his work here. I'm not suggesting, in such a short amount of time, Carla will be convinced he's not Ron, but I think it'll help for her to see him conducting his work. Maybe you've noticed she doesn't believe Ron left and became a doctor. That doesn't seem to be possible for her."

"That makes sense," Sabre said. "Anyone who knew Ron knows he would never choose medicine. He fainted at the sight of blood, and he didn't believe in taking prescriptions. He believed something existed in nature to heal anything ailing you and you didn't need synthetics in your body. He wouldn't even wear polyester because he didn't want it on his skin. His clothes had to be cotton, or silk, or something natural. Besides, he'd never have made it through med school. He squeaked by in college, not because of his intelligence, but because they didn't hold classes outside. He couldn't stand to be cooped up. No, the one thing Ron would never be is a medical doctor." Sabre looked at Dr. Steele and realized she was also convincing herself. There was hope for Carla.

Dr. Vincent put his hand on Sabre's shoulder. "I know this must be difficult, but we couldn't do it without you. Your insight is invaluable. Thanks again for coming. See you in a couple of days. "

"Anything for Carla." She stood up, smiled, and left the room.

~~~

Sabre drove to the beach, parked her car, and walked toward the boardwalk, hoping some time by the water would help take her mind off Honey. Fall was her favorite time of the year for the beach.

She approached the beach, smelling the salty ocean air and enjoying the breeze on her face. She wandered along the boardwalk, breathing in the air and admiring the magnificent ocean, the tide high and the waves crashing down. She loved the sound they made and the way the white caps of foam formed as they reached their crests. She took a deep breath, sucking in the majestic beauty before her. She imagined every one of her troubles being washed out to sea as the tide went out. She let them all go, and each new wave brought her more tranquility.

Reaching her favorite spot, she hoisted herself onto the concrete wall that acted as a breaker for the high tide. Feet dangling, she waited for the sun to set. About sixty feet away, she saw a man sit on the wall. He wore a black overcoat and a dark green knit cap, and he appeared to be looking in her direction. Within a few minutes, several other people sat on the wall between them. The sun started to set, and all along the boardwalk, people stopped to watch.

The bright yellow sun set, painting the ocean bronze, and the sky streaked with hues of pink, promising another breathtaking view. Sabre wondered if there would be a "green flash." Every so often, when the sun set on the ocean, the atmosphere was such that it created a flash of green light.

Sabre remembered the first one she had seen. During her freshman year of college, she and Ron were at the beach watching the sunset, unaware the flashes even existed until then. Just as the last bit of sun disappeared into the water, the horizon briefly flashed a bright green. Both she and Ron exclaimed, "Did you see that?" Sabre had only seen about half a dozen of them over the years, but every one she saw gave her brother back to her for that moment in time.

The rounded edge of the sun disappeared into the ocean, the sky fuchsia for miles around it. Sabre watched the last bit of yellow light meet the dark blue waters. She waited, watching for the flash of green. The sun sank, but no flash. She continued admiring the beautiful sky. Flash or not, it delivered a tranquil sight.

Before she descended from the wall, she glanced to her right and saw the man who had seated himself there earlier. As she rose, so did he. She walked toward him, in the direction of her car. After a few steps, he turned and went between some houses along the shorefront. She knew she was letting every little coincidence make her uneasy, and she didn't want it to ruin her beautiful evening at the beach. She had to let go of this crazy paranoia. She took a deep breath.

As she approached the spot where the stranger had been sitting, she smelled the familiar odor of Kantor cologne. Once again her heart skipped a beat. It was the only cologne Ron ever wore. The smell grew stronger the closer she came to where the man had been seated.

She peered around, but he seemed to be gone. She watched as she walked to her car, but no further evidence of him or the smell presented itself. More paranoia?

Frustrated, she drove home. Her relaxing time at the beach had lost its effect because she let her imagination run away with her again. The smell of the cologne, however, still bothered her.

She ate some leftovers and cleaned up the kitchen. She put in her favorite old movie, *When Harry Met Sally*, and climbed into bed. It made her laugh, no matter how many times she watched it, but her attempt to lose herself in the movie proved unsuccessful. Both the stranger at the beach and Honey occupied her mind. What happened to that poor little girl? She would try again to talk with Alexis.

After she tossed and turned for an hour, she fell asleep, but woke up several times thinking about the child whose world was void of sound. Where could she be? Each time Sabre fell back to sleep, she had a nightmare; either someone chased her or she dreamed of Honey, lost somewhere, wandering around by herself, scared and hungry.

After Sabre woke up for the third time, she went downstairs and warmed a glass of milk. As a child, if she had a hard time sleeping, her mother would bring her one. It always seemed to work when she was younger. Sabre couldn't be certain if it was because of the milk or because her mother would snuggle up to her and hold her until she fell asleep.

She sat on the edge of her bed and sipped her milk. She finished, crawled under the covers, and after lying there about ten seconds, she felt something move in the bed. She first thought she had moved the covers, until she felt it crawling on her leg. She screamed as she jumped out of bed. Her heart pounded. She trembled as she stood frozen in place trying to catch her breath. She just stood there with her body convulsing until she had the good sense to turn on the light. Her reluctant hand reached for the blanket, grabbed the corner of the covers, and threw them back. Something darted away. She screamed again, jumped back, and bumped her head on the wall. Finally, she saw it, a harmless, little lizard. She tried to calm herself. She took a step, but her legs felt like jelly. Her heart beat faster, as she inched her way around the bed, pulling the covers off onto the floor. He seemed to be alone.

Too frightened to get back in the bed or to lie down anywhere, she took a blanket from the closet and shook it out. She went downstairs, took the cushions off the sofa, and checked each crack and crevice. When satisfied there was nothing in it, she sat down on the sofa with the blanket wrapped around her, her knees pulled up to her chin. She sat in the dim light, still shaking. She wanted to call Bob, but it was three o'clock in the morning. For the rest of the night, she remained on the sofa in a state of fright, waiting for the sunrise.

CHAPTER 26

Sabre dragged herself into the courthouse on Monday morning with dark, puffy bags under both eyes. Between the lizard and the nightmares about Honey, she had only slept a few hours over the weekend.

Mike, her favorite bailiff, was working the metal detector. "Good morning," he said.

"Hi, Mike. How are you today?" she asked in a less than enthusiastic voice.

"Obviously better than you. Rough weekend?"

"You might say." She forced a smile.

"Well, you look like something the cat dragged in. I hope it was worth it."

"Absolutely." Sabre winked, as she exited the machine. She didn't want to talk about what was really on her mind, and complaining about her lack of sleep wouldn't do any good. So she left him with the impression she'd had a wild weekend.

She picked up her stack of files and walked over to her usual spot. Setting the files on the shelf, she spotted Bob at the front door. She walked over to greet him. His presence alone gave her comfort. "Mornin'," she said.

"Hi, honey," Bob said, putting his arm around her shoulder as they walked. "You doing any better?"

Sabre had called Bob as early as she thought appropriate Sunday morning. After sharing her lizard experience with him, he came right over and checked her house, but they couldn't find the little culprit. Bob tried once again to encourage her to leave her house, but she refused.

"I'm okay. I just need to catch up on my sleep. I'd sure feel better if we knew what happened to Honey Stone."

"Still no word, huh?"

"Nope. The police, both here and in Atlanta, are investigating, but no one seems to know where she is. They've questioned everyone involved and none of the stories have changed. Gaylord and Peggy say they left her with the cousin, Adelle. Adelle and her husband say she should be with Peggy."

"What about Alexis? Does she know anything?"

"Oh, I think she knows a lot, but she isn't talking. She has either blocked it out, or she's just too afraid to say anything."

"So what are you going to do at the hearing this morning?"

"All I can do is set it for trial. I can't let Alexis go home until I know Murdock isn't involved with Honey's disappearance."

"So the department hasn't changed their recommendation? They still want to send her home?"

"Marla doesn't, but she had pressure from her supervisor. They've decided Murdock is a good guy and Alexis should be able to go home. Marla was delighted when I told her I was setting it for trial. We're both hoping by the time we go to trial, we'll have some answers on Honey's whereabouts."

"Let's go get it done," Bob said.

They went to Department Four for the Murdock/Smith case. The other attorneys were already in the courtroom when she and Bob entered. Sabre informed everyone she needed a trial date on Alexis. The recommendations for Jamie and Haley to remain in foster care went unopposed by Sabre, but Peggy's attorney asked for the return of those children to their mother and Murdock wanted Haley in his custody. The attorneys took out their calendars and, along with the court clerk, agreed on a trial date of December 28, which placed the trial about a month out. Then they called the parents in for the hearing.

Tom Gilley, Murdock's attorney, argued for the return of Alexis to her father, pending the trial. Nevertheless, Judge Cheney denied his request since that was the crux of the contest by the minor's attorney. Gilley was not surprised; he didn't expect anything different. However, Murdock's disappointment was evident. He tried to maintain his usual calm demeanor, but his face reddened with anger. Sabre caught him looking at her with contempt. It only lasted a few seconds before he regained control. Although his look had sent a chill down Sabre's back, she thought about how he must feel. *What if he hasn't done anything except try to protect his unborn child? What if he is a victim like the children? How unfair, then, to him and to Alexis. Who am I to decide, to play God, if you will, and keep them apart, especially now during the holidays?* Nevertheless, she had no choice. She had to know what happened to Honey before she could let Alexis go home.

Her thoughts were interrupted when Judge Cheney spoke, ". . . the trial is set for December 28th; settlement conference, ten days from today. The parents are ordered to return for both hearings. All previous orders remain in full force and effect."

Sabre stayed in the courtroom until the parents had left. She didn't want to face Gaylord Murdock.

"What's the matter, Sobs?"

"I'm okay. I just hope I did the right thing. I hate to see families split up, especially for the holidays. And now Alexis will be in Jordan for Thanksgiving and Christmas."

"She'll be fine. She likes it there, and they love her. Besides, she'll be with Jamie, and that's important to her."

"True, it would be hard for her to be apart from him. But maybe they should both be with Murdock. He's doing everything the department has asked him to do," Sabre said.

"But what about Honey? There's a missing five-year-old no one can explain. They're all lying. Think about it. Why hasn't this child been reported missing? Why didn't anyone mention her until we brought it up? Why did Alexis need to make up a name for her and hide her identity?"

"That's exactly why Alexis needs to stay where she is until we know more. Besides, even if Murdock is not involved with anything illegal, he may not be able to protect Alexis from those thugs who snatched Elizabeth."

"You did the only thing you could do. Something surely will shake out by the trial, and if not, it won't be your decision any longer. Judge Cheney will make the call."

"You're right. Let's get out of here. I need some lunch," Sabre said.

"Okay, I'll drive. Where would you like to go?"

"You pick. I've made enough decisions for one day."

They chatted as they walked. Bob lit up a cigarette as soon as they stepped out of the courthouse. When he reached the car he took a few long, hard drags, and put it out. "So, what are your plans for Thanksgiving? Are you going to see your mother?"

"Yes, I'm driving up there on Wednesday, right after court. Mom would have a fit if I didn't go. Besides, I'm looking forward to a change of scenery."

"Good, you need a break. When will you be back?"

"Probably Sunday evening or late afternoon. Mom will insist I go to church with her on Sunday morning, and then she'll have to fix me a good meal before I leave. She's afraid I may starve to death on the long, one-hour drive. Then she'll pack me a care package of all the leftovers from the turkey dinner. Actually, that's my favorite part. I love the leftovers."

"My wife always makes a really big turkey so we can have sandwiches for a week, but after a few days, I get sick of them. Corey never seems to tire of them, though."

"So, are you going to the mountains this year?"

"Yeah, we're all going, the whole family, even 'the hippies,' my sister-in-law and her husband. It'll be a grand time," Bob said, in his usual sarcastic humor. "My mother-in-law will spend the whole time complaining; the hippies will make their own vegetarian dinner with their home-grown herbs; and their kids will run wild through the cabin, because the hippies don't believe in stifling them. Since there's no television, telephones, or video games, I'll pretty much be bored out of my mind."

"Sounds like a ball." Sabre, amused by Bob's reference to his sister-in-law and her husband as "the hippies," couldn't recall ever hearing their actual names.

"It's okay. When things become too crazy, Corey and I'll go skiing. He's getting pretty good," Bob said with pride. "I'm giving him some new ski equipment for Christmas this year. He's outgrown most of last year's stuff." He looked at Sabre, "Sobs, I'm glad you're getting away for a while. I feel better knowing you'll be out of town while I'm gone. That lizard thing bothers me. You should've called me when it happened."

"It was three o'clock in the morning. I didn't want to wake everyone up."

"I don't care what frickin' time it was," he scolded her. "You must've been scared out of your wits."

"It was a little spooky, until I realized it couldn't hurt me. The poor little thing was probably more frightened than I was. The way I screamed, it's a wonder I didn't scare him to death."

"Listen, Sobs, why don't you stay with us until you leave on Wednesday?"

"No. You don't need me intruding on your family."

"Then go stay with my friend JP, the private eye. He'd love the company. I'd sure feel better."

"Bob, it was just a lizard, a little lizard at that," Sabre said. "I just wonder how the poor little thing got into the house and into my bed." She saw the look of concern on Bob's face. "I'll be fine. You worry too much."

Sabre didn't tell him about smelling Ron's cologne at the beach. He'd never let her go home alone if she did.

CHAPTER 27

Detective Joe Carriage had the attention of Internal Affairs. The information Sabre provided from Ruby Sterling, coupled with the attempt on Joe's life, provided enough to spur them to open an investigation.

Brett and Joe left the department, walking together but not speaking. As soon as they entered the car out of earshot, Brett asked, "So, what's the latest from IA?"

"They've talked to Ruby, and she gave them the information they needed."

"Can she identify Davis?"

"She picked him right out of a set of photos. She also identified the thugs who took her daughter. The big guy is still in town. The other one is nowhere to be found, but they're looking for him."

"So are they going to make an arrest?"

"Not yet. They hope to find the second guy, and they're trying to find out who ordered the hit on Steve. There also appears to be a gambling ring under investigation that may be tied in with Elizabeth's disappearance and Steve's death."

"Well, I sure will be glad when this is over and things are back to normal at the office."

Before Joe could respond, his cell phone rang. "Joe Carriage," he said.

"Hi Joe, it's Howard Martin."

"Howard, nice to hear from you; I've been waiting for your call."

"I know and I apologize. I was waiting until I had more

to tell you, but I'm still chasing some loose ends. I can tell you this much, though. There's an FBI file on Elizabeth and Gaylord Murdock. It doesn't, however, include her disappearance. No one informed us. It should've been reported to us five years ago, but the liaison between the Atlanta PD and our department neglected to inform us. In fact, it looks like someone squelched it deliberately so we wouldn't know about it."

"So the FBI was working with the Atlanta Police Department, but we didn't keep you informed. Is that what you're saying?"

"Yup, but here's the kicker. The liaison . . . none other than your pal, Bill Davis."

"Bingo," Joe said.

"There's more. It appears your friend, Steve Parker, investigated thoroughly, in spite of the effort by Bill Davis to close the case. It looks like Steve must've gotten too close and that's why he turned up dead. And we have a pretty good idea where that may take us."

"Have you spoken to Internal Affairs about this?"

"No, I wanted to talk to you first, but I'll be glad to pass the info on if you say so. I'd have to do it eventually anyway, but I have a little leeway if you need some time," Howard offered.

"No, there's no reason to stall; in fact, the sooner the better. Thanks, Howard. You just made my life easier."

"Hey, it's the least I can do. By the way, I'm still working on the phone number. I should have something for you soon."

Joe hung up the phone and told Brett what he just learned. "That should add another nail to Davis' coffin. This is opening up their case, too, on Elizabeth and Gaylord Murdock. I wonder what that's all about."

"I don't know, but let's get back to the office. Adelle and Harry are coming in for the lie detector test this afternoon," Brett said.

"Do you think they'll show?"

"Who knows? Let's go find out."

Brett and Joe arrived back at the office a few minutes before the scheduled test. They tried to avoid as much time as they could at the department, but they walked in this time with the realization it would soon be over.

The examiner kept Harry in a separate room while they tested Adelle. He asked some preliminary questions and then delved into the questions about Honey. "Did Honey Stone ever live with you?"

"Yes, most of her life," Adelle answered; the needle steady.

"When did you last see her?"

"In October, just before Peggy left for California."

"Where did you see her?"

"At Peggy's boyfriend's house," she said. Still no suspicious activity on the machine.

"Have you had anything to drink today?"

"No." The needle went up.

"How much have you had to drink today?" the examiner rephrased the question.

"Just a beer, one beer; I had to settle my nerves. I was worried about the test. I drank it just before we got here. I didn't think one beer would hurt nuttin'." The needle steady again.

"Do you know where Honey is?"

"No." No activity on the monitor.

"Have you seen or heard from Honey since Peggy left for California?"

"No."

"Have you spoken with Peggy recently?"

"Not since she left for California." No movement on the machine.

"Are you in any way involved in Honey's disappearance?"

"No."

"Do you have any knowledge or information about her disappearance?"

"No." The needle did not indicate any misgivings.

The examiner looked at Joe and Brett to see if they had anything else they wanted covered. They both shook their heads. "Okay, Ms. Thompson, you're free to go. Just wait in the lobby; Detective Carriage will be with you shortly."

"Did I do okay? I told the truth, you know," Adelle said, her hands shaking. She looked like she could use another drink.

"You did just fine," Joe assured her.

When she left the room, the examiner spoke. "Well, the machine seems to think she's telling the truth. And it caught her immediately on the drinking question."

"Yup, I don't think she knows anything," Joe said. "Let's bring Harry in and see what the machine has to say about him."

They went through a similar series of questions with Harry and obtained the same results. In fact, the needle hardly moved. He showed little emotion about anything. At the end, when the examiner checked with Joe and Brett to see if they wanted to ask anything else, Joe asked, "Do you beat your wife?"

"Of course not," Harry responded. The machine went wild. "And this ain't sposed to be 'bout me and my wife; it's sposed to be 'bout Honey."

Joe nodded at the examiner, who unhooked Harry from the machine. "Okay, Harry, you can go," he said.

Joe thanked the examiner. He and Brett went to speak with Adelle and Harry. "So, how did Harry do? He didn't know nuttin' did he?"

"Harry did fine, Adelle."

"Peggy better not have done nuttin' to my little girl. I knowed I shouldn't of trusted her. Are you going to arrest her and her boyfriend?"

"We'll continue to investigate and we'll let you know if we find out anything about Honey's whereabouts," Joe said. He stood up and stepped towards the door.

Adelle ignored the implication to exit and went on,

"Those Murdocks will probably try to cover it up. All that money and all . . . ."

Brett walked over to her and directed her to the door, "Don't worry, Adelle, we'll take it from here. We'll find out what happened." He kept talking with her all the way to the door.

Before she exited, Adelle stopped and looked at Brett, "Don't let those Murdocks get away with this just cuz they got money. Ya hear?"

"We won't. We'll find out what happened, and we'll get the person responsible. You just go home and get some rest now," Brett said.

Adelle still would not leave. Finally, Harry grabbed her by the arm and gave her a yank pulling her off her feet. "Adelle, let's go. We're done here."

Joe did all he could to keep from popping Harry one for the way he treated Adelle. After they left, he said, "Boy, Harry's some piece of work, isn't he?"

"Yup, he'll probably go home and beat the crap out of her for making him go through this. He had little interest or concern about Honey. Say, if you don't need me right now, I have some paperwork to catch up on."

"Sure, I'll catch up with you later."

"Okay. I do want to stick around here for a while in case your friend Howard gets through to Internal Affairs. You know how they like to make their busts so everyone can see them. I wouldn't want to miss this one if it goes down at the department," Brett said.

When Brett left, Joe returned to his office, called Detective Nelson, and explained everything he knew so far. Then he called Sabre. He had several things he thought she ought to know for her own safety.

"Hi Joe. How was your weekend?"

"Not bad, and yours?"

"Interesting," she said without any further explanation. "What's up?"

"We just finished the lie detector tests on Adelle and

Harry Thompson, and they appear to be telling the truth. Peggy seems to be the last one who saw Honey."

"Does Detective Nelson know?"

"Yeah, I just spoke to him. He's going to go talk with Peggy again. Maybe even take her in for questioning."

"You don't think she'd hurt her own daughter, do you?"

"I don't know. It wouldn't be the first time a druggie sacrificed their kid for drug money. I've seen druggies do some pretty awful things."

"Yeah, me too, but she doesn't strike me as the type. Although, she is pretty self-centered."

"Well, we'll see what Nelson comes up with," Joe said. "Sabre, I think there's a connection between Elizabeth Murdock's disappearance and your attack by the bat."

"What are you talking about? What kind of a connection?"

"Remember, I told you Steve had a riddle on the case he was trying to solve. I found the riddle on the notepad Steve kept on Elizabeth's case. It read:

> *Color, a pretty, bright red*
> *In the darkness, toward the light;*
> *Circling, circling the head*
> *Blinding speed, causing sheer fright.*

Also, Steve left a note stating he had figured it out. He said it was a red bat."

After a moment of silence, Sabre said, "So you think whoever let the bat loose in my office has something to do with the Murdock case?"

"Well, you have to admit, it's a pretty strange coincidence. And another thing . . . . You don't find those red bats in California; they live east of the Rockies. Someone went to a lot of effort."

"I don't know what to think," Sabre said. "Maybe those thugs who took Elizabeth are after me. But why?"

"I don't know. Just be careful until we figure this out. One more thing – I found a phone number indented in the paper with the riddle. We're checking it out. It may be nothing, but I'll keep you posted."

Joe and Brett stayed at the office most of the day waiting for some action. Joe spoke with Howard Martin in the late afternoon. He had wasted no time contacting Internal Affairs. Martin provided them with the information on Davis and as much as he could from the FBI file. Between the FBI and Atlanta Police Department, they made twelve arrests, rounding up thugs connected to the gambling ring, but an arrest of Davis had still not been made.

CHAPTER 28

Sabre packed for the holiday weekend. Both her mind and body ached for some respite. She looked forward to playing with Ron's dog, Patches, sleeping in, baking pies, and spending time with her mother. The house would fill up on Thanksgiving Day. Uncle Chet and Aunt Victoria would be there with the twins. The girls, both married now, had five children between them. She looked forward to seeing the newest baby. Of course, she'd have to put up with all the remarks and questions about when she would follow suit. Nevertheless, she looked forward to the visit.

When she finished packing, she drove to see Alexis. She planned to visit with her, stop to see Carla, and then head out of town.

When Kathy, the attendant, brought Alexis out, her eyes lit up. "So nice to see you, Miss Sabre," Alexis said.

"So nice to see you, Miss Alexis," Sabre retorted. She turned to the attendant. "Thank you, Miss Kathy." Sabre looked around. "Where's Jamie?"

"He has a little stomach ache and is taking a nap. Did you want me to wake him?" Kathy asked.

"No, don't. I'll see him next trip."

Sabre and Alexis went into the interview room. Alexis told her all about the things planned at Jordan for Thanksgiving Day, including the special turkey dinner and the kids putting on a play. Alexis had a large part in the play and spouted off every word without a script. "Can you come to my play?"

"I'm sorry, Alexis, but I'll be out of town. I'm going to

see . . ." She didn't want to tell her about the visit to her mother. She imagined how many times Alexis must wish she could see hers. ". . . relatives in another city. They're fixing a big Thanksgiving dinner, much like you'll have here."

"It's okay. You've heard my part anyway," she said, but Sabre heard disappointment in her voice. "And it's the best part. Jamie and the other little ones are the turkeys. They have feathers for their tails and goofy beaks we made in art class, and they go around gobbling. They're sure funny . . ."

The door opened and Gaylord Murdock stepped in. "Hello, Alexis, Sabre," he said. "How are you two today?"

He reached out his arms for Alexis to come to him. She gave him a hug. "Hello, Father. I thought you weren't coming until tomorrow."

"Well, I missed my little girl, and so Kathy said I could come today."

Sabre was surprised to see him walk in. This was highly irregular and inappropriate. She'd have a talk with Kathy before she left, but right now she needed to deal with the situation without making a scene in front of Alexis.

"Hello, Mr. Murdock," she said. "Where's Kathy?"

"She's out there," he said, tilting his head toward the door. "She said since you were in here she didn't need to be, and she had a lot of other things to do this evening."

"Well, Alexis and I have just started our visit. Would you mind waiting outside for a little while so we can finish up?"

Murdock had his left arm around his daughter and his right hand in his pocket. "No problem," he said, as he walked toward her. "But first, I'd like you to do something for me." When he stood within inches of her, his eyes motioned to the hand in his pocket. He pulled his hand up so Sabre could see the tip of a handle on a pistol.

Sabre surveyed the room. She couldn't reach the phone without going through Murdock. If she screamed he might shoot and kill her and Alexis. "What do you want?" Sabre asked, trying to keep her voice steady.

"Alexis, get Ms. Brown's bag," he said. "Now, let's go out in the square," Murdock said calmly. Alexis looked confused. "Just do as I say, Alexis," he said firmly.

Alexis picked up Sabre's black bag and put it over her shoulder. She and Sabre moved toward the sliding glass door. As they stepped outside, the cold air hit Sabre, and she felt a chill come over her entire body. She saw Alexis shiver as well. Reaching for her, she pulled her close to keep her warm.

"Alexis, show me where you went the night you left here and went to Sabre's office. How did you get out?" Murdock said.

"Through here," Alexis said as she walked toward the outer door of another office, slowly opened it, and looked in. "Wait," she whispered. Alexis could see the clerk in the back room. As soon as the clerk turned her back, Alexis said, "Okay, quickly." She stepped inside the door, followed by Sabre and Murdock. They walked through the small room to the other side and out the door. A man came out of a room as they started across a hallway. They ducked around the corner, but the man turned the other direction and disappeared. Walking down the short hallway, they entered another room filled with old file cabinets and boxes. Alexis squeezed between a couple of boxes and behind a file cabinet to a door leading outside. Sabre and Murdock couldn't fit through. Murdock instructed Sabre to pick up one of the boxes. While she had her hands full, he grabbed the other one and moved it, allowing enough room for both of them to squeeze through.

As they stepped out into the cold air again, Sabre looked around for a way to escape. The sun had already set, but a street lamp illuminated the area. Murdock saw her looking around and stuck the gun in her back to remind her of his power. "Let's take your car, Sabre," he said.

"Where are we going?" Alexis asked.

"On an adventure," Murdock said, putting more pressure on the gun. "Where is your car?"

"Right there," Sabre said, pointing to the little green BMW.

Murdock looked at the car. "Never mind," he said. "I forgot you brought the Beemer. It won't hold all of us. We'll take my car, but you're driving." Murdock directed them about half of a block to his car. Sabre wondered how he knew she had more than one car. She always drove the BMW to court. What else did he know about her? Murdock opened the back door for Alexis on the passenger side. He held the gun above the roof of the car, aiming it at Sabre as she walked around to slide into the driver's seat. Then Murdock got into the car. "Don't forget to buckle up, sweetheart," he said to Alexis. "You, too," he told Sabre.

Murdock directed her to the freeway. They drove east toward the mountains, the traffic thick; many holiday travelers were already on the road. Sabre considered ramming into a car in front of her. Then they would have to stop and maybe she could get help, but it would just put more people in danger. "This isn't necessary, you know," she said.

"Oh, but it is," he replied. "Just drive where I tell you. No one needs to get hurt," Murdock said, sounding more like a statement of fact than a threat.

They drove for over an hour, twisting and turning through the back roads in the mountains. Sabre, unfamiliar with the area, tried to watch for every landmark she could, but everything looked the same, just trees and more trees. It had been a long time since she'd seen a street sign or a building. She tried to remember everything so she'd be able to return if she and Alexis could escape.

By the time they pulled off the pavement onto a dirt road, which seemed to lead to nowhere, it had been miles since they had passed any homes. Sabre glanced at the odometer: 32.2. She kept saying it over and over again in her head. They reached a little cabin, hidden by the trees, driving to within about sixty feet of it. She looked at the odometer and saw 33.8. *One point six miles, just over a mile and a half to the road.* She had no idea what direction they were going, though; without the sun, Sabre had no sense of direction. From the time they had left the freeway, she'd tried to keep her directions straight, but they'd made so many turns she really had no idea.

"Stop the car. Turn it off," Murdock said. He reached over and pulled the keys out of the ignition. "Just sit still. I'm coming around to open your door."

She was being held hostage and her captor wanted to be a gentleman. Alexis and Murdock climbed out of the car, and he walked around to the driver's side and opened her door. When she knew Alexis couldn't hear her, she whispered, "What are you doing? You'll go to jail for this."

"Come on," he said. "Let's go in. It's cold out here."

Murdock led them both into the cabin and turned on the light. The large room contained a living room, dining area, and kitchen. On the left, a six-foot-long counter separated the kitchen from the living area. An old, maple dining room table and four chairs sat across the room from the stove and refrigerator. On the right side were a sofa, a couple of easy chairs, and a huge fireplace with a pile of wood next to it. There was no television or stereo in the room, just a bookcase full of books. The old furnishings seemed to have fared well for their age. Across from the front door was a closed door Sabre surmised led to the bedrooms and bathroom. Sabre shivered. It didn't feel much warmer inside than out. She placed her arm around Alexis to keep her warm.

"Sweetheart, step away from Sabre," Murdock said. Alexis pulled away and moved to her father's side. Then, although speaking to Alexis, he kept his eyes on Sabre. "I know you may not like what I'm going to have to do right now, but I need to do it. You need to trust your father, and everything will be okay."

A chill went down Sabre's back. For the first time since

Murdock had brandished the gun, she feared for her life. *He's so calm and calculating. I'm going to die.* She looked at Alexis and saw her eyes open wide with fright. Her face solemn, she just nodded. Murdock said, "Good. Now, I may need your help. Come here."

Sabre looked for a way out, but Murdock stood between her and the door. She expected him to pull his gun and shoot her, or at least knock her out. He opened a drawer and pulled out some rope. He walked toward her, "Miss Brown, I'm not going to hurt you, but I need to tie you up or Alexis and I won't get any rest. Do you understand?"

As he came toward her with the rope, Sabre darted to the right. He reached out for her. She slipped back behind the table. He came closer. She moved around the table, getting as close as she could to the door. She yelled, "Alexis, run! Run for the door!" Sabre turned and moved toward the door. She glanced at Alexis and saw her standing frozen. She wouldn't or couldn't defy her father.

Sabre's hesitation cost her. Murdock tackled her. In spite of her efforts, she hit the floor. She tried to hold her head up, but she couldn't. She felt warm, wet blood trickle down her cheek.

Murdock grabbed her arms and put them behind her. Sitting on her hands, he tied the rope tightly around her ankles. He pulled her up by her arm, pushed her into a chair, and tied her hands behind it, as though he'd roped a calf in a rodeo – and he did it all in record time.

Sabre wiggled to free herself, but it only seemed to make the ropes tighter. She wanted to scream, but it would scare Alexis and wouldn't serve any purpose. She hurt from the fall, and the ropes cut into her wrists. She tried to stay calm and think rationally. "Gaylord, you don't need to do this. I won't try to run again."

Murdock didn't respond. He double-checked the knots.

"Gaylord, listen to me," she said. He ignored her. "Why are you doing this?" Her voice got a little louder.

He turned toward her slowly and deliberately. He leaned over and looked her straight in the eyes with the same piercing look he gave her in court when she set the case for trial. He stared at her for what seemed like minutes. Sabre could feel the hatred penetrate right through her. He stood up, smiled, and said, "I need to light a fire. It's cold in here." He walked over to the fireplace.

Sabre shivered from the cold dampness in the room and from the fear filling her. She took a deep breath, trying to calm herself. Alexis took a step toward her. She saw her sweet little face, her eyes veiled in sadness. She came closer.

"Alexis, are you okay?"

"Not too close," Murdock spoke up from across the room. "That's far enough."

When her father spoke, Alexis stopped. She stood about three feet in front of Sabre, "I . . . I'm okay," she said. "Are you?" Then, she mouthed with her quivering lips, "I'm sorry."

Sabre tried to compose herself for Alexis' sake. Her heart ached for her. "I'm fine," Sabre said. "I'm mainly cold, but I'll be better when the fire's burning."

Without saying a word, Alexis walked to the sofa, took a throw cover off the back of it, and took it to Sabre. She placed it around Sabre's shoulders and tucked in the sides so it wouldn't fall off. She looked up at her father, took three steps back, and stopped. "Thank you," Sabre said. "That's much better, and I'm already feeling the heat from the fire." When Alexis didn't respond, Sabre motioned with her head toward a chair a few feet from her and said, "Why don't you sit and . . . ."

Murdock, brushing his hands together to knock off any remaining debris, said, "Okay, the fire's going good. It'll be warm in here in no time." He acted as if they were a happy little family on vacation in the woods. "Let's have some dinner. You two must be starved. Alexis, give me a hand."

Murdock stood up. Alexis followed him into the

kitchen area. He leaned over and reached toward Alexis, put one hand on each shoulder and looked her straight in the eye. He lowered his voice, but not enough to keep Sabre from hearing. "Sweetheart, I know you like Ms. Brown, but remember she is one of *them*. We have to protect ourselves, so you need to do what I tell you. You need to trust me to keep you safe. Do you understand?" he said sternly, but with compassion.

Alexis looked him in the eye, and without speaking, nodded her head. "I've always kept you safe, haven't I?" She nodded again. Without hurting her, he tightened his grip on her shoulders and spoke a little louder. "Haven't I?"

Her response was meek, "Yes, Father."

"Okay, now you know you cannot untie her, right?"

Alexis nodded again and her father looked at her intensely. "Right," she said.

"What have you told Ms. Brown about our family?"

"Nothing, Father," she responded. He stared at her. "Honest, Father; I haven't told her anything."

Murdock put his arm around her and pulled her near, "That's my girl. I knew I could count on you. No matter what we go through, we always come out of it together, don't we?"

"Yes, Father."

"So I can trust you to do what I tell you, right?"

"Right, Father."

Sabre observed the two of them as they interacted in the kitchen. They were very efficient. She could see the strong bond between them. She had been hoping Alexis would be able to help her escape, but it didn't look promising. Whether out of fear or love for her father, Sabre didn't believe Alexis would defy him. It appeared Murdock felt comfortable in that belief as well.

"So what happens now?"

"Now, Ms. Brown," Murdock said with a little smile, "we eat our dinner. We get some sleep, and tomorrow I celebrate Thanksgiving Day with my beautiful daughter."

CHAPTER 29

"Are you sure? Could there be some mistake?" Joe asked the FBI agent.

"No mistake, Joe," Howard said. "I should have more information for you soon."

"Thanks, Howard." Joe hung up, stunned. He had to let Sabre know. She could be in more danger than they thought. He dialed Sabre's cell; when she didn't answer, he hung up.

He dialed her office and reached voice mail. "Hi Sabre, this is Joe Carriage. Please call me as soon as you receive this message. I have some information for you." He tried her home phone and again heard only voice mail. "Hi Sabre, Joe Carriage here. Please call me. It's important I talk to you right away." He waited for a few minutes and tried her cell one more time. "Hello, Sabre. Joe Carriage. I called you at your office and at home, but I just realized you may be traveling for the holiday and can't retrieve your messages. Please call me on my cell the minute you get this message, no matter what time it is."

Joe cooked a quick dinner and sat down to watch a movie. After a couple of hours without a call from Sabre, he tried her cell one more time. He fell asleep on the sofa with the television on, waiting for her call.

Leaves rustling in the wind awakened Joe at three-thirty in the morning. He still hadn't heard from Sabre. He shut off the television, and went to bed.

Joe woke again to the phone ringing.

"Joe, it's Brett. They arrested Bill Davis this morning.

Along with charges of tampering with evidence, accepting bribes, tax evasion, and several other things, they charged him with the murder of Steve Parker."

"So IA is finally doing something right. Do you know where they got the information to nail him?"

"Yup, it came from Ruby Sterling. She apparently gave them a mouthful. They also arrested both of the guys who nabbed Elizabeth Murdock."

"Do they have any information on her?"

"It doesn't appear so. Those goons aren't talking. I guess they're getting more out of Davis than they are those two."

"Well, that ought to make life a little easier at the office."

"It'll be a lot easier and back to normal before long. By the way, they also charged him with attempted murder on you."

Joe felt a weight lift off his shoulders. He took his shower, dressed for dinner, and tried Sabre again. By the time he reached his parents' house, he had called Sabre four more times. Although concerned, he decided to chalk it up to the holiday. *She's probably having a nice, peaceful meal with her family, in which case this information can wait. She'll call me tomorrow.*

~~~

Sabre heard her phone ringing in her bag in the other room. She wondered who might be calling, realizing no one would be missing her yet. Her mother didn't expect her until Thursday.

She turned to make herself more comfortable, her thoughts interrupted by the pain in her wrists and ankles from the rope holding them tied together. She had tried all night to shed the constraints, wriggling and twisting back and forth in an attempt to pull her hands out of the ropes, rubbing her skin raw. Between the ropes and her fear of

Murdock coming into the room at any moment to kill her, Sabre had little sleep and so many questions.

She could feel dampness on the bed from her burning, bleeding wrists. She ached from lying in the same position for so many hours. She was so cold. Sabre struggled, trying to move the blankets more tightly around her. With her feet tied to the bed and her hands tied behind her back, she bent over as far as she could, taking hold of the blankets with her teeth. Although she moved the blanket a few inches, she gagged from the mouthful of wool fabric and couldn't hold on to it. Dropping the two blankets, she tried again with just one. She pulled the blanket as far as she could with her teeth, but now it covered her face. Feeling claustrophobic, she lifted her chin to push it off. She had to get it off, no matter how cold she felt. After more twisting and turning, she nodded her head until the blanket fell down part way.

Though shivering, Sabre could at least breathe again. She thought about her nice, comfortable bed at home where she could fold the sheet neatly over the top of the blanket and keep it off her face, where she could tuck the blankets around her and keep warm. She shook from head to toe, her teeth chattering. She lay in frustration, her back now exposed to the cold air. The smell of pumpkin pie filled her nostrils.

Sabre heard heavy footsteps outside her door. It opened, and Murdock stood in the shadows. "Happy Thanksgiving, Ms. Brown," he said, as if nothing were wrong. Sabre stared at him, incredulous. She couldn't think of anything appropriate to say.

"Brr . . . It's cold in here. Come on. I've built up the fire in the fireplace." He untied her ankles from the end of the bed.

Free of the rope, Sabre stretched her legs and flexed her ankles. She stepped onto the floor, the blankets falling off her. The floor felt like ice under her stocking feet. She trembled, the cold cutting through her to the bone.

The fire enticed her. She walked in front of Murdock, down the short hallway to the living room. The smell of pumpkin grew stronger and stimulated her hunger. Sabre went straight to the fire, standing as close as she could.

"Is that better?" Murdock sounded concerned.

Sabre didn't get it. "Why are you doing this?"

In the same tone, Murdock responded with a question. "Why are you keeping my daughter from me?"

"It's my job to keep her safe. Unfortunately, I don't know enough about you to know if you are the best placement for her."

"You're right. You don't know me, and you don't know Alexis. We've done just fine for ten years without interference from outsiders." His voice grew louder. "You drive around in your little BMW and live in your fancy new condo. You come into our lives with your self-righteous attitudes. We don't need you to tell us how to live our lives."

Alexis walked into the room. Murdock turned to her and his voice became pleasant. "Good morning, sweet pea."

"Good morning."

"You ready to help your father with Thanksgiving dinner?"

"Sure," Alexis said. She looked at Sabre, as if to make sure she was all right.

Murdock walked over to Alexis, put his arm around her shoulder, and led her into the kitchen area. "I've already put the turkey in the oven, and I baked a pumpkin pie early this morning. You can cut up the stuff for the salad, but first you better have a muffin." They walked to the counter. Alexis put a blueberry muffin on a plate. She looked up at her father. He said, "Go ahead; take one for Ms. Brown. You never could let a stray go hungry. But she stays tied. You can feed it to her."

Alexis took the muffin to Sabre. Although it was awkward having someone feed her, she was thankful to be eating. Sabre forced a smile on her face, "Thank you,

Alexis."

"You're welcome, Ms. Sabre."

Sabre, feeling warm, moved away from the fire and sat down in the nearest chair. She watched as Alexis and Murdock prepared the Thanksgiving dinner. Alexis cut up the salad, making it ready for Murdock to toss. She peeled the potatoes. He cooked them and mashed them. She put the miniature marshmallows on the sweet potatoes after they were partially cooked, being careful not to burn herself on the hot pan. Murdock didn't like the marshmallows, but he didn't object since it was one of Alexis' favorites and one of the few dishes she remembered her mother making for her.

Alexis and her father conversed while they worked, but Alexis didn't behave like her usual chatty self. She would respond to his questions or comments and occasionally ask how to do something, but she didn't appear to be enjoying herself. Sabre wondered if this was her normal demeanor around her father. If not, Murdock didn't seem to notice.

As Alexis retrieved the plates from the cupboard, Murdock spoke, "Don't forget to set an extra plate. We have a guest coming for dinner."

For a moment Sabre thought there was someone else coming, but she realized he meant her. *A guest. How bizarre.* He acted as though she weren't in the room. She watched his every move to learn everything she could about him, to see his weaknesses, to see if she could use anything he said or did to help her escape. She spent most of her time trying to figure out ways to get away, but without Alexis' help and willingness to go with her, it didn't look hopeful.

Sabre sat in the chair for hours watching Alexis and her father create their masterpiece, like an old fifties movie, the warm room glowing from the fireplace and the smell of turkey in the air.

Her phone rang again. Was it her mother looking for

her? Marla? The police? Her mind raced with crazy thoughts. She worried about her mother and feared for Alexis; her wrists hurt from the ropes cutting into her, and she wondered if she would be alive tomorrow.

Sabre felt so tired. She had slept very little since her abduction. Sitting with her hands tied behind her wasn't easy. She tried to get comfortable in the chair, but she couldn't. She closed her eyes and tried to think pleasant thoughts until she finally dozed off.

Alexis startled her when she tapped her on the shoulder. "Ms. Sabre," she said. "It's time for dinner. Let's go wash up."

Murdock took a rope, and without saying a word, tied Sabre's ankles together, leaving them loose enough for her to shuffle along. He untied her hands. When she pulled her arms back in front, Alexis gasped at the sight of the blood and open cuts on Sabre's wrists. She looked up at her father, her eyes wide with concern and disbelief. Murdock glared at Sabre for a second, and said, "Now look what you've done, Ms. Brown. You need to quit trying to get loose. If you'll just hold still, you won't hurt yourself." He turned to Alexis, "Take Ms. Brown into the bathroom and rinse off her arms. I'll get the first-aid kit."

Once inside the bathroom, Sabre pleaded, "Alexis, you need to help me. We need to get out of here."

"Shh . . ." Alexis said, putting her finger over her mouth, "you'll upset Father."

Alexis helped Sabre clean up, and they returned to the living room. Murdock took bandages out of the first-aid kit and wrapped her wrists. "There now, Ms. Brown. That better?"

He directed each of them to their seats at the table. He bowed his head and said, "Let us pray." He glanced at Alexis and Sabre. Their heads bowed, he began, "Oh Lord, I want to thank you for keeping my daughter safe and for bringing her back to me." He paused. "Please bless this wonderful food we are about to eat. Bless all of us gathered here today. Bless those who don't have the good fortune to spend this great day of giving thanks with their families. And dear Lord, please bestow a special blessing on Alexis' mother and Sabre's brother, wherever they may be." He looked up, caught Sabre's eye, and winked.

"Amen," he said. "Let's eat."

CHAPTER 30

Due to the holiday, it was particularly quiet at the office when Joe arrived on Friday morning. Since he didn't have a family demanding his attention, he had offered to work for someone who did. Many of the officers came to him, shook his hand, apologizing for his or her behavior.

He was anxious to reach Sabre. It was nearly ten now, which made it almost seven on the west coast. He couldn't wait any longer. Sabre needed to know who the phone number belonged to and about the note he had found in Elizabeth Murdock's locker. He also wanted to inform her of the latest on the investigation on Honey.

He tried calling her cell phone, only to get her voice mail again. The only connections he had to her were Marla, the social worker, and Gregory Nelson, the detective who had handled the bat incident. He decided to try Marla first.

"Marla, it's Joe Carriage from Atlanta. Got a minute?"

"Sure, Joe. Do you have some information on Honey Stone?"

"Actually, I do, but I called to see if you knew how I could reach Sabre. I've been trying to call her for two days. I keep getting her voice mail. And she hasn't returned any of my calls. That's not like her."

"Joe, Sabre's missing."

"What do you mean, missing? What happened?"

"On her way out of town to visit her mother, she stopped to see Alexis at Jordan Receiving Home. Gaylord Murdock came in and sweet-talked one of the attendants into letting him into the room with Sabre and Alexis."

"Oh, no! Did Murdock kidnap them?"

"Well, we think so. No one saw any of them leave the building, but Murdock's car was gone and Sabre's was still in the parking lot. Someone at Jordan reported them missing when Alexis didn't return to her room. Some kid from teen housing who had sneaked out to have a cigarette said he saw a man, a woman, and a young girl get into a car fitting the description of Murdock's. The kid couldn't tell us much because the lighting is terrible there, so it's hard to tell if he saw them or not."

"Marla, I have some information that may shed some light on this. You know I've been doing a little investigating on the Elizabeth Sterling-Murdock case, right?"

"Yes, Sabre told me they investigated a police officer in conjunction with the case."

"Yes, Bill Davis. My best friend, Steve Parker, partnered with him on the force. Steve got too close to exposing him, and Davis killed him before he could talk. They arrested Bill Davis today and charged him with Steve's murder. Anyway, in the process of snooping around, I came across a note in Elizabeth's locker at the gym – a riddle about a red bat."

"A red bat? You mean like the one that attacked Sabre in her office?"

"Yes, that's what started me looking, because I remembered something Steve had told me about the case and a puzzle he couldn't solve."

"So you think there's a connection between what happened to Sabre and the Elizabeth Sterling case?" Marla sounded a little confused.

"Oh, there's definitely a connection, all right. I found a Dallas phone number indented in the note. I had an FBI friend of mine check it out for me. Five years ago it belonged to Ronald Adrian Brown, Sabre's brother."

"Oh, my God!" Marla gasped. "Do you think Murdock knew Sabre's brother?"

"It looks like it. I have no idea what Murdock is up to,

but I think he has an agenda far beyond anything we know about yet. I think Sabre is in serious danger. We have to find her."

"The police are looking for her. They've been searching since Wednesday evening. Since Alexis is a minor, they didn't have to wait twenty-four hours to begin their search. At first, they thought maybe Alexis had run away, but they realized Sabre hadn't checked Alexis back into Jordan. Sabre would never have left without checking her in. And then Murdock showed up. It's the only thing that makes any sense. But why would he kidnap Sabre?"

"Maybe she got too close to something, like what happened to Honey Stone, perhaps. By the way, Adelle's story checks out. It appears Honey never made it back to Adelle's from Peggy's. Adelle and her husband, Harry, both passed their lie detector tests. I don't know if Murdock had anything to do with Honey's disappearance, but at the very least, Peggy must know something. Have you learned anything new?"

"No, my immediate concern has been Alexis and Sabre, so I haven't had a chance to do much else. I know Detective Nelson is working on it, though. You may want to talk to him."

"I'll give him a call. By the way, things are heating up back here."

"How?"

"Adelle decided to go to the press, and she stirred up quite a bee's nest. Honey's picture has been plastered in the paper and on the local news, which is good in a way because someone might see her and report it. It is especially newsworthy here because of the Murdocks' political connections. But the phones have been ringing like crazy with false reports, and it has us all jumping." Joe thought about Sabre again. "I wonder where they are. I sure hope she's all right."

"She's a survivor, Joe. If anyone can get through it, Sabre can."

"Is there anything I can do to help?"

"Just keep us informed, and I'll do the same."

"Thanks, I'd appreciate it."

Joe couldn't keep his mind off Sabre. If he had just known this information sooner, maybe she could have avoided Murdock. Joe checked his messages and saw he had a call from Howard. He called him back.

"Sabre, Alexis, and Murdock are all missing," Joe told him when Howard answered the phone. Joe gave him the details.

"Do you think Murdock has them? Or maybe one of the thugs you're trying to round up has them all?"

"Well, we've stirred up a lot of commotion here with the arrests we've made, but the timing wouldn't be right. They were already abducted before we arrested anyone. So, unless something leaked out, Murdock's taking them is the most likely scenario, but why would he?"

"Based on the information I've gathered here, I think it has to do with the connection between Ron Brown and the Murdocks. When Elizabeth and Gaylord moved to Dallas, Elizabeth joined a gym, the same one Ron Brown used. They became friends, and shortly thereafter she introduced him to Gaylord. The three of them socialized some. They took a weekend trip together to Atlanta once, but other than that, they usually just went to the local races. Gaylord loved the ponies and anything else he could bet on. He gambled pretty heavy and sank deeper and deeper into debt."

"And Ron, did he gamble?"

"No. He bet occasionally, but he didn't have the sickness. He went to the races just because Elizabeth asked him to. They'd gotten pretty close."

"Were they lovers? Ron and Elizabeth?"

"I don't think so, but they were real tight. They saw each other almost every day at the gym and often had coffee together. She confided in him, told him things no one else knew."

"Was Gaylord jealous of Ron?"

"It appears so, but he never confronted either of them. Instead, Gaylord found a way to use Ron to his own benefit," Howard said.

"How?"

"Our theory is he knew enough about Ron to know he was a rescuer and he cared about Elizabeth, so he set him up. Gaylord was in debt to two different crime bosses, one from Atlanta and one in the Dallas area. The Dallas group had been trying for some time to spread their territory and wanted to take over the Atlanta area, but in order to do so, they had to get rid of the leadership there. Because of Gaylord's family connections and his own dealings underground, he had a lot of information on the Atlanta group."

"Was his family involved or aware of any of this?"

"No, they're as clean as a whistle. They did know he gambled, but I think they just looked the other way. They didn't disown him or anything, but they saw a lot less of him."

"I'm sorry; I interrupted you. So how did he use his information against Ron?"

"Well, Gaylord couldn't do anything himself because he knew the Atlanta group would take him out. So, he leaked the information to Ron through Elizabeth. The weekend trip to Atlanta took place so Ron could meet some of the guys and later be able to identify them. Of course, Ron didn't realize it at the time."

"What purpose did that serve?"

"As I said, Gaylord had Ron pegged as a rescuer and he turned out to be right. He knew Ron would try to save Elizabeth if something happened to her. Gaylord had some thug nab Elizabeth and force her to call Ron. As she had been instructed, she told him she was being held hostage by the Atlanta guys and to go to the police and tell them everything he knew about them."

"And he did?"

"Exactly. As a result, we had enough information to cease the operation in Atlanta, which in turn gave Dallas a chance to take over."

"It all seems so hopeless sometimes, doesn't it? You work so hard to get rid of one criminal element and another just takes up where they left off."

"Yes, it does. In this case, they moved in there before the convictions came down. We were their pawns, too, just like Ronald Brown."

"So why wasn't Gaylord ever arrested?"

"We could never pin anything on him. He knew a lot of people, but he had no involvement in their operation. We couldn't prove he had his wife held hostage. He made it look like the Dallas bunch kidnapped her. It probably was their thugs, but we're pretty sure Gaylord planned the operation. We tried to force him to testify against Dallas, but he couldn't see any advantage to it. I expect the Dallas group would've killed him if he had. I'm sure it also helped clear up his gambling debts."

"So he cashed in his wife for some gambling debts?"

"Not exactly; I think he just used her to help wipe out Atlanta. He had become pretty jealous of Elizabeth's and Ron's relationship by then, and he blamed Ron for the problems in their marriage. By setting Ron up to squeal on Atlanta, he evened the score with Ron, and at the same time, taught Elizabeth a lesson."

"Some lesson, getting rid of your wife," Joe said.

"I don't think he initially planned to get rid of her. We're not sure what happened there. But it got real messy, mostly because Steve had figured out too much, I think. So they had to get rid of him and probably her as well."

"So with Steve and Elizabeth gone, and with Murdock and Davis in their pocket, Ron could testify against the Atlanta leaders, Dallas could swoop in and take over, and no one would be the wiser."

"Exactly."

"So what happened to Ron?"

"Keep in mind, I wasn't a part of this operation. I'm receiving all the information secondhand, but from a reliable source. The file reads he was on his way to Montana to go fishing. They found his car at the airport with his fishing gear still in it. Nothing further is reported."

"So what does it mean?"

"It means he's either dead or in the witness protection program, but at this point I don't know which. That kind of information isn't easy for even us to get into, but I do have a way, and I'll let you know as soon as I find out."

"Thanks, Howard. I can't tell you how much I appreciate your efforts."

"Hey, it doesn't come close to what I owe you. I'll be in touch."

CHAPTER 31

Sabre spent another night with virtually no sleep. She woke so exhausted she couldn't think clearly, and her wrists and ankles felt like someone had sliced them with razor blades. At first she'd been terrified, but her fear turned to anger. She sat in the armchair near the fire as Alexis fed her oatmeal. She didn't feel like eating, but forced herself in order to keep her strength up. She put her head against the fold at the top of the chair attempting to get comfortable, not an easy task with her hands tied behind her back. Her body wanted to sleep, but her mind rebelled. She replayed everything she could remember from the moment Murdock walked into the room at Jordan. Maybe it would help her to understand what he wanted and, in turn, somehow help her escape.

Sabre sat straight up in her chair and gasped. Murdock had said yesterday she "lived in a new condo." How would he know? She had never told him or Alexis. She remembered something else he had said, and it took her breath away. When he gave the blessing, he'd said, "Bless Alexis' mother and Sabre's brother, wherever they may be." Terror returned and she gasped. How did he know she had a missing brother?

She looked up; through tired, blurred eyes she saw Murdock and Alexis cleaning the kitchen. They did everything together. She thought what a good father he appeared to be in so many ways. What a shame he insisted on destroying his life, a life he'd likely have been sharing with his daughter in a few short weeks. Why would he be willing to risk it all at this point? Nothing made any sense.

Her thoughts were interrupted by Murdock's voice. "Alexis, I'm going to go outside and gather some more firewood. You keep an eye on Ms. Brown. You know the rules."

"Yes, Father."

As soon as Murdock went out the door, Sabre said, "Alexis, we need to get out of here. We need to get away. Please help me."

"I wish I could, Ms. Sabre, but I can't. Father would be very angry. Besides, he'll let you go soon. He promised me."

"I don't think he will, Alexis, because then he'll go to jail. He'll have to get rid of me. Do you understand?"

"No, he won't. He won't hurt you. He promised." Her voice raised an octave.

"Alexis, come over here a little closer to me," Sabre coaxed, thinking it might be easier to get through to her if she could look her straight in the eye.

"I can't, Ms. Sabre. When Father is out of the room, I'm not allowed to get too close."

The door opened and Murdock came in, carrying a load of firewood. "It's a beautiful day out there. Alexis, why don't you go out and play a little. The fresh air will do you good."

Alexis picked up her jacket and started for the door. "Have fun," Murdock said. "Just stay in the front where I can keep an eye on you. I don't want anything to happen to my little girl."

"Yes, Father." Alexis seldom ever said anything to him except, "yes, Father" or "no, Father." She seemed complacent, almost comfortable in the role. Murdock didn't seem to notice any difference. Sabre knew a different Alexis, the one who wouldn't stop talking.

"Don't try to influence her. It won't work," Murdock said. "I know the minute I turn my back you're trying to convince her to help you. Don't waste your time. Alexis will never defy me."

TERESA BURRELL

"Why? Because you have her scared to death?"

"No, Ms. Brown, because Alexis loves me. We're a team. We've been close since she came into this world, and we only got closer after her mother left us."

"What do you know about my brother?"

"Plenty," Murdock said smugly.

"Why, when you gave the blessing yesterday, did you say 'wherever he may be'?"

"Well, you don't know where he is, do you?"

"No, I don't."

"So he's missing, just like Elizabeth. I just asked the Lord to bless them both. I'd think you'd appreciate it." He added, "A good looking chap, that brother of yours."

"How do you know what he looks like?" She knew full well he was playing her, with no way for her to stop the game. She knew he wouldn't let her stop at this point anyway.

"You have his photo on your credenza, in your office."

"But you've never been to my office."

"Oh, right. It must've been in your condo on the mantelpiece. Or upstairs in the hallway?"

Sabre jolted, spooked. He'd not only been in her office, but in her home. "Have you been stalking me?"

"Oh, I wouldn't exactly call it stalking. I just like to keep an eye on the enemy."

"Why do you think I'm the enemy?"

"Why? Because you ruined my life, that's why. First you take my wife and then you take my daughters."

"Your wife? You mean Peggy?"

Gaylord sneered. "Don't be ridiculous. I'd never marry that little chippie. She's worthless. She's been nothing but trouble ever since I met her. If she hadn't been carrying my child, I'd have dumped her a long time ago."

"So you mean Elizabeth?"

"Of course I mean Elizabeth. What a lady." Sabre saw him slip away for a second to what must have been a better time.

"I didn't even know her. How could I take her from you?"

He didn't answer the question, continuing with his game of cat and mouse. She could see he had something big to taunt her with. "You're just alike, aren't you? You go around acting like you want to save the world, but instead you destroy people. You destroy families. Well, I'll destroy his, all of it." Gaylord paced now, speaking louder.

Sabre didn't bite. "Did you put the bat through my mail slot?"

Murdock's mouth turned up in a smile, apparently proud of the maneuver. He quoted a riddle, in an eerie Vincent Price tone.

Color, a pretty, bright red
In the darkness, toward the light;

He took his hand and he swirled it around Sabre's head, like a bat zooming in and out, saying "*Circling, circling the head.*" He brought his hand back and swooped in with one quick move. He took a step back, then leaned his body towards her. His face inches from hers, he said, "*causing sheer fright.* Boo!"

Sabre knew he wanted to see her squirm, so she tried her best not to show just how frightened she felt. "Alexis was at my office when you did that. She could've been hurt."

"Yes, that was unfortunate, and I scolded Alexis for running away. She shouldn't have been there. I never would've done it if I'd known, but I think it taught her a good lesson. Don't you?"

Sabre didn't answer his question. "The lizard – did you put it in my bed?"

"Cute little things aren't they? Boy, did you scream!"

A chill went up her spine. "You were there the whole time?"

"No, not the whole time. I slipped out after you parked yourself on the sofa for the night."

"You did it all – the flat tire, the beach?"

Murdock walked into the other room and returned with a bottle of cologne. He sprayed a little in the air in front of her nose. "Maybe this'll help."

"*Kantor*," she whispered, recognizing the cologne. "Why *Kantor*?" She already knew the answer. What she didn't know was how he knew or why he was doing all this.

"Well, your brother loved this cologne. Didn't he?"

So much swirled through Sabre's mind, frightened and confused. The thing striking her hardest . . . Murdock had just used the past tense. Did he know something she didn't? "How did you know? What do you know about my brother?"

"Oh, I know plenty about Ronald Adrian Brown." He said the name with contempt. "I know he lived in Dallas. I know he worked out at the gym every day at ten o'clock. I know he drank espresso and drove a Porsche." Murdock watched and seemed to enjoy every twitch in her face as he delineated his knowledge of her brother in a quicker tempo. "I know he had a dog named Patches, a mother who still bakes his favorite pie on holidays, and a sister named Sabre, who worshipped him."

He leaned over Sabre's chair and put a hand on each shoulder. She could feel him tremble. He looked her straight in the eye, saying very slowly, "I know he pretended to be my friend, and he loved my wife." Murdock remained in that position – looking directly into Sabre's eyes – for several seconds, in complete silence. Finally, he let go and stood up.

"Gale and Beth," Sabre said in disbelief. "You're Gale, and your wife is Beth." She remembered Ron talking about this wonderful couple he had met. The last few months before he disappeared, he had spent a lot of time with them. She knew he shared a special relationship with Beth, but she never suspected any kind of romantic interest. Besides, it wasn't Ron's style. Although quite the lady's man, he had strong convictions about not messing with another man's woman. Whether or not something went on between Ron and Beth didn't matter at this point, Sabre decided. *What matters is what Murdock believes.* Sabre felt sick. "Did you kill my brother?"

"No, of course not." Murdock smirked. "I just helped him become the savior he wanted to be. It's not my fault he talked too much."

"What happened to him?"

"I don't know for sure. I just know there are some circles where if you talk too much, you don't live to tell it."

"Am I going to live to tell this?"

"Now, what do you think, Ms. Brown? You're a smart lady."

"Did you plan this from the beginning? Did you come to California to kill me?"

"I needed to leave Atlanta for a while. California seemed like a good idea. I remembered Ron telling us about you, so I decided to have some fun, pay him back for what he did to me."

"But the juvenile court case – how did you get me on your case?"

"Pure coincidence. I didn't even realize it was you until after we'd left the courtroom. I heard someone call you Sabre." Murdock smiled. "You got thrown right into my lap. I didn't even have to track you down."

"So what happens now?"

"Well, you're not much good to me anymore, Ms. Brown. Yes, you and yours will definitely have to go, but you won't know when."

Sabre remembered Honey. "What did you do with Honey?"

"You don't need to know about Hon . . . ." Murdock stopped as Alexis walked in. "Alexis, did you have a good time?"

"Yes, Father."

"You must be hungry. I'll start dinner. Go wash up and then come help me," he instructed.

Alexis followed his direction and went to the

bathroom to wash her hands. When Alexis left the room, Sabre tried to pick the conversation back up where they left off, but Murdock, not responding, strolled into the kitchen area and started dinner.

After dinner, Murdock and Alexis cleaned up the kitchen and then sat down at the dining room table to play some games. Alexis convinced her father it would be more fun to play with three so he untied Sabre's hands, but he left her feet tied. Everything seemed so crazy to Sabre. She didn't have any experience with kidnappers, but she was pretty sure this was not the norm. She sat at a table eating pumpkin pie and playing games with her captor, the whole experience bizarre. Most of the time she had her hands and feet tied, and she was in excruciating pain and suffering from sleep deprivation. The food, on the other hand, tasted four star, but every time she ate she felt like an inmate on death row having her last meal.

There were no clocks in the room. Sabre, uncertain of the time, thought they retired earlier than usual. The bed beckoned Sabre, her exhaustion taking a toll. Her eyelids had been heavy all day, but as soon as her head hit the pillow, her eyes popped open. Murdock had tied her feet to the bedpost again, leaving her stuck in one position, and she couldn't get comfortable. Every sound she heard startled her. She wondered if this night would be her last, and as much as she wanted to sleep, she struggled to stay awake and live every moment.

After about two hours, Sabre fell asleep. She awakened abruptly when she heard her door creak. Her heart skipped a beat, certain it was Murdock coming in to kill her. She scooted as far as she could to the opposite side of the bed. The footsteps tiptoed toward her. She muffled her scream when she saw Alexis' silhouette. "What are you doing here?" she whispered.

"Shh . . . ." Alexis said. "He's asleep." She walked softly around to the back of Sabre's bed and untied her from the bed. Alexis handed Sabre her shoes and she slipped them on. Sabre stood up, making as little noise as possible. They walked to the door and Sabre looked out. She didn't see anything in the hallway, and no lights were on. They crept down the hallway. Just when they reached Murdock's bedroom, the floor creaked. They stopped and waited. After what seemed an eternity, they moved on. Every couple of steps, the floor creaked. Sounds never noticed during the day pounded out in the quiet of the night. They continued to the front door. Sabre reached up and slowly unbolted the lock. She turned the handle and opened the creaky door. It seemed so loud in the still darkness. No lights came on and they didn't hear anyone coming. Alexis picked up a bundle and a backpack near the door and followed Sabre.

They had made it outside. They hurried off the porch and toward the dirt road when Alexis spoke. "Here, I brought us each a coat." Sabre, so glad to be getting out, hadn't thought about how cold it would be.

"You're a smart cookie." She gave Alexis a little hug.

Sabre took a step, glanced back at the house, and saw the lights go on. Murdock flipped on the porch light and yelled, "Alexis. Alexis, where are you?" They stood still, watching him. He looked around, dashed back in the house. He returned moments later and ran to the car. Sabre grabbed Alexis by the hand and they ran off the road into the woods.

The utter darkness made it difficult to see. Suddenly a light beamed through the trees. They could hear the engine from Murdock's car as he drove around in a circle, using the headlights like a searchlight.

The light came toward them. "Get down. Lie flat," Sabre said. They dropped down. Sabre hit her face on a stick protruding from the ground. It poked her hard in the lip. She muffled a cry. The lights came closer. She didn't dare move. The lights passed them. When Murdock had made a complete circle, he drove down the road toward the highway. Alexis and Sabre slipped deeper into the woods.

CHAPTER 32

Sabre and Alexis stumbled along in the darkness for about an hour, trying to put some distance between them and the cabin, not knowing which direction they were going. Sabre feared she could be leading them in circles and they'd end up back at the cabin, or worse, deep in the woods where they would either starve to death or be eaten by some ravenous animal.

The leaves rustled. Sabre stopped, put her arm around Alexis and held her still. Something moved a few feet away. Sabre could feel Alexis trembling. She held her tighter. All of a sudden it scurried away. "Just a squirrel or something," Sabre said, whispering. She had no idea what kind of animals lived in these woods, or in any woods for that matter.

Finally, Sabre felt comfortable enough to speak. "What's in this backpack, Alexis? It's heavy."

"Just some stuff I thought we'd need, like some water, your cell phone . . . ."

"My phone?" Sabre said, pulling the pack off her back. "You have my phone? Why didn't you tell me?" She sat down right where she stood, opened the backpack, and dug out the phone.

"I forgot," Alexis whispered.

"It's okay," Sabre said, elated. She could just call the police, and they'd be rescued. She snapped the phone open and started pushing buttons, but nothing happened.

"What's the matter?"

"It's dead. The battery's dead."

"I'm sorry, Ms. Sabre, I thought it would help us."

"Sweetie, you were so smart to think to bring it. Don't worry. We'll get out of here just fine. Let's see what else you stuck in this bag," Sabre said, going through the backpack. "A flashlight – that could come in real handy, but we better not use it right now because it could draw attention to us. Two water bottles – good – muffins, a roll of toilet paper, and what's this?" Sabre pulled out a small tin box.

"A first-aid kit. We could clean up your face, Ms. Sabre. You're bleeding."

Sabre had been too cold and scared to think about her face. Besides, it didn't hurt as much as her ankles and wrists. "You're right. We should clean it up so it doesn't get infected."

Sabre placed the kit and the flashlight deeply into the backpack and turned on the flashlight, propping it so the light wouldn't show. She reached into the backpack and poured a little peroxide onto a cotton ball. Dabbing it on her face, she felt the peroxide fizzle and sting. Sabre flinched. She removed another cotton ball from the kit and dabbed it on her face again. She wiped the dried blood off the best she could without a mirror. Before she closed it up, she looked through the kit. Besides the usual supplies, band aids, cotton balls, an ace bandage, and the peroxide, she saw some matches and a compass. She pulled the compass out, gave Alexis a great big hug, and said, "You're a genius!"

"What is it?"

"It's a compass. It'll keep us from going in circles, and as long as we go west we'll be headed for the ocean and not deeper into the mountains." They each took a small drink of water. Sabre repacked the bag. "Here, hold the backpack so I can shine the light inside on the compass." Sabre looked inside. "It looks like we've been going south. We'll make a turn and go west."

Sabre carried the flashlight in her hand, even though

she didn't dare turn it on; the flashlight and compass gave her a sense of power. She had a plan.

They continued on their journey, mostly in silence, stopping occasionally to check the compass. "You okay?"

"Yeah, I'm fine. Just a little cold, and it's kind of spooky out here," Alexis replied.

Sabre felt her anxiety. She wanted to stop and hold her and keep her warm, but she didn't dare. They had to keep moving. Murdock could be anywhere, looking for them in the woods. Sabre didn't know what else might be out there waiting to hurt them. She had to take their minds off the dark, frightening woods. "Alexis, why did you decide to help me escape?"

"I heard you and Father talking today. He wasn't going to keep his promise to me, was he?"

"No, I don't think he was. That's when you decided to help?"

"Yes. I didn't want him to hurt you."

"When did you put the things in the backpack?"

"When I was in the kitchen helping with dinner, I set the muffins and the water bottles aside. When I put the games away, I picked up the flashlight, the first aid kit, and the toilet paper. I've been camping with my father lots of times, and you always need toilet paper in the woods," she digressed. "My father tucked me in on the sofa and then he went to the bathroom before he went to bed. That's when I took your phone out of your bag, put the things in the backpack, and lay back on the sofa. He came out after he used the restroom and kissed me goodnight, but I pretended to be asleep."

"You are the bravest little girl I've ever met. Thank you."

They stopped and checked the direction on the compass. They were off course, heading north. Sabre made the adjustment, and again went due west. The night was silent again, except for the noises from the forest, the occasional owl hoot, or a coyote howl in the distance, but every noise took their breaths away.

Although it had been only a few hours, it seemed like they had walked for days and still saw no signs of civilization. Sabre wondered what time it was. Just then she saw a light in the distance. She couldn't tell what the light came from. Inching their way forward, they kept low to the ground and behind trees as much as they could. She heard a car engine. Through a small clearing, Sabre could see the road and a car creeping north along the highway with a light shining outside the window and into the trees. It must be Murdock.

Sabre's heart pounded as she quietly turned Alexis around and headed deeper into the woods. When Sabre thought they were far enough away from the light, they turned and went south, trying to stay parallel with the road without getting too close. Sabre felt a little relief. Murdock continued to search for them, but from his car and headed in the opposite direction, not on foot in the woods. For now, their biggest concern was the wild animals, the thought squelching any relief she had felt.

They continued along in the quiet winter air. "They killed Honey," Alexis blurted. The words echoed in Sabre's ears, making her shudder. "They shouldn't have killed her. They didn't need to, you know."

Alexis spoke quickly, as if she needed to say it all before she changed her mind. "It was the night we left for California. Father said we were going to go anyway, but I don't think so. He had never mentioned it before. Honey was visiting us. I loved it when she came to visit. We would play with our Barbies. She had more than me, and she had lots of clothes for them. Adelle liked to sew and she made her lots of Barbie clothes." Alexis paused for a moment. "It's my fault, you know."

"What's your fault?"

"That she's dead. She wouldn't be dead if it wasn't for me. I'm the one who should be dead. I'm the one who heard them. She didn't hear them. She couldn't hear them. She was deaf."

"Alexis, I'm sure it's not your fault Honey is dead. You didn't kill her. Tell me what happened, what you heard?"

"We were playing with our Barbies on the back porch. Honey had just put the mink coat on one of her Barbies, a coat Adelle made. It wasn't real mink or anything, but it was real pretty. I got tired of playing with the dolls and wanted to play school. I wanted to teach Honey her ABCs. I had learned how to sign each one of them. I had to get real good at it so I could teach her. Anyway, Honey lined up her dolls, like in a classroom, and ran inside to get the blackboard. I followed her, but she ran into the room first.

"I heard a man yelling at my father and he sounded real angry, so I stopped. I could see inside the room. The man said something about killing a cop and that my father would go to prison. He spotted Honey and I saw him charge at her. I tried to scream, but nothing came out."

Alexis talked faster, her voice cracking, tears running down her cheeks. "He picked her up with one arm and grabbed her by the neck with the other and just twisted." Alexis spoke lower, breathing heavy and sobbing. "Her head just flopped over . . . like a d-d-dead b-bird. Then he j-just . . " Alexis sobbed, "d-dropped her and she lay there on the floor real still."

Alexis started to cry hysterically. Sabre sat down, pulled Alexis close to her, and wrapped her arms around her for comfort and warmth. Alexis pressed her head against Sabre's bosom and sobbed. Sabre couldn't think of any words to comfort her. Although concerned Alexis might be heard, she couldn't interrupt her mourning. She held and rocked the scared, sad, little girl while she wailed in the quiet forest.

Alexis sat up, still whimpering, but quieter. Sabre reached in the backpack and pulled out some toilet paper for Alexis to blow her nose. "You're right," Sabre said. "The toilet paper did come in handy in the woods."

Alexis responded with a quick smile. "Thanks." She

wiped her nose, turned to Sabre, and said. "We better get going, huh?"

"Yup, we better. Are you okay to go?"

"Yeah." She stood up. Sabre marveled at Alexis' strength, as she took her by the hand and they walked on.

They had only taken a few steps when Alexis spoke again. "I was so scared. I wanted to go help Honey, but I was too scared. I just wanted to get away before they saw me."

"So what did you do?"

"I sneaked back to my bedroom and crawled in bed and pretended to be asleep. A little while later, Father came in the room and gave me a kiss on the cheek and went back out. I think the men had left by then."

"The men? Was there more than one?"

"Yes, I saw two of them, but I only recognized one. There may have been more, but I don't think so. That's all I saw, anyway."

"You recognized one of them? You mean you had seen him before?"

"Yes, a long time ago when I was little, but I know it was the same man. He was real big and had tattoos and was the scariest person I ever met. I could never forget his face."

Sabre knew, too. He fit the description from Ruby. "Alexis, was he the man who kidnapped your mother?"

Alexis stopped. She tugged at Sabre's hand and said with surprise, "You know about my mother?"

"I know two bad guys took you and dropped you off at your grandma's house."

"I never told anybody, not even Father. I don't even think I remembered it myself, until Honey . . . ." Maybe it made it too real when Alexis said it out loud. "Then, I began to remember a lot of things." Alexis paused. "Do you know what they did with my mother? Did they k-kill her too?"

"I don't know, sweetheart." Sabre squeezed her hand. "I don't know."

They were silent for a moment. Alexis continued. "I lay in bed for a while, trying to go to sleep, but Father and Peggy kept yelling at each other. Then it got quiet and I heard Peggy drive off. I know it was Peggy because my father came into the room and told me to get up and start packing for a trip. I didn't ask any questions. I just got up and started to take my things out of my drawers. He came back a few minutes later with two cardboard boxes, and he told me I could take whatever I wanted as long as it fit in those boxes. I mostly put in clothes and my Barbies, and I made sure I had room for the album my mother made for me. I carried Dogwog, so he didn't have to go in the box. He's my stuffed animal I sleep with. My mother gave him to me when I was real little. I couldn't have him at Jordan because too many things disappear around there, and I didn't want to lose him. I sure miss him, though," Alexis said, slipping off track with her story as she so often did.

"Tell me about the album your mother made you. What does it look like?"

"It's bright pink and it has my pictures in it from ever since I was born. It even has one of me in her stomach. She put in all my awards, and every year she put in a picture of me on my birthday. My favorites are the ones with her. On the outside it says . . . ."

"My Pride and Joy."

"You've seen it?"

"Yes, I have. It's a lovely keepsake. Your mother must love you very much. I saw a photo of her. She's a beautiful woman, and you look a lot like her. I noticed the album had pictures and awards for the later years, too. Did your father keep the album up for you?"

"No, I did. I just thought about what my mother would have put in there, and then I did it. I think she'd like it if I kept it up."

"I'm sure she would." Silence followed. Sabre stopped, put the flashlight inside the backpack, and checked her direction. They were headed southwest, primarily downhill. Every so often she would lead them west, close enough to see the highway, and then they would turn back into the woods, trying to stay on course along the road. The road twisted and turned so much that sometimes they ended up a long way from it. It had been awhile since she had checked her mark, so she lined up her compass and they went west again.

They came to a little clearing. She could see some headlights in the distance, on the other side of a huge ravine. Sabre and Alexis were a good distance from the highway. They'd either have to backtrack or cross over the ravine and climb back up the mountain. Sabre, tired, cold, and her feet blistered, knew Alexis must feel the same. In addition, she feared at any moment they would come face to face with a coyote or a mountain lion or something she couldn't even name. They kept walking, aware of the increased danger from animals the further they walked from the highway and the danger from Murdock if they got too close.

Exhausted, Sabre wanted to lie down and sleep, but she didn't have that option. Still holding hands, they started down the mountain toward the road. Sabre determined it was less risky to cross the ravine than to go back the way they had come. Most of the time the trees blocked their view, but every once in a while they could see a light on the highway.

"You doing okay?"

"Yeah," Alexis answered.

"You're such a trooper. I couldn't ask for a better traveling companion." Sabre, amazed at Alexis' stamina and strong will, never heard her whine or complain. "Most adults wouldn't do as well."

Alexis squeezed her hand. She seemed to be pleased with Sabre's praise. "Mother would be brave. I want to be brave like her."

Sabre squeezed back.

They kept walking down the mountain. Sabre dreaded

the thought of climbing back up. She wondered how long they had before daylight, estimating a few more hours. She wanted to be close to the road when day broke. There would be more animals coming out in the early morning, so they trudged on.

Once again Alexis broke the silence. "Father said Peggy went to take Honey back to Adelle's. I remember saying, 'But I have to teach her the ABCs.' I don't know why I said that. I just didn't know what else to say. My father said I didn't need to worry about her ABCs anymore." She sighed. "When Peggy came back, she had a large, green plastic box and a whole bunch of ice. She put some of the ice in a little cooler and put some food and water in there for the trip. Father kept yelling at her to hurry. He wanted to get going. They loaded some of their stuff in the car, including the green plastic box. Then Father told me they had to run an errand, and I needed to watch Jamie. He said they wouldn't be gone very long and I needed to be ready to go when they got back."

"Do you know where they went?"

"No."

"How long were they gone?"

"About an hour, I think. I was all ready to go and Jamie had fallen asleep, so I sat down and watched television. I watched *The Brady Bunch* twice."

"Did they still have the green box when they returned?"

"Yes."

"Then what happened?"

"We finished loading the car and we left for California."

"Alexis, did you see what they put in the green box?"

"I know it had ice in it because I touched it once and it felt cold. We left in the night and we kept driving for two days. Peggy and Father took turns driving and sleeping, but neither of them slept very much. Mostly they just argued. In the afternoon, we finally stopped in a town called

Phoenix. We got something to eat and then we went to a movie. We never go to movies at home, but it was real hot and they told me it would be a lot cooler driving through the desert at night."

"What did you do after the movie?"

"We started driving again to California. It was real late and I fell asleep once we started moving, but then we stopped somewhere and I woke up. They were whispering so I pretended to be asleep. Peggy and Father got out and walked to the back of the car. I peeked over the seat, and I saw them moving things off the green box. I almost got caught once, so I ducked back down again. Lying down, I could see through the window in front of me and I saw Father walk away carrying the green box. He was gone quite awhile. Peggy stayed outside, smoking her cigarettes, one right after another."

"When he came back, did he have the container?"

"Yes, but it was empty. I could tell by the way he carried it. He yelled at Peggy to help him wipe it off. Then they got back in the car and we drove off. Father stopped the car again when we got into some other town. He pulled in behind a big grocery store, and they stuck the box in one of those big things where you put the trash."

"Alexis, do you know what your father left in the desert?"

Silence ensued for a moment. Alexis said, "I really miss her."

CHAPTER 33

They continued to climb the mountain toward the road. It was steeper than Sabre had anticipated and they were both exhausted. It had been difficult enough walking on flat ground. As they climbed, they had to stop every few steps to catch their breath. They moved along in silence; talking took too much effort. In the darkness, they could hear every noise. Sabre had never realized how noisy the quiet woods could be. She wanted to lie down and sleep, but every noise in the night told her she couldn't or they'd be an early breakfast for some rapacious animal.

They kept moving slowly but methodically toward the highway, with Sabre encouraging Alexis. Sabre saw what effort it took her, but she never complained.

"Ahh..." Alexis grabbed Sabre's coat as she stumbled, and pulled her down. Down the mountainside they went, grabbing to hold on to something . . . anything. Down, down . . . Sabre finally caught hold of a branch and braced herself against a rock to steady them both. They had slipped back about halfway down the mountain.

"I'm sorry, Ms. Sabre. I slipped." Alexis began to cry.

"Hey, it's all right. You're okay, right? You're not hurt, are you?"

"Nope."

"Well, neither am I, so we're fine. Let's just rest here for a few seconds, and then we'll be on our way." They positioned themselves to get comfortable, hugging each other to keep warm. Sabre couldn't decide which bothered her most – the cold, the pain, the exhaustion, or the fear.

Any one of them was difficult to deal with alone; all of them together made it almost impossible. She couldn't think about any of that right now; she had to take care of Alexis. She wondered what she would do if she were alone. Would she just lie down and die, or would she keep going? *Scarlett O'Hara would keep going.* She laughed to herself about the odd things coming into her head. *Whatever it takes. Thanks, Scarlett.*

She gave Alexis a squeeze, "Ready to move on, partner?"

"Yeah," Alexis said and stood up.

"Why don't you lead the way? I'll aim you in the right direction, okay?"

"Okay."

They checked the direction on the compass. They were going south, but Sabre caught a glimpse of a headlight every now and then providing her the location of the road. They had to get to the road – away from the animals and hopefully not into the hands of Murdock. She wanted the daylight so they could see better and make better time, but it would also make them more visible and easier for Murdock to spot. Sabre knew if they encountered him, they wouldn't stand a chance. Sabre had no fight left in her. *One step at a time. Just put one foot in front of the other.* They kept moving, every step a chore.

"Alexis, look." Sabre reached her arm across Alexis' shoulder and pointed toward the road. They could see a headlight on the highway. They reached the road just as dawn broke, offering little traffic on the road. Sabre and Alexis found a spot behind a rock where they could sit unseen until they determined it was safe to flag down a car. Sabre's mind raced again, trying to figure out the best way to do this. If she attempted to flag a car and it didn't stop, Murdock might see them. Even if they stopped someone, how safe would it be to go with a stranger? They could be putting their fate in the hands of a serial killer, a rapist, or who knows what.

Sabre saw a car coming around the curve, slowly heading downhill. She stood up to flag it down, then threw herself back down, bringing Alexis down with her.

"What is it?" Alexis asked.

"It's your father," Sabre whispered. "Stay down."

Sabre sat in the bushes, behind the rock, holding Alexis and afraid to breathe. She could hear the engine of the car as it crept along the highway, moving closer and closer. She didn't dare look for fear they would be seen. The car stopped, though the engine noise remained. A car door opened and closed. It appeared to be about thirty feet away. Sabre turned her head slowly in the direction of the car. She could see the top of Murdock's head. She stretched up just a little to see what he was doing. She saw the profile of his face, looking out over the canyon with a pair of binoculars. As he turned his head toward her, Sabre slid her body down and wrapped herself around Alexis. She felt Alexis squirm. She whispered in her ear, "Sit real still." The sun had not yet come over the horizon, and with the sky slightly overcast, Sabre hoped enough darkness remained to keep them safe. As they sat holding each other, Sabre hoped he wouldn't see them.

Honk! A car sped around the corner, just missing Murdock's car. Sabre and Alexis both jumped from the noise of the horn as the car whizzed by. She heard Murdock yell obscenities at the passing car.

They sat still again, trying to stifle the smallest movements of their bodies. Even their breathing seemed too loud. She heard footsteps. Alexis gulped. Sabre held on tighter, doing her best to alleviate Alexis' fear, but certain Alexis could feel Sabre's heart beating against her back. Finally, she heard the sound of the car door open and close and the car creeping past them. Murdock drove away.

Sabre took a deep breath, let go of Alexis, and glanced over the rock. She could see the rear of the car inch down the hill. She waited until it disappeared out of sight before she let Alexis up. Tears of frustration welled up in Sabre's eyes. They'd made it this far, but she didn't know what to do from here.

Alexis saw her tears. "Are you okay, Ms. Sabre?"

"I'm fine, sweetheart." Sabre forced a smile on her face. "Hey, we're out of the woods and the sun is almost up."

"So, what do we do now?"

Sabre summoned the courage she needed to make her next move and to make the right decision. She had to show a decisive front for Alexis. "Here's what we're going to do," Sabre said, still not certain what might come out of her mouth. "We're going to catch the next car that comes by here and go home."

About five minutes went by with no traffic. Sabre became more anxious. She didn't expect Murdock to go far before he came back. She didn't dare stand out by the road in case he did, so she had to stay behind the rock and jump out when she saw a car come around the curve from the north. She missed the first one. It went too fast and had already passed her before she reached the road. She knew she'd never make it out there in time to stop a car, so she crouched down trying to watch both directions – the south for Murdock's return and the north for what she hoped would be their ticket out.

Two more cars went by. Sabre waved, but neither of them stopped. The sun shined over the horizon now and the traffic had picked up. "Please, someone, please," she said, "stop and get us before Murdock does." Another car zoomed by. Sabre knew she had to do something more. She looked at Alexis, sleeping on the ground behind the rock. She dreaded having to wake her up. She touched Alexis on the shoulder and she jumped. "Sweetie," Sabre said. "They aren't stopping for me. I'm thinking if they saw you with me, they may realize we're in trouble and stop and help. Do you mind?"

Alexis stood up and stumbled to the road with Sabre. Alexis' eyes only halfway open, she stood next to Sabre waiting for help. Every car in the distance coming from the south prompted them to jump back behind the rock, and every car from the north had them waving frantically. Finally, an old, green, dented Ford Pinto with a red door pulled off the road just past them. They ran to meet it. The car looked like it would barely make it down the mountain. The driver, a man around fifty, reached over and rolled the passenger window part way down, and asked, "You need help, lady?"

"Yes, please," Sabre said. "Can you just drive us down the mountain so we can get help?"

"What happen?" The man had a heavy Spanish accent.

"Our car broke down and we've been out here most of the night. My daughter's not well. I need to get to a phone."

"Come in," the man said, as he unlocked the doors. Sabre got in the front seat and Alexis in the back. They pulled onto the highway, rounded the first curve, and saw a blue car slowly coming toward them. As the cars passed each other, Sabre turned to Alexis, her eyes wide with fear. It was Murdock. They both watched as he drove on, hoping they hadn't been seen.

Within a few miles, Alexis fell asleep and Sabre breathed easier. "My name is Ricardo," the driver said, startling her. "Ricardo Servantes." He reached out his hand to shake hers.

"Sabre Brown," she said, shaking his hand. "I'm so glad to make your acquaintance. Thank you for stopping. We were about to give up hope; so many cars had passed us by."

"It's scary to stop. It's a shame, but there are so many crazy peoples out there. You must be very careful."

"So why did you stop, Ricardo?"

"I seen you standing there with the little girl. I think about my childrens. I figure you are in trouble. Maybe you have a gun or knife or something. You could rob me, but I don't think so. I just think you need help. Sorry, my English not too good."

"Your English is great. In fact, I've never heard the English language sound so good." She smiled.

Sabre asked Ricardo about himself and his family. He told her about his five children and how he had come to California to earn a living. He had applied for citizenship and seemed very proud his children were Americans. His eldest had just begun medical school at the university. He continued to talk about his family until they reached the edge of the city. "Where you want to go?"

"The first place with a telephone will be fine."

Ricardo stopped at a restaurant. When Sabre tried to thank him again, he said, "I go in and wait for someone to come for you."

Sabre, though pleased with his offer, did not feel safe yet. She woke Alexis up and they all went into the restaurant. "I wish I could buy you breakfast, or at least coffee or something, but I don't have any money with me. I don't have my purse or anything. I feel terrible," Sabre said.

"No problema," he said. "You just call."

Sabre and Alexis went to the phone and called 911. "My name is Attorney Sabre Brown. I have with me a ten-year-old girl, Alexis Murdock. We were abducted from Jordan Receiving Home on Wednesday," Sabre told the dispatcher. "Please contact Detective Gregory Nelson and let him know where we are." After some questions about Sabre's whereabouts, the dispatcher told her someone would be there immediately.

Sabre and Alexis went to the restroom, washed up a bit, and returned to Ricardo, who sat sipping a cup of coffee. Although Sabre objected, Ricardo insisted on buying them each something to drink. "Decaf coffee for me," she told the waitress. "Alexis?"

"Milk, please." The waitress stared at Sabre and then at Alexis. Looking nervous, she scurried off.

Sabre kept a close watch on the door, waiting for the police, and watching for Murdock. "Ricardo," she said, "I haven't been honest with you. Our car did not break down.

I was afraid if I told you the truth, you might not give us a ride." He waited for her to finish.

"Alexis and I were kidnapped on Wednesday evening. We escaped last night and spent the night in the woods."

"I know. I seen you on the news. Everyone look for you."

Sabre hadn't really thought about that. They'd been so far from civilization she'd forgotten about the real world. It would explain the reaction from the waitress, as well. She looked around the restaurant. Although there were only a handful of people in there, all eyes focused on their booth. "Why didn't you say something?"

"You don't need to tell stranger. You say what you want. I listen. I help if I can."

Within minutes, the place crawled with police, Sabre wasn't the only one who had called them. Reports from others in the restaurant thought Ricardo was their captor. Sabre, Alexis, and Ricardo walked out with police officers surrounding them, herding them to a police car. A crowd of people had gathered in the parking lot, all straining to see the commotion. Three news trucks from different television stations pulled into the parking lot, all about the same time. Reporters and cameramen jumped out and ran toward them trying to get footage. The police hustled Sabre and Alexis into one car and Ricardo in another and drove to the station.

CHAPTER 34

Sabre awakened on Sunday morning, initially confused by her surroundings. She glanced around, and found a small clock radio on the nightstand. It read 9:54 a.m. *Surely, that's not right. I haven't slept that late since college.*

Sabre dressed and wandered out to the living room, looking for JP, Bob's private eye friend. Finding no one, she stuck her head in the kitchen. She felt strange wandering around someone else's home, but more uneasy at the thought she might be alone. She spotted the sliding glass door open to the patio and looked outside.

"Good morning, Sabre," JP said. "Did you sleep well?"

"Yes, I did. Thanks so much for putting me up and for bringing my things from my house."

"My pleasure; I'm glad I could help. Bob told me some time ago he tried to arrange for you to stay with me. Apparently, he feared something like this might happen."

"I guess I should've listened to him, but who would ever expect Bob to be right about anything," she mocked.

"Good point. By the way, is he coming home today?"

"Yeah, he should be here shortly. I left him a message to call me on my cell when he gets home."

"Want coffee? I'm afraid it's decaf. I'm trying to cut back on the caffeine, so my second pot in the morning is unleaded."

"Decaf would be perfect."

JP went into the kitchen and brought back a cup of coffee, a container of cream, and a couple of bagels. "Sorry I don't have any cream cheese, but I do have some jam if you want . . . and peanut butter."

Sabre's mind elsewhere, it took her a second to respond. "No thanks; plain is fine."

"You okay?"

"Oh yeah; I'm fine. Just wondering where Murdock is right now and how long it'll take to find him. I can't stay hiding forever, and I don't want to take advantage of your hospitality."

"Hey, America's finest is looking for him. They'll get him. Besides, his picture is plastered everywhere. Where's he going to go? In the meantime, don't worry about me. You can stay here as long as you need. I enjoy the company, and you're safe here."

"Thanks, JP," Sabre said, just as her phone rang. Bob's name came up on the caller ID. "Hello, Robert."

"S-o-o-bs," Bob said excitedly, stretching her nickname out as he often did when he hadn't talked to her in a day or so. "Where are you? I tried you at home, but got voice mail."

"I'm at JP's house."

"Where?"

"Your friend, JP. You know – tall, handsome guy, with a beard and a really big . . ."

"Big what?"

"Gun, really big gun."

"Pray tell, what are you doing there?"

Sabre remembered they had no television at Bob's cabin. Apparently, he hadn't heard about her abduction. "It's a long story. Can you stop by? I'll tell you when you get here."

"Sure thing. See you in a jiff."

When Bob arrived, Sabre greeted him with a big hug. They all went out to the backyard.

"So," Bob said, "you're back from your mom's kind of early. How was your holiday?"

"Oh, uneventful."

JP laughed, and Sabre joined him.

"Okay," Bob said, "what's going on? Are you two having an affair or something behind my back?" That struck them both even funnier, and they laughed louder. "And what the hell happened to your lip?"

"You *have* been shut off from the world," JP said.

Sabre decided she'd toyed with him enough. "Remember Wednesday, when I called you from my cell phone?"

"Yeah, on your way to see Alexis before you left town."

"Well, it all went downhill after that." She told him the story, explaining in detail about being kidnapped, her Thanksgiving dinner, the escape, the night in the woods, and their rescue.

Bob shook his head. "You're sure you're all right?"

"Oh yeah, I'm fine. My wrists and ankles are a little sore from the ropes." She raised her sleeves and her pant legs so he could see her bandages. "And my body is a little beat up from the hike, but otherwise I'm okay."

"And Alexis?"

"She's fine, too, at least physically."

"Wow," Bob said. "The most exciting thing to happen on my vacation was Corey spilling his milk at the Thanksgiving dinner table and one of the hippie in-laws contracting diarrhea. I guess you topped mine."

The phone rang. JP went in the house to answer it. Bob walked over and gave Sabre another hug. "Sobs, I'm so glad you're okay. I'm just sorry I wasn't here for you."

"Hey, there's nothing you could've done. Besides, you were here for me. You left your pal JP to take care of me, didn't you?"

They sat and visited until JP returned. "That was Greg on the phone."

"Greg?" Bob queried.

"Gregory Nelson, the detective on this case. He's a friend of mine. We spent time together in the same precinct back in our rookie days. He's a good guy."

"Did they find Murdock?" Sabre asked.

"No, I'm afraid not, but they did pick up Peggy Smith. I guess she's pretty high, but they're about to interrogate her. He said we can go down there and listen if we'd like. We'd be in an adjoining room, and she won't know we're there. Want to go?"

"You bet," she said. "Besides, I want to get Ricardo Servantes' address and number from Greg so I can thank him properly. I was so rum-dumb yesterday, I didn't think to ask him. I'm not even sure I thanked him for saving our lives. Let's go."

Detective Nelson greeted them when they arrived at the precinct, and directed them to a one-way window in which they could see Peggy sitting in a room with a police officer. She twitched and wrung her hands, and every few seconds she'd stand up and pace. The officer kept telling her to sit down.

"We're just about to start. Don't worry, she can't see you. Enjoy the show," Nelson said as he left. They watched him walk into the room with Peggy. Nelson turned to the officer. "Has she been Mirandized?"

"Yes, sir," he said.

"Did she decline to speak to an attorney?"

"Yes, sir. She said she wants to cooperate."

Nelson turned to Peggy. "Is that right, Ms. Smith? Are you willing to talk to us without an attorney present?"

"Yeah," she said, "let's just do it."

Nelson asked her a couple of preliminary questions and then asked about the night Honey was allegedly killed. "Where were you that night?"

"At home," Peggy said.

"Tell us what happened," Nelson said.

"We had just finished eating when these two guys came to the door. They didn't knock; they just walked right in. They were real mad at Gaylord. One of them said he got in too deep again and he better start paying. He said Boss wasn't going to let him slide forever."

"Did you know what he meant by that?"

"Yeah, when he lived in Dallas he had done some favor for this guy everyone called 'Boss.' Gaylord had helped him set up some gambling kingpin in Atlanta so Boss could take over his territory. Then he set up some patsy who took the fall." Sabre felt a knot form in her stomach. She knew the "patsy" referred to Ron. Bob squeezed her hand.

"It erased a lot of debt for Gaylord, but he wouldn't stop. He just kept on betting those ponies and football games and anything else he could bet on. He spent his trust money every month and anything else he could borrow," continued Peggy.

"So what happened next?"

"Well, the big guy kept blabbering on, saying something about how he had to kill a cop five years ago because Gaylord had screwed things up. I never knew the whole story on the cop, but I know it had something to do with Gaylord's wife disappearing." Peggy started pacing. "Do you have a cigarette? I really need a cigarette," she begged. Nelson nodded at the officer, and he left the room.

"So, what happened then?"

"It all happened so fast. Honey darted into the room. She grabbed her little chalkboard off the chair and turned to go back out. The big guy yelled at her, but she couldn't hear him on account of she was deaf, so she just kept going. He got mad 'cause she didn't stop and he just kept yelling and acting all crazy like. Then he reached down, snatched her up, twisted her neck, and dropped her on the floor." Her voice held little emotion. Almost as an afterthought, she sniffled. "He took my sweet little Honey from me. Why me?"

Sabre rolled her eyes, "That was real touching. A little work and she might sound like she cared. I don't know about you two, but I can't muster up any sympathy for her. Even now, it's not about Honey; it's about what they did to poor Peggy."

The police officer returned, carrying a pack of cigarettes, a lighter, and an ashtray. He handed them to

Peggy. She tore the pack open and lit one, shaking so hard she missed the end of the cigarette the first time she tried to light it. "He thought Honey had heard what he'd said about killing the cop and she'd be able to identify him. He had no idea she couldn't hear anything." Peggy took a deep drag on the cigarette. "Then he told Gaylord to clean up the mess, and they left."

"What did you and Gaylord do?"

"Well, I was pretty upset. You know, my baby dead and all, so Gaylord gave me something to calm my nerves. He told me to go to Wal-Mart and buy the biggest plastic bin I could find and to stop and pick up about ten bags of ice, or as much as I could get."

"And did you?"

"Yeah."

"What did you do when you got back?"

"Gaylord was packing our stuff. He said we were going to California. He told me to pack up only what I really needed 'cause there wouldn't be much room. So I did."

"When you left, did you call the police?" Nelson asked.

"No."

"Why not?"

"I was too afraid. Gaylord said if I told anyone, I'd go to jail. He said he'd tell them I was high and that I did it. He said Alexis would back his story, and since I had a criminal record and he didn't, I'd go to jail."

"If neither of you killed her, why wouldn't you just tell the truth?"

"Gaylord said if we did, we'd both die, and after I saw what that guy did to Honey, I believed it."

"So then what?"

"Gaylord put Honey in the container I bought and put ice all around her. He put her in the back of the car. He got in the passenger side and told me to drive to Adelle's, so I did. He made me stop just before we reached the trailer. I think he planned on leaving Honey there, but changed his mind because the dog kept barking. Instead, he waited in the car and told me to go tell Adelle we were leaving for California and taking Honey with us. Then we drove back home, finished packing the car, and left."

"Where did you go?"

"We started driving to California. When we got to Phoenix, Gaylord said we needed to drop Honey off in the desert, but we had to wait until real late at night. It was still early in the day, so we went to see a movie. We'd been taking turns driving and we hadn't slept much, so we both slept through most of it. Then we left and Gaylord turned on some road he'd found on the map. After a while, he drove off the road and across some dunes and stopped the car. He carried Honey out somewhere in the desert, dumped her out, and came back with the empty container. When we got to Yuma, he pulled up behind a grocery store near a trash bin. He told me to get out and throw it in the trash. So I did."

Sabre felt sick to her stomach. "That's pretty much the way Alexis told it."

"I hope they nab the monster who killed Honey," Bob said.

"They already have," JP responded. "I spoke with Nelson earlier. He said they arrested him a couple of days ago. He's the same guy who abducted Elizabeth, Murdock's wife. He's the goon with the tattoo, 'Mama tried,' on his arm. They need to give him another tattoo on the other side that says, 'and failed.'" Everyone chuckled. "By the way, they charged him with Elizabeth's murder and the murder of the police officer who investigated her case. Now they can add another murder rap."

"Steve Parker, the police officer he killed, was Joe's best friend." Sabre jumped up. "Joe! I need to call Joe. Will you two excuse me for a moment?"

"Sure, go ahead," Bob said, reaching for his cigarettes. "I'm going out for some fresh air."

Sabre looked at him and raised her eyebrow. "You mean contaminate the fresh air, don't you?" Bob smiled and left.

"I'm going to talk to Nelson for a minute. I'll be right outside," JP said.

Sabre dialed the phone.

"Joe Carriage."

"Two-syllable Joe. How are you?" she asked, teasing about his accent.

"Sabre, are you okay? Where are you?"

"I'm fine. I'm at the precinct with Detective Nelson. They rescued us yesterday morning. I'm sorry; I should've called you sooner."

"It's okay. Nelson called to let me know they found you, but not before I saw it on television. It's big news here because of the Murdock family," he said, his voice smiling. "How's Alexis?"

"She's safe and sound."

"Are you sure you're okay?"

"Yes, I am, although I'll feel better once they catch Murdock. Say, I understand things have picked up for you as well."

"Yes, they arrested Bill Davis a few days ago. But Sabre, there's something else you need to know. It's about your brother. Murdock knew him."

"I know, Joe. Murdock told me all about it," she said. "Look, I need to get back in. Let's talk tomorrow after you've read the police report, and we can fill in the missing blanks for each other."

"Sounds good." He paused. "Sabre, I'm so glad you're safe."

CHAPTER 35

The next morning Sabre woke up in JP's house for the second time, still adjusting to the strange room. She missed her bed, her personal things, and her familiar surroundings. JP had been kind enough to go pick up some of her belongings, but she still didn't have everything she needed. He had brought her red notebook for her, though, and that pleased her. It had been some time since she'd been able to write in it or read it. She picked it up and held it in her hand for a second. It seemed so small. She thought back to when Ron gave it to her for her sixth birthday; it seemed to have so many pages then.

She read through the list, beginning with *Marry Victor Spanoli* right through to her last entry, *Peace Corps*. She wondered if Victor had married and if he had children. She wondered if he even remembered her. She realized she probably wouldn't remember much about him if it weren't for the reminder in her notebook every day.

Sabre had another entry to make. When she had been out in the woods, walking for miles up and down the mountains, she'd wished she had stayed in better shape. She vowed to become more physically fit if she ever made it out. She needed a goal to keep her motivated, something tangible to drive her. She smiled. She knew what she wanted to do, something she had thought about before but had never taken too seriously. She loved to run. She picked up her pen and wrote, *Run a Marathon*.

Sabre spent the day trying to keep busy. She returned some phone calls and e-mails, and worked on some files

Bob had brought her from her office. She hated using JP's dining room table for her desk. Although he didn't seem to mind, she still felt in the way. Imposing on others made her uncomfortable, and she missed having her own space. She felt guilty for being ungrateful for all the help he had given her. She wanted to go to court, go for a run in the park, or just sit in her own house and do nothing, unsure how long she could take being a prisoner, no matter how comfortable the surroundings. She couldn't continue to let Bob do her caseload, either. She had made up her mind. "JP, I'm going to court tomorrow." He laughed. "What's so funny?"

"Bob said you wouldn't last more than a day. Are you sure I can't talk you out of it?"

"Nope, I can't do this. I'll be in the loony bin by the end of the week."

"Okay, but here's the deal. I'll drive you to court. You'll be safe while you're there. The bailiffs will keep an eye on you. After your hearings are completed, I'll pick you up and bring you back here. You're not going to your office or your home. Understood?" He sounded like a drill sergeant.

"Yes, sir!" She saluted him and clicked her heels together. "Whatever you say, sir!" She laughed. The idea of returning to the real world made her giddy.

"What say we order a pizza and watch a video, something nice and easy, like a good comedy?"

"Sounds good; I'm hungry. You call and order the pizza. I'll pick out the movie." She looked through his collection of movies. She had no trouble picking one out. "Here we go," she said, as she put *When Harry Met Sally* in the machine. "I love this movie."

"Me, too." JP smiled.

About twenty minutes into the movie, someone knocked on the door. "That was quick," JP said, as he stood up to answer the door, expecting to see the pizza delivery person. Nevertheless, he looked through the peephole before he opened the door.

"Nelson," he said in surprise, "what are you doing here?" The detective didn't respond. JP opened the door and stepped back, making room for him to enter. "Come on in. You can join us for some pizza. It should be here any minute now."

"No, thanks. I'm not hungry," Nelson responded, trying to be pleasant, but he had an edge in his voice. "Hi, Sabre."

"Hi Gregory, what brings you here?" She perked up and added, "Did they find Murdock?"

"No, I'm afraid not," Nelson said. He sat down in front of Sabre and put his hand on top of hers. She knew something was wrong, but was afraid to imagine what it might be. Her stomach felt queasy. She heard the detective speak, but the words didn't register. "Listen, Sabre, I'm sorry, but there's a fire. Your condo is burning."

"What?"

"I'm sorry," he repeated.

"How bad is it?" JP interjected.

"It's still burning. They're doing everything they can to extinguish it, but right now it's out of control."

Sabre looked at him, shaking her head from side to side. "My house is burning?"

He nodded.

"No," she said, "this can't be happening. How . . . What happened?"

"We don't know yet. One of the condos next to yours is burning now, too, but it started inside yours."

"Oh my God, there's a baby next door and an old couple on the other side. Is anyone hurt?"

"No, they're fine. A police officer detected the fire while patrolling the area. Consequently, the neighbors evacuated. Everyone is okay."

The pizza man knocked on the door. Nelson sat up, turning toward the door like a lion ready to pounce on its prey. JP checked the door, then opened it. He paid him, took the pizza, and set it on the table. No one felt much like eating.

Sabre didn't cry, partly because it hadn't all sunk in, and partly because she wouldn't allow herself the luxury in front of people. "Do you think Murdock did it?"

"We don't know. We don't know yet what caused it. It could've been some electrical thing or something. As soon as the fire is contained, they'll be looking for the cause. We'll know more then."

"Objection, non-responsive," she said, as if in the courtroom. "I didn't ask you what you know; I asked you for your opinion. Do you think it was Murdock?"

"If it's arson, he's our prime suspect."

Sabre stood up. "I'm really exhausted. If you two don't mind, I'm going to go to bed."

"Go ahead. Goodnight," they both said.

She walked toward the bedroom, stopped after a few steps, and turned. "Oh, JP, I think I'll pass on court tomorrow. I haven't a thing to wear."

Sabre lay down on the bed, trying to comprehend the magnitude of what had just happened. She realized all her personal belongings were probably destroyed; every treasure, every memory, and every photo of Ron, all gone. She started to cry – a deep, loud wail. She couldn't keep it inside any longer. *Everything is gone! I have nothing of Ron left. That's what he wants. He can't hurt Ron any more, but he can still hurt me.* When she remembered her notebook, she reached for it, clenched it in her hand, and tucked it under the covers. She pulled it to her heart and held it tightly with both hands. Her wailing turned to sobs. Eventually, she fell asleep with the notebook secure in her arms.

CHAPTER 36

Bob walked into Sabre's office after court to gather up some of her files, once again amazed at her organizational skills. Everything Sabre had asked him to pick up was exactly where she said it would be. He noticed, however, something missing in the room. "Elaine," he called to the receptionist, "did you do something with the photo of Sabre's brother?"

"No," she answered, as she walked down the hallway to the room. "It should be sitting on the credenza where it always is."

"Hmm . . . well, it's not here. Do you know if Sabre did something with it?"

"No, I don't think so. In fact, I remember seeing it on Tuesday when I put some things on her desk."

"Maybe she took it with her when she left for her mother's house for some reason. I'll check with her. I'm going over there right now."

~~~

Sabre welcomed Bob, and the antics he shared about the daily courtroom drama. A pro tem had yelled at one of the new social workers and had her in tears. Bob said, "She made a bonehead call, but he didn't have to embarrass her. Granted, she was a rookie and didn't know much, but he could've cut her some slack. Since he didn't know anything either, he decided to take it out on someone who knew even less."

"Gee, I miss all the fun stuff," Sabre said jokingly.

She tried to keep a smile on her face, but it slipped away on more than one occasion during their conversation.

"Sobs, I'm so sorry about your house. You know you're welcome to stay with us if you'd like."

"Thanks, but I'm fine. JP said I can stay here as long as I want, but I'll be out looking for an apartment once they catch Murdock. I just need to regroup. I'm okay, really," she said, trying to convince herself as much as Bob.

Bob didn't want to bring up the photo, but if it was missing, then Murdock had probably been in her office and he had to let the police know. "Sobs, did you do something with your brother's photo in your office?"

"No, why? What's wrong with it?"

"It's not on the credenza where it usually is."

"Where is it?"

"I don't know. I looked around the office, but I couldn't find it. I thought maybe you had taken it with you when you left on Wednesday."

"No, I didn't. Did you ask Elaine?"

"Yes, the last time she noticed it was on Tuesday."

Sabre fell back in her chair. "It's like he's trying to take everything from me. At least anything connected to Ron. He said we were just alike, that we destroy families."

"Don't be silly, Sobs. You can't take anything he said seriously. He's a madman."

JP chimed in, "Bob's right, Sabre. That's ridiculous."

"No, guys, that's not it. It's what he said afterward. He said, 'You destroy families. Well, I'll destroy his, all of it.' Don't you see? He's not talking about just *me*? When he said I would die, he meant more than just me. He said, 'you and yours.' My mother," Sabre shouted. She ran to the phone. "I need to get my mother out of her house!"

"Sabre, what are you talking about? What are you thinking?" JP demanded.

"He knows my mother," she said, as she dialed the phone. It rang once, twice, three times, but no one answered. She let it ring. "She's not answering. I can't be too late. I just can't."

"Sabre, why do you think he knows your mother?"

"Why didn't I realize it before? I'm so stupid!" She banged the phone down.

Bob grabbed her by the shoulders. "What are you talking about?"

"Murdock said my mother still made Ron's favorite pie for the holidays. How would he know? He couldn't hear that from Ron." Sabre grabbed her coat and her car keys and headed for the door.

"One second, young lady," JP said. "I'm driving. Just point the way." The three of them jumped into JP's car. The tires squealed as he pulled out of the driveway. JP zipped in and out of traffic like a video game. "Bob, call Nelson and let him know we're going to get Sabre's mother. Tell him we're going to bring her back to stay with us for a while. And tell him why."

"Sure thing," Bob said. He tried to dial the number, but every time he tried to push a button, JP would take a sudden turn. "How the hell am I supposed to dial with you flopping me all over the place? Can't you go straight for just one minute?"

JP laughed. "Do you mind if I follow the road, chum?"

Sabre didn't say much. She didn't seem to notice how JP swerved in and out of traffic, or when he reached speeds well over ninety-five on stretches of the freeway. Nor did she pay any attention to the men bickering in the front seat. She just kept trying to reach her mother, hoping she still had time.

It normally took Sabre just over an hour to drive to her mother's house from her condo, but JP made it in forty-three minutes. Sabre kept checking her watch and dialing her phone. "Turn right at the second light," she instructed JP. He stepped on the accelerator and sailed through the first light, glowing orange. "Left at the stop sign." He squealed around the corner. "The third street, make another left and it's the second house from the next corner on the right."

JP followed her instructions. Just before he made the last left turn, he slowed down. He handed Bob a baseball cap and said, "Here, put this on and put your hand up so it covers your face. Sabre, scoot down. I'm going to drive past and see what we can see." As he approached the house, he reported back to Sabre. "There are only two cars on the street; the rest seem to be in garages. There's a Mercedes Benz on the right and a Dodge van on the left at the end of the street."

"They both belong there," she said.

"There's a light on in the living room, but there don't appear to be any other lights in the house. There's a white Honda in the garage and the garage door is open."

"That's her car, but she wouldn't leave the garage door open. There's something wrong." Sabre started to shake. A lump formed in her throat.

"Maybe she just got home," Bob said.

"She closes the door first thing, and she's not answering her phone," Sabre said.

"Is there a back way in?"

"Yes, but it's fenced. You can climb on up the neighbor's fence and drop down right behind the peach tree. There are two back doors: one is a sliding glass door into the family area, and the other goes through the laundry room. I have a key for the door to the laundry room, but you'll have to cross the patio to get to it."

"Is there a dog?"

"Yes, his name is Patches, and he's probably in the house. Even if he's not, he doesn't have a clue he's supposed to guard the place. He won't bark, much less bite."

JP pulled around the corner and stopped the car. "Here's what we're going to do. I'm going in through the back." He turned to Bob, "You drive around front and park a couple of houses down, but be sure you have a good view of the house. If I don't come out or you don't hear from me in five minutes, call the police and report a burglary." Sabre's hand shook as she passed him the key. They synchronized the time.

JP checked his gun and hopped out. He climbed up on the neighbor's block wall and dropped into Sabre's mother's yard just behind the peach tree. The half-moon gave out light and more came from the house, making JP an easier target as he sneaked along. He stayed close to the fence until he reached the end of the house. Crouching, he cautiously stepped along the hedge to the patio to keep from being seen through the windows. He had to cross the patio to reach the door. His only other option was to navigate through a patch of rose bushes. He opted for the patio. He crept across, careful not to bump into anything. As he reached the end of the patio, he saw movement in the house. He stopped and listened, but he couldn't hear anything.

JP carefully put the key in the door and unlocked it. He held his gun ready and pushed the door slowly open, peeking inside, unsure what he might encounter. Satisfied he occupied the space alone, he stepped inside the dark room and crept along past the washer and dryer to the slightly open door leading into the family area. He could hear voices. He moved as closely as he could to the door, and tried to peer through the crack. He couldn't see anyone, but he could make out most of what was said. He heard a man's voice say, "Where is she?"

"I don't know," came the response from a woman JP assumed must be Sabre's mother. She spoke softly and her voice trembled.

"She's history, no matter what, just like your asshole of a son, so you may as well spare yourself."

"I don't know where she is. She wouldn't tell me."

JP wanted to barge in and save her, but he couldn't be certain she would be safe. He didn't know if Murdock had a gun or maybe a knife on her. He heard Murdock say, "Well, then, you're not much good to me, are you?"

"Bang!" The gunshot deafened JP's ears. He flung the door open and dived toward Murdock, bringing him down. They struggled and Murdock's gun went flying across the room. JP could see Sabre's mother lying on the floor.

Sabre and Bob heard the shot ring out through the neighborhood. Sabre jumped out of the car and ran for the house, Bob close behind, yelling at her to stop, but she kept running. She had to reach her mother. Nothing else mattered at the moment. She could hear sirens blaring close by as she dashed across the grass and up the walk to the front door. She threw open the door and charged into the family area. Tears burst from her eyes as she threw herself on the floor and enveloped her mother in her arms. "Mom, Mom, are you okay?"

"I'm fine, dear. Just help me up."

Sabre put her arm around her and pulled her up from the floor. Turning, she saw JP had his gun to Murdock's head. She didn't look at Murdock. She didn't want to feel the hatred. Instead, she smiled at JP and whispered, "Thank you."

Within minutes, the police swarmed the house. "What happened?" an officer commanded.

Her mother replied, "I went out to visit someone in the hospital, and when I returned, Murdock was waiting in the garage for me. He grabbed me from behind when I got out of my car and dragged me into the house. He held a gun to my head and tried to make me tell him Sabre's whereabouts. I didn't know exactly, but I wouldn't have told him even if I did. No, I would've died first. I wanted to spit in his face and tell him that, but I was too terrified to say anything else. I don't have the spunk my beautiful daughter has. She gets it from her father."

"What happened when he shot the gun?" the officer continued.

"He made me sit in the chair and he stood over me. He pointed the gun at my head. I could see the evil in his eyes.

He threatened to kill me. For a moment, my fear left and I got angry. I couldn't see any reason not to fight back. Besides, I owed him one for saying those nasty things about my children. I figured I had the perfect angle so I pulled my foot back and kicked up as hard as I could right between his legs. The gun went off and I think the bullet went through the floor as he doubled up. Just then, this nice gentleman charged through the door and tackled him."

CHAPTER 37

Sabre hopped out of bed, took her shower, put on one of her new outfits, and ran out the door, yelling goodbye to JP as she left. Breakfast at Clara's Kitchen awaited her, and she was delighted to be engaged in one of her routine activities. She wore a huge smile as she enjoyed her newfound freedom. She was devastated by the loss of her house, but determined not to let it bring her down. *Heck, if Scarlett O'Hara could rebuild Tara against all adversity, I sure as heck can replace a little condo.* Sabre, elated Murdock had been caught, still wore the smile it generated as she greeted Bob at the restaurant.

"You look happy this morning, Sobs. It's nice to see your beautiful smile."

"Thanks, it feels good to be free. Don't get me wrong – I'm really bummed about my house burning and losing all my little treasures, especially my photos of Ron, but it could've been so much worse. I could've lost my mother. Heck, I could be dead, and then how would you ever survive?"

"You're right, but I'd still like to kill the slime bag. Not only for what he did to you and your mother, but for dumping poor, little Honey in the desert. That's reason enough to off him. JP should've done it when he had the chance."

"He'll get his," Sabre said. "Enough about Murdock. What does your day look like?"

"I'll be in court all day. I have a pretty heavy calendar."

"Need some help? I owe you big time."

"No, it's mostly just review hearings. Why, is your calendar light?"

"I have one case this morning and then the Smith/Murdock settlement conference this afternoon. I thought I'd go by and see Carla for a bit after my morning calendar. I haven't seen her since before Thanksgiving. Even though I don't expect any real problems on the Murdock/Smith case this afternoon, I still want to go through the file one more time."

"There's nothing either Gaylord or Peggy can do at this point. They're both in jail. The trial will have to settle. Their attorneys will make them see the light. I must say I'm looking forward to seeing Murdock in silver bracelets."

"I don't want to see him at all, handcuffed or otherwise," Sabre said. "I'd be happy to never lay eyes on him again."

They enjoyed the Clara's Kitchen flower garden and each other's company while eating their breakfast. When they arrived at court, they were greeted by a new bailiff, working the metal detector with Mike. "Good morning, Mike," Bob said. "How goes the war?"

"Same ol', same ol'," he said. "You know, Sabre, you really ought to keep better company. Bob is not good for your reputation."

"I know, but someone has to keep an eye on him."

"Who's the new guy, Mike?" Bob nodded toward the bailiff behind the metal detector.

"Oh this is Stimson, Mike Stimson. He has my given name, but don't let that fool you. He's not nearly as smart or as good looking as I am," he said. "Stimson is our brand new rookie, fresh from the classroom. It's his first day, so we thought we'd throw him into the really tough stuff, like watching the screen on the metal detector. After this, we're going to teach him how to fetch donuts."

"Nice to meet you, Stimson," Bob said. "You'll do just fine, if you can live with the harassment this bozo gives you."

"Nice to meet you both," Stimson responded, looking nervous.

Sabre felt like a celebrity at court. Everyone gave her special consideration. She knew it wouldn't last long, so if they wanted to give her case priority she wasn't going to argue with anyone. As a result, she finished early and headed out to see Carla.

She poked her head into Carla's room and saw her sitting on the edge of the bed.

"Sabre," Carla shouted. She stood up and gave Sabre a hug.

Sabre, surprised at her behavior, couldn't remember the last time she received such a greeting. "Carla, you look great, so full of energy."

"Yeah, they changed my medication, cut it back, actually. It doesn't make me so groggy."

"You must be doing really well for them to reduce your meds. Are you having fewer episodes?"

"I haven't had one in almost a week," Carla said. "And it's a good thing, too, since you've been on vacation and not around to help me."

"Yeah, vacation."

Carla looked at her and smirked. "I know what happened. They told me in session because they were afraid I'd see it on television. I got pretty upset, but I knew you'd want me to be strong. So I tried harder . . . for you, Sabre." She sounded like a little girl trying to make her mother proud. Sabre was proud – proud of Carla's efforts and her obvious improvement.

Carla and Sabre visited the rest of the morning. They both needed to laugh, and found humor in the least little thing. They chatted like two school girls enjoying each other's company. Sabre was so pleased with the change in Carla. She had had moments like this before, but it had been a while since she'd experienced hours of lucidity. As the morning went on, Carla began to tire. She sat down on her bed, leaned back, and said, "Sabre, tell me about the butterflies and green pastures." Sabre spoke to her softly like she had in the past, but she could see Carla was not desperate for her narration as she'd been so many times before. She could see some light in Carla's future . . . and hope.

Sabre drove back to court, her mind turning to the possibilities ahead. She would face the last demon on this case. It would be the last time she'd need to be in the same room with Gaylord Murdock.

As she drove into the juvenile court parking lot, she spotted three news vans with their antennas stretching into the sky. The reporters, lying in wait, began filming as she exited her car. Sabre wished she had prepared for this. She and Murdock were big news. For days during her absence, her face had been plastered on television and in the papers, followed by Murdock's face as the police in turn searched for him. Sabre's condo fire had created more suspicion and a news story they couldn't resist. Questions came at her from all directions. "Ms. Brown, how do you feel about Murdock being captured?"

"Naturally, I'm pleased," Sabre responded, wondering where they came up with these lame questions.

"Do you think Murdock burned your house down?"

"I have no idea, but I'm sure the police will figure it out." She hurried across the parking lot toward the front door of the courthouse, dodging microphones stuck in her face. She'd be provided a safe haven from their questions inside juvenile court, where the reporters weren't allowed.

"Ms. Brown, I understand Murdock dumped Honey Stone's dead body in the desert. Is that true?"

"The case is under investigation. I'm not free to discuss anything at this point." She reached the door, and saw Mike working the metal detector. She waved at him and he motioned her to come forward. She walked past the line waiting to go inside, around the metal detector, and into the lobby. "Thanks, Mike." She smiled.

"My pleasure," he said, as he went back to his machine.

Sabre looked through the crowd for Bob. She spotted him across the room and walked over. She glanced around at all the people. "Wow, this sure is busy for a Thursday afternoon."

"Yeah, it's been a crazy day. Half my morning calendar continued to the afternoon, most of them in Department Four. I know at least two other courtrooms didn't complete their calendars, either, so it's going to be a while before we do the Smith/Murdock case."

"No problem, I'll just hang out and wait. At least I'm away from those vultures outside."

"Who?"

"Oh, the place is swarming with news reporters. They attacked me when I drove up, asking a bunch of stupid questions."

"I'm sorry. I didn't even realize they were there. They must've arrived after I did," Bob said. "It's not a surprise, though. Murdock has taken up a lot of news time."

"Have you seen Marla? I'd like to talk with her a bit."

"Yeah, she just went in the interview room to see Murdock. He's been in there since they brought the prisoners in. There's not enough room in the back, so they stuck him in there."

"Great, I'll watch for her. When I'm done, I'll come hang in Department Four with you."

~~~

Marla, uncomfortable sitting in the interview room with Murdock, wasn't about to let him know. She felt safe enough; she just didn't want to be near him. The room, about eight feet wide and ten feet long, was divided down the middle by a three-foot high wall and a heavy plastic window reaching from the wall to the ceiling. A thick wire mesh lay over the plastic, and a shelf protruded out on the top of the wall on either side. Marla sat in a chair with her papers on the shelf. Murdock sat on the other side of the wall, handcuffed to his bench.

A door led out of each side of the room. On the visitors' side, it opened to a small hallway and the courthouse lobby. On the prisoner's side, the locked door led to the back hallway, away from the lobby, just in front of the bailiff's station.

Marla continued with her interview of Murdock. He turned on the charm, but failed to have any effect on Marla. He had burned her once, and she wouldn't let it happen again.

After finishing, she stepped out into the lobby. "Hi, Sabre, how are you doing?"

"Not bad," she said, with a tense smile. "I'll be glad when we're done here today, though."

"Yeah, me too," Marla said. "Hey, can you wait here a minute? I need to give something to County Counsel. I'll be right back. I'd like to chat with you a bit, if you don't mind."

"Sure, take your time. I promise I won't wander off and get lost in the crowd."

The bench along the wall was filled with people waiting for their hearings, so Sabre stood with her back against the glass leading into the hallway by the interview room, waiting for Marla. Suddenly she felt cold metal against her throat and hot breath on her neck. A shiver shot down her spine. She felt the chain tighten around her neck and heard Murdock's voice in her ear. Murdock was back in control.

A hush came over the crowd as people stepped back. The silent alarms went off in the courtrooms. Judges descended from their benches, hastening into their chambers for safety. The bailiffs ran through the lobby from every direction, pushing people out of the way. Murdock scooted along the wall toward the door leading outside, keeping Sabre in front of him. The crowd had moved back and the bailiffs gathered around. One of them moved toward Murdock.

"One step closer and I break her neck," Murdock said

coldly. The bailiff stopped. Murdock continued toward and through the door, dragging Sabre with him.

The news reporters aimed their cameras as Murdock exited the building. The bailiffs filtered out and strategically positioned themselves around the parking lot. People ran toward their cars. Others tried to move in as close as they could while the officers struggled to keep them back. Sabre, terrified, didn't want to be imprisoned again. She'd rather die. He dragged her toward her car. She looked around and saw her friend, Mike, not far away with his gun drawn. She yelled out to him, "Shoot him! Shoot him, Mike!" She screamed as she struggled to get out of the way so the Bailiff could get a shot, but Murdock tugged tighter on the chain he had around her neck and pulled her closer to his body to provide a shield for himself.

"Shut up," he snarled at her.

"Shoot him, Mike!"

"I'll do it. I'll kill you," Murdock said.

"Go ahead. Give Mike a reason to shoot you."

"Sabre, don't push him," Mike said, staying with them as they moved across the parking lot, keeping the same distance between them.

"Mike, just shoot him. Don't let him take me. I'd rather die," Sabre screamed. Murdock squeezed tighter on the chain. She felt faint, hardly able to breathe. She heard Mike trying to talk Murdock down, to reason with him, but he would have no part of it. Murdock kept pulling Sabre slowly across the parking lot.

She yelled again, "Shoot him, Mike!" Off to the side she heard a deafening sound. An excruciating pain shot through her body. She felt herself falling, the force on her neck releasing. As she fell to the ground, the people and buildings seemed to turn sideways; she saw both the sky and pavement. She heard another shot before she felt her body hit the ground. The lights went out.

~~~

"Sobs!" Bob yelled, as he pushed through the crowd. He ran past Stimson, the rookie bailiff, just as Stimson hurled. Bob heard him coughing and hacking, saw yellow and red chunks spew from his mouth. Bob dodged to the right to avoid the flying vomit. He finally reached Sabre, lying on the ground next to Murdock, in a pool of blood. "Call an ambulance!"

"It's on the way," Mike said.

"Oh my God," Bob yelled. He threw himself down onto the ground and pulled Sabre's head onto his lap. Her limp wrist lay in his hand, but he could feel a faint pulse. "Hang on, Sobs, you hang on." His breathing heavy and his heart pounding in his chest, he sobbed as he held his friend in his arms. "You're strong; you can do this. You can't let him beat you, Sobs. You just can't."

Mike dropped down on one knee, level with Bob. "How is she?"

"She's breathing." Bob's voice cracked.

"What the hell happened?" the Sarge yelled as he walked up to Mike.

Mike stood up. "It was Stimson. We were closing in on Murdock as he moved toward the car. All of a sudden, Stimson starting shooting."

"Why in the hell would he do that?"

"He heard Sabre yell, 'Mike, shoot him.' He thought she was talking to him and freaked."

"Stupid rookie," Sarge said. "Where is he now?"

"He's over there by the car, puking his guts out."

"How did Murdock get out of custody, anyway?" Mike demanded.

"Somehow, he managed to remove the handcuff from the chair, climbed up on the shelf, pushed the ceiling tile aside, then climbed across, and dropped down on the visitors' side of the wall. From there, he walked out the door and grabbed Sabre," the sergeant responded before walking off.

Mike knelt back down. "Stay with us, Sabre. We need you."

Sabre lay in Bob's arms, covered with blood. Bob felt helpless. He took his handkerchief and wiped the blood from her splattered face. He knew some of the blood belonged to Murdock, and she would want him to wipe it off. He looked down at her blood-soaked clothes. He didn't know where Murdock's blood stopped and hers began or where she had been hit. From all the blood on her chest it looked like she had taken a bullet on the left side of her body, just below the shoulder. Bob told himself to breathe, to keep from hyperventilating. Afraid she'd been hit in the heart, he checked her pulse again. She still had one, but fainter than before. The sirens grew louder as the paramedics neared the courthouse.

"They're almost here. Just hang on, Sobs." He leaned over her, murmured, "Sobs, I tell you what I'll do. If you'll just come through this for me, I'll quit smoking for you. I will. I promise." He half expected her eyes to pop open with shock. Maybe that's why he did it. He didn't know, but he had made her a promise and he would keep it. All she had to do was live.

The paramedics jumped out of the ambulance and went to Sabre. They took her out of Bob's arms and placed her on the stretcher. Bob watched as the paramedics loaded her in the ambulance, hoping they'd be able to stabilize her. For the first time, he looked over at Murdock just in time to see them pull the sheet over his face. Bob didn't feel good about it, as he had imagined he might. Nor was he upset because someone had just died. He felt nothing.

Bob slid into his car, lit up a cigarette, and drove to the hospital. "She's going to have to live if she wants me to quit."

CHAPTER 38

Sabre was groggy. She wanted to wake up, but her eyelids seemed too heavy to open. Unsure of her whereabouts, and afraid to find out, she opened one eye and then the other. Through the haze, she saw a doctor sitting on the side of her bed. She looked around the room, satisfying herself she was in a hospital.

"Good morning, sunshine."

"Hello, Dr. Steele," she replied. She smiled up at him, "You sounded just like Ron. That's the way he always greeted me in the morning."

He looked back at her and smiled a sheepish little smile, making his eyes twinkle. Sabre's heart skipped a beat and her stomach fluttered. He looked so much like Ron.

"Sabre, it's me, Ron. Dr. Steele's in his office."

Sabre pinched herself on the wrist. She closed her eyes for a second and reopened them, this time filled with tears. "Am I dreaming?"

"No, you're not dreaming. I know this seems strange, but I'm really here. Now if you'll just give me a hug, I'll tell you what's going on."

Sabre reached up. Ron leaned over and hugged her, being careful of her shoulder. Tears streaming down her face, she asked in disbelief, "Is it really you, Ron? I'm not hallucinating?"

"It's really me." Ron smiled his devilish smile.

"You're not Dr. Steele?"

"No, I'm just lucky enough to have someone who looks

TERESA BURRELL

a great deal like me." He picked up her hand and held it in his. "Where do I begin?" he paused. "Sabre, I've been in the witness protection program for the past five years. I couldn't contact you or Mom because it would've put you both at risk. I couldn't even tell you about the program because the mobsters I testified against think I'm dead. That's the only way this would work. I'm so sorry. I know you've gone through hell, but I just couldn't put you in danger."

"You're here now. It's all that matters."

"Sabre, I can't stay. I only have a few hours and then I'll have to go back." He watched the smile leave her face. "I'm sorry. I didn't know which was worse, to let you go on thinking I had died, or to take this opportunity to see you. I'm afraid I was selfish. I just had to see you again."

"Oh, I'm so glad you did. I'm selfish, too. I want to keep you with me." She fought back the tears.

"Who knows? Someday I may be able to return. You never know."

"So what happened?"

"Well, you already know about my relationship with Gaylord and Beth. I met Beth at the gym. We became very close friends, nothing more. Oh, don't get me wrong; I loved her, and had she been single, we may have had a chance. But nothing ever happened, not even so much as a kiss."

"Did Elizabeth, I mean, Beth, love you?"

"I don't know. I'd like to think so, but we never discussed it. I do know she cared a great deal for me. We shared a lot of secrets."

"Gaylord thought there was something between you?"

"Apparently, although I didn't realize it at the time. He never gave any indication he had a problem with our relationship. Instead, he fed me information through Beth so he could set me up."

"Yeah, I heard about that, but wouldn't it have been simpler for him to testify against Atlanta himself?"

278

"Sure, but Gaylord never did anything the simple way. Besides, he didn't want to be the one to testify and end up dead or in my situation. So he devised a plan where Atlanta would fall, Dallas could move in, and wipe his slate clean. If he used me as his pawn, he got a bonus by getting rid of me at the same time."

"So you testified and put some sharks in prison?"

"Yeah, quite a few of them. Gaylord made sure we wiped out their leadership. Then the FBI put the word out on the street about me being dead and faked a cover. So, it appeared they tried to protect themselves from looking like they screwed up, a pretty ingenious plan actually."

"Is Beth with you?"

"No. I didn't even know she was missing until this morning, but I'd bet my life Gaylord had something to do with it."

"Don't be doing that. You can't have too many lives left," Sabre said. "Enough about the Murdocks. Tell me about Ron Brown, or whatever your name is now. Are you married? Do you have any children?"

"None of the above," he responded. "Unfortunately, my life doesn't really lend itself to an honest commitment. When you live a lie, it's hard to build trust in a relationship." Ron didn't sound bitter. Instead, he sounded as if he had come to terms with his plight and accepted it.

"I do have a dog, a yellow lab. He's a great hunter. I have a good job, something I really enjoy doing. I told them when I signed up for this gig I'd only work out of doors. And I have some very dear friends." Ron paused, "Yes, all in all, my life has been good the past five years. Except for the fact I don't have you and Mom around, it's a life I would choose for myself." He chuckled a little. "I guess, in a way, that's what I did. Not many people have the opportunity to do such a thing."

"Mom. Does she know?"

"Yes, she knows. I spent the morning with her in Dr. Steele's office. She'll be in here shortly. She wanted to give us a little time alone."

"Just like Mom, always giving."

"Yeah, she's the best," Ron agreed. "Sis, I'm so sorry about your house burning down."

"Hey, it's only material things. I'm safe, Mom's safe, you're alive; the rest doesn't really matter. Besides, I retrieved the most important thing from the house the day before it caught fire . . . my little red notebook you gave me for my sixth birthday."

Ron laughed out loud. "Are you still writing in that old thing?"

"Every day I either write in it, or at least review what's already there. Every day I think of you when I do it. Look at all the things I've accomplished because I put them on my list."

"Like what?"

"Like getting my law degree."

"Yeah, and it nearly got you killed," he said.

"Well, like buying my own home, with a view."

"And that lasted what? Six weeks? You certainly have a view now."

She laughed, "Okay, I have one. Remember the roller coaster? It took me six months after I wrote it in the book to work up the nerve to actually go on it."

"Yes, and when you finally did, it got stuck at the top and you sat there for over three hours before they brought you down." Ron laughed. "Oh, and let's not forget the love of your life, Victor Spanoli. That one worked well. Not only did you not marry him, you haven't married anyone. Why is that, by the way?"

"Just waiting for Victor, I guess." Sabre thought about how much she had missed the banter only she and her brother could do. He had been teasing and cajoling her as long as she could remember. When she reached about ten or eleven years old, she started to give it back to him, and by the time she reached her teen years, she held her own.

Sabre couldn't take her eyes off her handsome

brother. "Wow, it's so good to have you here with me." She sighed. "Do you ever hear about what's going on in our lives?"

"I receive reports from time to time on you, Mom . . . and Carla." Ron paused. "I feel so responsible for Carla. I should've taken her with me, but it all seemed too risky at the time."

"Hey, you did what you had to do. It's not your fault Carla has problems. Besides, she's doing much better now with the help of Dr. Steele."

"I know. He told me about Carla's progress. He sounded real promising."

"He's right, Ron. She's come a long way. I believe she's going to make it. By the way, how were you able to come home to us?"

"It seems you made an impression on someone who wanted to return a favor."

"I don't understand."

"You retrieved some information from Beth's mother, which in turn helped clear the name of a cop in Atlanta . . . Courage or Carriage or something like that."

"Carriage, Joe Carriage."

"Yeah, that's it. Well, he has a friend in the FBI who owed him big time, so he called in a marker. Even with all that, it wouldn't have worked except for my outlandishly handsome look-alike, Dr. Corbin Steele. I must say, he has been a prince through this whole thing. I have to tell you, it's really strange looking at someone who looks so much like you."

"He's a pretty great guy," Sabre said.

"And a handsome devil, wouldn't you say?"

"I don't have to. You've said it plenty."

The door opened and Mrs. Brown looked in. "Can anyone join this party?"

"Hi, Mom, come on in," Sabre beckoned.

The three of them spent the next few hours sharing their lives and reminiscing. They talked, they laughed, and they cried, always touching, trying to hold on to each other and to the few precious moments they had together. They feared the moment the door would open and they would be split apart.

When the US Marshal walked in, he was greeted with three very disappointed faces. "Sorry folks," he said. "I hate to do this to you, but it's time. You have a few minutes to say your goodbyes and then here's what you need to do. Ron, when you leave here, remember you are Dr. Steele. Nurses and such may be vying for your attention to ask you things. Sabre's friend Bob will be out in the hallway. He'll be asking you questions about Sabre and acting crazy, if he has to, in order to keep others distracted. You'll lead him to your office where Dr. Steele's waiting. From there you'll slip out the back and we'll be on our way. Any questions?"

"No, I've got it," Ron said. He hugged his mother for the longest time, both holding on. They had all agreed earlier they wouldn't cry when it came time to leave, but it didn't work. Mrs. Brown bawled as she gave him some last minute motherly instructions on how to take care of himself. Tears rolled down Ron's cheeks as he agreed to be careful. He turned to Sabre, gave her a hug, and whispered in her ear, "Don't ever forget how much I love you, Sis."

Sabre couldn't fight back the tears. Sobbing, she replied, "I love you, too, Bro." As he turned to leave, she and her mother squeezed each other's hands watching Ron transform into Dr. Steele and shuffle out the door.

CHAPTER 39

"Come on, Sobs, you're going to miss your flight," Bob yelled.

"Relax, Grumpy, we still have plenty of time," Sabre said, as she walked out of the bedroom with her suitcase. "By the way, how are you doing with the smoking? You still clean?"

"Absolutely," Bob said, looking at his watch. "Twenty-seven days, three hours and thirty-two minutes . . . but who's counting?"

"I'm really proud of you."

"I promised, if you lived, I'd quit. I have to admit there were a few times when I first stopped that I wanted to kill you myself just so I could smoke again." They laughed as they got in the car and left for the airport. "Well, Sobs, things haven't turned out so badly after all."

"Yup, you're right. Howard, the FBI agent, sure came through, finding Elizabeth and all."

"How did that come about? I never heard what happened to her."

"More of Gaylord's doing. Elizabeth decided she had had enough of his abuse and his gambling, and she told him she was leaving him. He threatened to kill her mother and Alexis if she left. He told her, if he couldn't have Alexis, no one would, especially not her. He kept getting worse and worse. Crazy things started to happen to her, including a red bat appearing in her bathroom during her shower.

TERESA BURRELL

Imagine that. A few days later, the riddle about the bat showed up in her purse. Things escalated to the point where she couldn't take it any longer. When he left for work one morning, she packed some things for her and Alexis, and went to tell her mother goodbye. He must've been having her followed because those thugs intercepted her and she never made it to her mother's house. Somehow, though, she managed to escape. She hid for a while, and then she went to the police station. When she arrived, she saw one of her abductors in the parking lot. She hid behind some cars and saw him talking to a police officer. She was too frightened to go in after that because she didn't know who to talk to. Murdock had lots of friends in the police department.

"She left, went to Boston, and hid out. She had a friend in Atlanta who kept her informed about Alexis. Her friend discovered she knew one of the investigating officers on the case, named Steve Parker. She assured Elizabeth he could be trusted. Steve was Joe Carriage's best friend, remember?"

"Yeah, the cop they killed."

"Yup, so Elizabeth's friend called Steve. She planned to meet with him and tell him about Elizabeth and what had happened. She went to the meeting, but Steve never showed. She read in the paper the next day he was killed in a car accident. That clinched it for Elizabeth, too afraid she would put her mother or Alexis in danger if she came forward. She didn't want to leave Alexis with Gaylord, either, but in many ways he was a good father. She knew he wouldn't hurt her as long as she stayed away."

"So she sacrificed a life with her daughter to save her life?"

"And her mother's," Sabre added. "She's quite a woman. I can see why Ron loved her."

"Oh, by the way, do we need to pick up Alexis?"

"No, Marla's bringing her to the airport."

"I'll bet she's anxious to see her mother."

"Yes, she's excited. They've been talking on the phone every day, getting reacquainted. Everyone is anxious for Alexis to return to Atlanta. And Alexis is excited about seeing Jamie."

"Where is Jamie?"

"Didn't I tell you? Jamie and Haley were placed with a maternal great aunt in Decatur, Georgia. Peggy has an aunt who is a nurse. She was estranged from the rest of the family and so she didn't know what was going on for quite a while. She saw the news story and contacted Marla. It sounds like a good placement for them and the aunt has agreed to continue the contact with Alexis."

"Do you think it will be a long term placement?"

"They want to keep him, so if parental rights are terminated, they plan to adopt him. If not, I'm sure they will do a guardianship at the very least."

"That's great," Bob said. "How are the Murdocks reacting to what happened?"

"They're upset, of course; after all, they lost a son. They also feel terrible about all the suffering he caused. I expect they are terribly disappointed in his behavior. They made a public apology on behalf of the Murdock name, but other than that they're keeping it within the confines of their home and family, like well-bred southern folks do. They appear to be good people and they love Elizabeth like a daughter, so I'm sure it'll all work out," Sabre said. "They bought us all tickets for some big shindig at the country club for New Year's Eve. It might be fun, hobnobbing with the rich and famous." She laughed.

They arrived at the airport, and Sabre and Alexis flew to Atlanta, where Alexis would begin her new life. The Murdocks, Elizabeth, and Ruby were waiting in baggage claim when they arrived. The grandparents held back and let Alexis greet her mother alone. Alexis saw her flaxen-haired mother in a periwinkle blue cotton dress standing across the room, and said, "She looks like an angel."

"She sure does," Sabre said.

Alexis ran to her with open arms. "Mother, Mother," she yelled from across the crowded corridor.

ABOUT THE AUTHOR

Teresa Burrell has dedicated her life to helping children and their families. As an attorney, Ms. Burrell has spent countless hours working pro bono in the family court system. She continues to advocate children's issues and write novels, many of which are inspired by actual legal cases.

Teresa Burrell is available at www.teresaburrell.com.
Like her page on Facebook at
www.facebook.com/theadvocateseries

Dear Reader,

Would you like a FREE copy of a novella about JP when he was young? If so, please go to www.teresaburrell.com and sign up for my mailing list. You will automatically receive a code to retrieve the story. Or you can email me at teresa@teresaburrell.com.

Thank you,

Teresa

Please send an email to Teresa and let her know what you thought of THE ADVOCATE. She would love to hear from you. She can be reached at: teresa@teresaburrell.com.

If you like this authors writing, the best way to compliment her is by telling your friends. Reviews are nice too.

THE ADVOCATE SERIES

THE ADVOCATE (Book 1)

THE ADVOCATE'S BETRAYAL (Book 2)

THE ADVOCATE'S CONVICTION (Book 3)

THE ADVOCATE'S DILEMMA (Book 4)

THE ADVOCATE'S EX PARTE (Book5)

THE ADVOCATE'S FELONY (Book 6)

THE ADVOCATE'S GEOCACHE (Book 7)

THE ADVOCATE'S HOMICIDES (Book 8)

THE ADVOCATE'S ILLUSION (Book 9)

THE ADVOCATE'S JUSTICE (Book 10)

THE TUPER MYSTERY SERIES

THE ADVOCATE'S FELONY
(Book 6 of The Advocate Series)

MASON'S MISSING (Book 1)

FINDING FRANKIE (Book 2)

If you liked THE ADVOCATE, there are ten more books in The Advocate Series, and more to come. Below is the Prologue for the second book in the series, THE ADVOCATE'S BETRAYAL.

Prologue

Pain, from a sharp knife plunged into his chest, yanked John out of a deep sleep. He forced his eyelids open. The only thing worse than the pain was the shock when he saw who was standing over him. It wasn't until the blood dripped on his face that he realized it was not a dream.

"No, no, not you...." John reached out, hitting his hand against the wall. He tried to speak again, but could only mumble. *"Our Father, who art in heaven..."*

The killer mockingly said, "Are you praying, old man? Here, use this....," tossing John's rosary at his open hand near the floor. It caught on his fingertips and dangled there. John felt his air diminishing as his lungs filled up with blood. He fumbled his fingers until his thumb and index finger clasped the first large bead, the words no longer audible. *"...hallowed be Thy name..."*

His attacker stepped back, gazing at him lying there, holding the knife dripping with blood, his blood. John reached for his chest, but his arm wouldn't move. *"...Thy kingdom come..."* The naked walls of the trailer felt like a box. They were so close on every side. It was stifling. This was his box, his cage, his coffin. The only illumination came from the front room. He listened as the footsteps echoed back and forth at the end of his queen-size bed that filled the room, leaving less than a foot on each side. And then he heard the rubber soles of the shoes exit the bedroom.

He heard water run. His backside felt wet. Was it water? No, the water came from the kitchenette; blood pooled around his body. John heard his assailant washing away his blood in his kitchen—his murderer washing away the evidence. "...*Thy will be done, on earth as it is in heaven...*"

Footsteps returned to John's bedroom, and with them returned his fear. Was the attacker returning to finish the job? John couldn't protect himself; he couldn't even move. Then the fear subsided. It was too late. The damage already done. "...*Give us this day, our daily bread, and forgive us our trespasses...*"

The floor creaked all the way to the front door. Click—door unlocked, opened. The lights went out in the front room, completely dark, or was it the light in his mind that ceased? The pain in his chest intensified. His body felt lethargic. The front door closed. John listened carefully—no lock. The trailer shifted when the last step was vacated. He was alone, left to die alone.

John tried to move, to struggle, to fight, but his body wouldn't budge. He saw his life—the despicable parts when he was a kid, the pain he inflicted on others—but mostly he thought of the man he had become. The man who tried his whole life to fix what he had done as a child, that's who he really was. It pained him to have to think he would suffer eternal damnation for the crimes he committed so long ago. Was this his punishment— betrayal, death, eternal damnation? "...*as we forgive those...*"